Ruined

TEAL ROSE

Contents

Acknowledgment   VI

Author's Note   VII

Prologue   1
Kyndall

1. Chapter 1   16
Kyndall

2. Chapter 2   21
Kyndall

3. Chapter 3   32
Melissa

4. Chapter 4   45
Melissa

5. Chapter 5   57
Kyndall

6. Chapter 6   65
Kyndall

7. Chapter 7   73
    Melissa

8. Chapter 8   79
    Kyndall

9. Chapter 9   84
    Melissa

10. Chapter 10   99
    Kyndall

11. Chapter 11   106
    Melissa

12. Chapter 12   117
    Kyndall

13. Chapter 13   124
    Melissa

14. Chapter 14   136
    Kyndall

15. Chapter 15   146
    Melissa

16. Chapter 16   157
    Kyndall

17. Chapter 17   165
    Kyndall

18. Chapter 18   174
    Kyndall

19. Chapter 19   183
    Kyndall

20. Chapter 20   192

    Melissa

21. Epilogue   195

I dedicated this book to my best friend and sister, Noura. To my aunts Christene, Julie, and my uncle Courtney, thank you for the love and the support.
Thank you for anyone whose help to push me to release this labor of love!
And to my readers and new followers, the best is yet to come.
Peace, Love, and Keep *Beyoncé* in your heart!

Author's Note

This book explores themes around emotional trauma, relationship issues, homophobia, dubcon, and mental health issues; but most importantly, this book touches on forgiveness, second chances, and love.

Prologue

Kyndall

I RUBBED MY HANDS on the side of my jeans as sweat fell from my back. It made my t-shirt stick to my skin. I had rubbed the clear lip gloss I brought from the beauty store off my lips. I'd not felt this way about anything since I started high school three years ago, in which I became the laughingstock of my class.

It's now or never! This will be my only shot to ask her to prom.

The other students whispered; Nathan Thomas planned to ask Melissa to the prom in our English class next period, which made me sick. While I waited for Melissa to get out of class, I wondered whether waiting until the day before prom would benefit me. I could only hope it did. I admitted that my desperation stemmed from everyone else making last-minute prom dates. The thought of attending prom alone or with anyone who didn't appeal to me disheartened me.

I paced the floor until I heard the loud creak of the classroom door as it swung open. With each step Melissa made, the words I practiced disappeared. My body was like the vending machine in the cafeteria that wouldn't stop humming.

Melissa was my confidant, my safe harbor when I was down. I remembered when she gave me clothing out of her closet, which helped me out tremendously. Because of her drive, we stayed up into the early morning hours studying, binging on bad snacks, and watching videos during our study breaks.

It wasn't until our junior year of high school that I dreamed about Melissa in intimate ways. Some nights, the need to relieve myself was overwhelming. I would wake up in the middle of the night with my hands down my panties, as one of my hands caressed my clit. The other two fingers would be deep in my core, moaning out Melissa's name while imagining her kissing and touching my soft skin until I exploded all over my hand. Afterward, whenever we were together, I would lower my head as if she had known about my dreams.

As I took a deep breath, I steadied my trembling hands. I met Melissa in the middle of the empty classroom. She tapped her feet to the pace of my steps. Her signature vanilla perfume infiltrated my nose, which made my tongue dry up like sand at that exact moment. *Great.*

Melissa swayed back and forth. I watched as a smile touched her lips. "Kyndall, you wanted to talk. What's up?"

I rolled my tongue around my mouth to get the saliva circulating. I spoke, "Melissa, we have been friends since we were freshmen. You're my best friend. Actually, more than a best friend to me, right?"

"Yes... what's going on, Kyndall? We have to be quick. Our next class is about to start, and I can't afford to be late," Melissa responded, fiddling with the pencil behind her ear and the straps of her bookbag, as we stood in the empty classroom.

"Yes, umm, well, shit," I trailed off, as I grabbed my hands in an effort to keep them steady. But I went blank. Until I met Melissa, I had never felt a spark for any of the girls at my school. Simply put, she was everything I wanted, plus more. She was gorgeous. Melissa's golden-brown skin was soft with a dewy touch today, her heart-shaped lips coated in her favorite clear lip gloss, her long eyelashes framed her almond-shaped, hazel eyes, and her small, rounded nose had a new gold nose piercing. Today, her hair was in black braids down her back. Her favorite black skinny jeans that showed off her perfect ass were paired with an old Beyoncé t-shirt. Her ample breasts strained against the shirt, and I could see the outline of her bra.

"Kyndall, we're going to be late for class—" Melissa started, but I couldn't help myself. Something unexplainable happened to me. I was supposed to ask her to our senior prom, not shove my tongue down her throat. But I did the one thing I had been dreaming about for one year, seven months, five days, six hours, and twenty-five minutes.

Not that I was counting.

I kissed her!

I must have been hallucinating, because she opened her mouth and kissed me back. Me! Kyndall Williams. Melissa Stella Brown was kissing me. This kiss was what dreams were made of, as we explored the warm, wet insides of our mouths. All I hoped for was that she had enjoyed it as much as me. As she pulled me closer into our heated embrace, I felt her tongue slip into mine and she moaned into my mouth. We both pulled away from the kiss, panting. Before I could even open my mouth to say anything, she turned and hurried out of the room, as I stood in the classroom like an idiot. My legs wouldn't move. It was as if someone told me I would die if I moved from that spot.

After a couple of minutes, the bell rang. I snapped out of my daze and hurried to class. Luckily, the teacher had stepped out for a minute, and I slipped in without her noticing my tardiness. I slumped down into the chair, my hair stuck to my forehead, and I glanced at the desk next to me, where Melissa normally sat. It was empty. I instantly felt like shit. I couldn't help thinking that I had made the biggest mistake of my life, and not only did I lose the last chance to ask Melissa to prom, but it disrupted my friendship with her.

But she must have liked the kiss since she kissed me back, right?

After class, I asked her cousins Sage and Mercedes and their friend Bella, who had always disliked me because of our friendship, if they had seen Melissa today.

"Melissa is always with you, I don't know why, or she is always in class even if she's sick," Sage stated jokingly. As usual, she was the one with the sharp bite to her words for me. "What did your geeky ass do to our cousin?"

"Nothing! I haven't seen her since lunch," I lied. If they found out something happened between us, I knew they would make the last month of my senior year a shit show.

"Well, we'll check on her after class, anyway, since we're going to her house today," Mercedes told me, backing up her cousin.

"Okay, whatever. I'll see y'all later!" As they walked out the door, I mumbled. I didn't know that I wouldn't talk to my best friend again until prom night.

It was Saturday, senior prom night. I went because I didn't want to miss out on any of my senior year milestones. My mom and I had searched several stores to find a dress, which was hard because of my size. I wore a size twelve and was tall, about a little less than six feet, but I had an hourglass figure. I am what people would call thick, and any other time, I would own my curves. However, my mind kept returning to the kiss from yesterday. Focus proved impossible. I grew even more frustrated when my mom didn't understand that getting the perfect dress could make or break your prom night.

"I should have taken that other dress in and made it fit for you. You're too blooming picky, especially since nobody is taking you to prom," my mom scolded me in her Jamaican accent as she helped me into the dress we had purchased.

Leave it to my mom to make me feel bad for not having a date.

I sighed. "Mom, I want to make this night memorable in a good way, and I don't need a date to have fun." A total lie, but I didn't want to feel like a complete loser.

She kissed her teeth and retorted, "It would have been better if I fixed it up."

I rolled my eyes and gritted my teeth because that's my mother for you. She would never give a compliment without making it about her.

I threw up my middle finger when she turned her back to leave my bathroom to get ready for work. An intense heat of shame washed over me. With a second huff, I shook my head and walked over to my vanity.

After what felt like an eternity of getting ready, I stood in front of the mirror. My honey-brown skin looked radiant in the sky blue t-shoulder dress that stopped at mid-thigh because of my height. I got my mom to spend some money on cute, sky blue peep-toe shoes I found at TJ Maxx for cheap. I also wore the one necklace my mom owns and some diamond stud earrings. My kinky hair was silk pressed to within an inch of its life and placed in a half-up hairstyle. I just hoped I wouldn't sweat it out in this Florida heat. I did the bare minimum with my makeup because, frankly, I had no clue how to put on makeup or if I was doing it right. A light foundation, nude lipstick on my heart-shaped lips, and winged eyeliner in black. I carried the white Coach clutch my mother had purchased when times were better.

As I stood up and grabbed my phone, my foot tapped to the beat of the Destiny's Child song that I played.

Me: Hey, we're still riding together, right?

Me: K cool, see ya soon.

Melissa the diva: Yeah, that's cool. Just FYI, Nathan is driving since we're going together.

Great, there goes my night!

Me: Great, I'm ready whenever you're ready. Oh, you have a date?

Melissa the diva: We'll be there in ten minutes. My mom is taking about a hundred pictures of us. Yeah, he asked me at the last minute, and no one else had asked me, so I accepted.

It should have been me, but I messed up.

Mom reappeared in the bathroom, and I watched her frown in the mirror. I chucked my phone in my purse.

"You're gorgeous, Kyndall. Why are you fixin' your face like that?"

"It's nothing. Just a little disappointed, is all," I grumbled.

"Ah, boy trouble, isn't it? I can tell," She said and winked.

I watched as my mom gave me a sympathetic smile. If only she knew my disappointment was over Melissa or how I repulsed my best friend with my kiss. She would have dropped dead.

My head shook as I held back a laugh. "Yeah, something like that. I'm okay, Mom, really," I said as I hugged and kissed her goodbye while I hurried her out of my room and watched her walk to the front door.

"Have a good night at work," I yelled.

She stopped before shutting the door and yelled, "Forget those boys, Kyndall! Have a great time and take lots of pictures. This is your last night together, rude girl." She slammed the door shut.

"Huh, okay." I shook my head because my mother was forgetful.

Graduation would be the last event, and then college.

After ten minutes of walking a hole into the carpet, I got a text from Melissa saying they were waiting downstairs for me. As I walked out into the balmy Florida night, my mood flipped like a light switch. Gone were my nervous ticks. In their place growled the heated green-eyed monster. When I walked to the car, I noticed Melissa looking at me, her lips slightly parted. I saw her eyes roam my body, and the tip of her tongue swiped over her red lips. I paused, and her eyes found mine. It was like time slowed down.

Nathan popped out of nowhere, greeted me with a compliment, and opened the door for me. Nathan Thomas wore a black tuxedo with a red-accented dress shirt and bow tie to match Melissa. He looked handsome, but I was too bitter to admit it. I rolled my eyes and got into the car.

Melissa greeted me and kept everything neutral as I fought the urge to press my lips into a thin line. As we started driving, Nathan kept the conversation going. He was so nice that it made me sick. I stuck with scrolling on my phone as I acted like it was the most interesting thing on this planet. I would glance up and catch Melissa staring at me through the side-view mirrors.

Maybe my eyes were playing tricks on me.

After the ten minute drive to the gymnasium, we found a spot to park, and I wracked my brains for ways to flee the stifling sunny dispositions of Nathan and Melissa. As I exited the car, I wanted to leave them there, but I wasn't trying to be rude since Nathan was nothing but pleasant to me.

Nathan helped Melissa out of the car and I gasped as the warmth pooled in my stomach. She was an angel. Melissa's red strapless dress hugged all her curves, and her dress was so short that if she bent over, you would see everything. She had diamond earrings and the birthstone necklace I bought her for her birthday two years back. Her hair was in a top bun with loose hair that framed her face. Makeup was barely present other than her black winged eyeliner, and her golden skin shimmered. Her shoes and purse matched her dress.

Self-preservation aside, the way her body looked in that dress had me clenching my thighs together as my clit throbbed.

This was pure torture.

"You look amazing, Kyndall. I love that dress on you, and your hair is gorgeous." Melissa finally acknowledged my attire. As she enveloped me in her warm French vanilla essence, I felt like a pervert because her nipples hardened through her dress, which made me flush. Melissa pulled away abruptly, and I had seen the same heated gaze flash in her eyes, but it disappeared as soon as she blinked.

"Thank you, and you look amazing. I see you're wearing the necklace I bought you. It looks beautiful on you." She turned to Nathan, but not before her cheeks turned light pink, which left me scratching my head. But then I looked down and noticed my nipples fought with my dress to gain attention. I blushed and moved to cover them.

All that from a hug, pathetic!

As we neared the gym, we heard the DJ playing Rihanna's "Birthday Cake" as we got closer. Nathan and Melissa were ahead of me, and I hung back a bit to scrutinize them. I prayed they wouldn't turn around because they would see my lips twisted at just how good they complemented each other.

When we entered the gym, dim lights and chatter amongst the attendees greeted us. Melissa and Nathan stopped at the makeshift gold, white, and black photo booth as we entered. I didn't want to seem like a weirdo who waited for them, so I walked further into the main gym area and looked like a weirdo anyway, by the way I had gawked at the decorations. The gym had been transformed into a vibrant dance hall, with colorful lights illuminating the walls. The air was thick with the heavy scent of perfume that had replaced the usual musty smell of sweaty students. A definite improvement from smelling like a sweaty locker room. They boldly outlined our school colors, black and gold, everywhere throughout the gym. Gold and black balloons decorated the DJ booth, and when I looked closer, I noticed someone had filled the gold balloons with black glitter. I stood in front of the giant room with my mouth agape.

My arms stuck to my sides, as I tried my hardest not to look like a loner by going to find Melissa's cousins and Bella's table. I searched for them in the open gym amongst the sea of students. My search didn't last long since they took up residence at the refreshment table. Student volunteers worked around them, filling drinks, passing out napkins, and re-stocking snack bowls. I walked over and noted gold-covered tablecloths and black balloons on the tables surrounding the dance floor.

When I got to their table, I said my hellos and ignored them when they told me they're shocked I looked good and fashionable for once. My eyes rolled of their own accord as I took my once-in-a-lifetime half-assed compliment. "Hey guys, y'all look good," Melissa remarked, as she walked to the table and gave the group a hug.

They chatted while I observed as my classmates danced, and a few, like me, sat out. I wished I could be as carefree as them. Melissa glowed while she spoke with her cousins; instant guilt followed. She looked at her cousins as if they were the only people in the room. A remnant of jealousy seeped through my body. A feverish heat touched my cheek, and I played with the soft gold cloth on the table that reminded me of the one my mother had at home.

I should have told her the kiss was a mistake and preferred having her friendship rather than losing her as my best friend. I blinked fast to stop the tears threatening to fall as everyone but me hit the floor. My loneliness fed my depression. When Sage got tired and returned to the table, I asked for some of the alcohol she had snuck in to calm my nerves. I chugged the drink down and regretted it as the heat and bitter aftertaste followed.

I will get used to it because I need something to get me through the night.

Throughout the night, Melissa and I met up twice at the refreshment table. I blocked any view of her when she snuck alcohol into the punch. Melissa grabbed my hand, which caused an electric bolt to my core, and we went to take pictures at the booth. I almost broke my neck when her hand palmed my ass, causing the photographer to yell at us, and as we retook the photo, this time with her hand on the small of my back. Melissa looked on like she hadn't just groped me, which made me wonder if Sage had brought extra-strong liquor tonight.

Am I going crazy?

I wanted to return to my post on the sidelines, but a group from my English class hoarded the space. We chatted, and they dragged me to the dancefloor so I could embarrass myself even more. The DJ changed the music to Neyo's "Let Me Love You" and I let loose. As I closed my eyes, I dipped and maneuvered my body into the music. The music faded to another song as I opened my eyes. That's when I noticed I somehow glided over to our little group during my drunken dance fit. When I turned to Melissa, her eyebrows were almost in her hairline, and her almond-shaped eyes were wide.

It wasn't until I chugged my third cup of Sage and her friends stash that I thought I may have pushed my limit too far. I couldn't tell if everything in the gym was swaying or if it was my mind playing tricks on me. I promised never to drink that much again if I made it home. As I tried to make sense of everything, I squinted around, but it was fruitless. The red dress that Melissa wore called my name, as I locked onto her as she headed toward me. She stumbled into my arms.

"Let's get out of here," she shouted over her hiccups.

I nodded, and she grabbed me by my arm. She pulled out her flask, chugged whatever she was drinking, and offered me some. I took a sip, gagged, but swallowed because I didn't want to seem weak. As we stumbled out of the gym, we looked like a mess. The warm heat of the night washed over me.

Poor Nathan looked on as he watched us stumble into the car.

I don't remember how long it took to get back to my house, but the next thing I knew, my body had dropped onto my bed. When I sat back up, I froze. I had only dreamed of the scene in front of me. Melissa was naked. This wasn't the first time I had seen her naked, but the stirring, heated look she gave me was new.

I shook my head, which made the room spin. I raised my hands to grab my head, but Melissa beat me to it, as she held my face between her hands and started kissing me. This kiss wasn't the one we shared in the classroom, which was messy and rushed. No, the kiss was filled with enough heat to scorch my apartment building. As Melissa deepened the kiss, she stroked my entire mouth with her tongue. I didn't even remember when Melissa grabbed the zipper of my dress and pulled the dress to my hips. I finally broke the kiss, and we both sounded like two panting, drunk fools.

"A-Are you sure you want to do this with me?" I squeaked out. If she answered no, I would burst into tears.

She helped me get up to remove the rest of the dress and my panties. Standing this close, her body heat radiated against my skin. She pushed me onto the bed, straddled my thighs, and leaned over to whisper in my ear. "All I've been thinking about tonight is how I want to fuck you until you scream my name, Kyndall."

Is this really happening?

"O-Ok," I responded, dumbfounded, and my core became a slick, heated mess.

I was at a loss for words, and my mind failed to come up with the right move. Was this real, or was my cruel mind punishing me again? I waited too long to be with her. As she adjusted her position over me, my cheap dildo rolled out from under my pillow. With a smirk and a raised eyebrow, she grabbed it. Something about her look made me grow wetter between my thighs.

She gave me a quick kiss on the lips and continued to place kisses down my neck until she got to my breasts, which weren't as big as her C-cups, but were perfect for her, or so I assume because the next thing I knew, she stuck one of my sensitive, hard nipples in her mouth, and released it with a pop—wetting the dry and tender peak. She wrapped her mouth over my other nipple while squeezing and pulling the wet one. Whimpers and moans escaped my lips. My back arched, making it easier for her to devour my breasts. Midway through her torture, she switched nipples again. Melissa sucked and lightly bit, as she teased with her hand.

Everywhere she touched—with her lips, fingers, or even the soft inside of her forearm that grazed my stomach as she cupped my breast—I ached for more. I came, releasing control over my body altogether. I moved to sit up and something cold was under my ass. Fuck, my arousal was making a wet spot on the bed! I squeezed my legs together, hoping to hide it as best I could, but when I glanced up, I found Melissa staring me down, her eyes lit with fire.

Melissa chuckled and bit back a smile. "Don't worry, baby. I'll make you come again."

My clit throbbed with my heartbeat as her words sent another wave of heat to my burning core. Until now, my only sexual experience had been with my ex-boyfriend about a year ago. This was all new to me. I whimpered, "Please, Melissa." She continued to press kisses from my wet nipples to my mound.

Moisture formed on my top lip. I uttered the first thing that came to my mind, "Please, Melissa, I want you to make me cum."

She smirked against the top of my mound, making me bite back my smile while I lifted myself onto my elbows. Just in time for Melissa to drag her tongue the entire length of my pussy. I thanked God that my mother worked at night because no adult needed to hear the pleasure-induced scream I let out.

I needed to feel more of her. I scooted myself closer to her, and Melissa took that moment to clamp her mouth onto my engorged clit. A scream ripped through me again, and I hoped the neighbors didn't hear me. She giggled while she continued to suck and flick my sensitive clit, and my hand gained a mind of its own and grabbed onto the back of her head. The next thing I knew, she stuck her tongue right into my burning core as she used her right hand to continue to work my clit until my legs buckled. I tried to close my legs, but Melissa's hands flew up and wrapped around them with an iron grip on my thighs to keep them from moving. The building sensation was too much, and I screamed Melissa's name with my next release. I dropped to the bed; spent from my release. But Melissa was apparently determined not to be done as she grabbed my hip and pulled me closer to the edge of the bed, as she bit her bottom lip.

I felt clammy from my neck to my lower back, and she grabbed my dildo from my bed. "I want to fuck you with your dildo. Can I do that, love?" She leaned over and nibbled on my lips as she waited for my answer.

Shit. My exhaustion dissipated with the promise of another round. While, by some magic, I pulled myself together, my following words came out as a whimper: "Yes, you can."

She smiled against my lips, and I almost came undone again, right there from her excitement.

I widened my jellified legs, and Melissa centered the dildo at my entrance. She was about to push it in, but she stopped. She turned to face me with misty eyes. "You know I love you, right? You're the best thing that's ever happened to me, no matter what I do. That will always be true, Kyn, right?"

I felt overwhelmed by the swirling thoughts and sensations that filled my head. Melissa gave me a soft kiss, and I declared, "Yes, I love you more than you know, and I want us to try this new relationship—"

The next thing I knew, she pushed the dildo in slowly. She waited for me to adjust to the size, and when I was ready, she fucked me with slow steady strokes while she kissed, licked, and held me. I never wanted this to end.

See, I'd had sex multiple times with my ex-boyfriend, but this sex was beyond pleasure. This was like heaven on earth.

Melissa moved from kissing and licking me to whisper how much she loved me; how beautiful I was and how I was hers forever.

She moved her free hand to rub and pinch my clit as I moved my hand to help get her off. She grabbed my wrist and announced, "No, not yet, love. I will let you know when I'm ready."

I turned to holding her head as she brought me to the edge again. I swear I was two seconds away from a meltdown, from all the emotions and lingering warmth from the alcohol.

She removed my dildo right before I was about to have another orgasm. I protested, but she silenced me with a scorching kiss before she pulled away. I asked, "Why did you stop—"

She pushed the toy back in and fucked me fast. She grabbed the hand closest to her and guided it to the soft warm wetness between her legs. I stuck two fingers in her and was going to thumb her clit, but she pressed her hand into mine, flattening it against her wet pussy, and rode my fingers to the beat as she fucked me with my toy.

She was such a fucking sex goddess. My eyes followed her as she chased her release until I couldn't take it anymore. My release hit me hard as black dots painted my vision. After two more seconds, Melissa tightened around my fingers. All I could do was stare as her beautiful face twisted with pleasure when she did. I gave her time to recover from her release, then withdrew my wet, sopping fingers.

"Open up, Ky," she purred.

I opened up, and she stuck my fingers in my mouth. Her essence's sweet and salty taste burst into my mouth. My mouth memorized it, determined to never forget. She removed the dildo from my core and licked off my juices, and we shared one last kiss that tasted like a mix of both of us.

I chewed my lower lip. Cleared my throat and asked, "Would you stay with me?"

She paused. "I have to leave super early. Maybe I should go home," Melissa stated.

"I will set the alarm and wake you up," I asserted.

She nibbled on her lower lip, smiled wide, and said, "Alright. Kyndall?" She slid in and spooned me naked.

"Yeah."

"I love you," and she kissed me on my shoulder.

"I love you more, Melissa,"

As I fell asleep to her favorite French vanilla perfume on my pillow, I couldn't help but smile at our new beginning.

To my surprise, I woke up alone. Not even the alarm woke me. As I held my phone in my hand, I could see the alarm I had set had been switched off. My room looked like nothing had happened the night before. I pushed the negative thoughts to the deserted corner of my mind.

Today was a new day. I was beyond cloud nine right now. I was up and dressed, feeling energized. The craziest thing happened when I texted if she got home safely while I made breakfast. The text bounced back. I called her number and got the disconnected phone number message. My mouth turned down. I checked her social media. The last update was before our prom started. A prickly sensation crept up and down my back.

This isn't like Melissa. She's generally up by now.

Abandoning my food, I ran up the block to her house at the end of our road and rang the doorbell. No one answered. I looked inside of her window, even though I hated being seen as a Peeping Tom, and the place was empty.

What! The! Fuck!

Feeling used and confused, I headed back to my house and bumped into my mom returning from work. We climbed the stairs into the apartment together.

"Hey Kyndall, how was your big night?" she inquired sleepily.

"It was good," I lied, and my face heated because I couldn't comprehend anything at that moment. The small talk would kill me, especially when the voice in my head nagged me to find Melissa.

"I bet, especially since it was Melissa's last day here in Orlando," she added coolly, as she headed to the kitchen to make something to eat.

"Excuse me? What did you say, Mom?" I looked at her with wide eyes. My head was still foggy from my hangover.

"Melissa's mom told me they were moving to California. They're leaving early in the morning, at around three A.M., I think. Did you not know?"

My mom stared at me with her eyebrows scrunched up. I didn't even stay to respond as my mom called my name. I ran to my room and back to bed, feeling like an idiot.

My mom found me in my bed. "Do you want to talk about it?"

"No, I don't," I choked out because my mother wouldn't understand.

"Well, if you want to talk about it, then let me know." She stood in the door frame for a bit before leaving the room.

All the things she said about loving me, about how I was hers, were lies.

The following Monday, Melissa's cousins re-confirmed what my Mom told me. Melissa had moved away and would finish her last month through virtual school.

"You mean your best friend, your third nipple, didn't tell you she was moving?" Sage pestered. I pretended not to care. Exhaustion from being unable to sleep seeped in from the long nights of crying.

My mother recognized that I had no energy to do anything. I couldn't tell anyone about my feelings for Melissa, especially my mom, because she would kick me out of the house.

If there's one thing she can't stand, it is homosexuality.

Recluse became my middle name. School was the only thing I came out of my room for. I spent my free time in bed with my door shut, in hopes I could cry without my mother hearing. Graduation became just another day for me. It was no longer a joyous moment for me. Not when the person I loved and trusted the most had hurt me in a way I never expected, leaving me feeling emotionally broken.

It was my fault for having a dream about us being together. Like anyone would want someone like me.

Such a big freaking dummy, Kyndall!

After graduation, I thought I could block my issues, but my depression worsened.

I notified the Florida A&M University registrar that I wanted to give up my freshman spot, even though I would lose the admission fee. Bitterness welled in my heart. Melissa and I had applied and accepted our spots together. We had promised to be roommates and support each other financially and emotionally. If she wasn't going there, there was no way I could afford to go to FAMU.

Instead, I went to a local community college. Performed poorly in my first two semesters, which led to me failing my first year. My concentration was shot. I wasn't motivated. The hope that I would ever become a teacher, my dream career, was over. Even if I got my certification now, would any job interviewer hire a teacher with a history of failing grades?

It would take almost two years to get my life back together. I was mentally tired of being tired. So, when I got my first job, I started therapy.

As a part of my recovery phase, I had to come out to my mom, who took the news as well as I thought she would. She cursed me out and kicked me out of her home for being "possessed by the devil." Later, I found out she told everyone who would listen about my wicked ways. They also turned their noses up at me.

And I also wrote *her* a letter, per my therapist's homework. It was extremely short. It went like this:

Dear Melissa,

Fuck you and your shitty ways.

Kyndall

My therapist stated this was not the type of letter she meant for me to write. I told her that's all Melissa's worth. I kept the letter even though I knew Melissa would never see it. It reminded me to never fall in love.

Love ruined you.

Chapter 1

KYNDALL

Ten years later

I AM A STRONG Black Woman!

I am strong!

I am worthy!

I breathed in slowly as I repeated my daily affirmations. Those words have kept me grounded and sane. Well, for the past eight years, after they had deemed me okay enough for my therapy sessions to be reduced.

As I sat on the bed, I glanced at my clock. My post-slumber ritual had taken too long. My ass needed to get up and move or I might as well lay right back down and cancel today. In the back of my head, I heard my wallet chew me out and my tattered Betsey Johnson bag glared at me. I groaned as I hauled my ass up.

With a sigh, I shuffled into my bathroom and turned my shower to the hottest level my home plumbing would allow. I stepped in.

When I exited the shower, I stopped to look at myself in the mirror.

My twenties had been good to me. My skin had cleared away the few childhood blemishes, which made me gleam. The art of makeup was something I had finally learned. I stopped critiquing myself because I had nitpicked to the point that I drove myself insane. Having mastered complex techniques and the intricate use of many products, I just decided less is more. Like my talented sister Queen Beyoncé sang, "Comfortable in my skin, cozy with who I am." I typically stuck with clear lip gloss, and maybe if I was feeling adventurous, I might apply a winged tip eyeliner. After losing my patience , I relaxed my 4C natural hair. It had become a tremendous burden to maintain. I now wore my hair loose and falling to my mid-back and dyed honey blonde. The hair dye was one adventure I wanted to continue.

I threw on some of my favorite black skinny jeans and a white cami with a built-in bra because my boobs look amazing in it. I went to my little shoe closet by the kitchen and dug out my black leather thigh boots. Afterwards, I slipped on my badass leather jacket, and munched on the spinach wrap sandwich I grabbed from the kitchen. I was in heaven as I shoveled the wrap into my mouth when my phone rang, and thank goodness it did, because I would have left it on the bed from when I was scrolling through my social media page. I got to the phone just in time to answer the call.

"Hello," I panted.

"Hey K, you, okay? You sound like you just ran a marathon." Alex, my cousin, said.

"I'm good. I left my phone in my room and had to haul ass to get it. What's going on?" I inquired.

"Oh, I was checking on you to see if you wanted to come out with the girls and me tonight. We're celebrating Maxine's birthday," she inquired. I would have told her yes, but some of the ladies she hung out with were questionable. When I was twenty-one, I made the mistake of attending one of Alex's girls' nights. I ended up knocked out in front of my cousin's boyfriend's house, with nothing but my panties and a man's tank shirt on because I mistook the front lawn for a bedroom. When I awoke, Alex's best friend, Jody, huffed out, "I'm not going to watch a grown woman when she's drunk off her ass."

That was the last time I had over two drinks.

Yes, I'm a lightweight, and I recognize that.

"No, Alex, it's Sunday. I'm going to relax after doing some errands."

She huffed. "Come on, Kyndall. You never want to go out with me or the girls anymore."

"Did you forget I haven't been a drinker in seven years?" I asked, a little too vigorously.

"I know, but you can come to The Little Hut and just hang out with us," she appealed. I love my cousin, but Alex sometimes has her priorities mixed up.

My foot beat a rhythm on the floor. "Okay, but I won't stay long."

"Thank God I can finally get you out of the house."

"Don't thank Him just yet," I barked out. "I can still change my mind." I knew I sounded bitchy, but I gave up the bar and club scene a while ago.

"Okay, cranky pants. I will see you at nine at the Hut. Love ya." She hung up before I could even form the word goodbye.

Jeez

Alexandra Grant saved my life after my mother threw me out for being bisexual. During my Orlando years, I worked for one of the major theme parks, and I had about five dollars to my name after I paid my bills and insurance each month. I slept in the local mall parking lot and used their bathroom to get ready for work when I couldn't afford a room at a motel. When the park let me go, I lasted two weeks couch surfing. After those lonesome fourteen days, I called Alex and begged for help. I had no one else to call. My mom had called all our relatives and told them I was the devil reincarnated, that I wanted to live like the people of Sodom and Gomorrah.

The most hurtful rejection had come from my aunt in Houston. All my life up to that point, she was the only aunt who sent me anything on holidays and my birthday, the only one who seemed to care about me, besides my Mom. After Mom's phone call, she told me she would never in this world, or the next, have someone as vile as me in her home. I cried and didn't stop until the plane landed in New York City.

I'd visited Alex in New York once before, a long time ago. I fell in love with the city after that one time. It excited me to start this new chapter in my life. But when I arrived, I found that city living on minimum wage was damn near impossible. Yes, I lived with my cousin for a short time, which allowed me to save a bit, but I found that if I didn't work every hour of every day, it was next to impossible to survive living in the city.

My cousin, meanwhile, wore the latest designer clothing, bought a new Lexus SUV, all cash, and spent excessively. One night, she ordered enough lobster for me, herself, and her four friends. I gaped at the total when the meals arrived. Suddenly, my naivety gave way to suspicion, and I heard the tiny voice in my head to ask her about her income.

"Alex!" I yelled, barging into her room on Sunday afternoon.

"Is there a fire? Robbery?" She ran out of the bathroom, half-dressed.

"No, please put some clothes on. You're blinding me!" I blurted, as she stared at me.

Alex rolled her eyes. "You came into my room when the door was closed."

I beamed lovingly. "Yes, I did, and I am sorry, my favorite cousin—"

"What do you want? You know I hate when you try to butter me up," she demanded as she continued to get dressed.

"Okay, I'm going to be straightforward and ask you. What the heck do you do to afford this house and all the shit in it?"

"You're noisy, Kyn." She wrinkled her nose. "I hustle to make ends meet."

"Okay, that's very ominous. Explain more, and this better not be some crazy mob shit."

"It's not that bad. I am what you would call a kind of falcon for Marcus' gang. Nothing heavy, just light work and lots of money." She shrugged, like it was normal to work for a gang.

"Are you mad?" I suggested, bug-eyed.

Marcus was Alex's longtime boyfriend and an attractive man on the outside, but ugly as sin on the inside. I had the displeasure of meeting Marcus once, and that was one time too many. He was a bit of an asshole to me from the moment Alex introduced us, but I let it slide because even if I had mentioned it to Alex, she would have ignored it. Sometimes it's good to mind your own business.

"Listen, Kay. I recognize you like to be Ms. Goody Two-Shoes. If you want to live paycheck to paycheck and be poor your whole life, that's on you. But what I do is simple, and mostly, I am in and out before any shit goes down," she answered.

"Okay, this is crazy. What does a falcon do?" I inquired, confused.

"Well, I scope out places. Normally, at a bar or a club, the day before or the day of, I get a picture of the place and report anything that seems suspicious to Marcus or whoever I'm working for. In and out. Just have to make it look like I'm a regular customer."

"All you do is case the place and return the information? You don't handle any product or have to shank anyone?" I asked. This seemed too easy.

"Kyndall, grow up," she crossed her arms. "I would never do anything to endanger my life. The world would cry 'cause I am too sexy to leave this earth early." She twirled around.

Humph, that is debatable.

Did Alex lie, though? No, she was a beauty. She had deep mocha skin, round light brown eyes, and wide lips that fit her round face. All of that wrapped in an athletic body.

"No, you wouldn't do anything like that. How much do you make?" I urged.

"It depends on the job. I can make five to ten thousand per night."

"Excuse me? Just for scoping out a place?"

"Yes, sometimes I get in and out within an hour, and I am home by midnight."

"How much do you make in a month?"

"Anywhere from fifteen to thirty thousand, depending on how much I work that month."

I gawked. "Can I get in on this?"

It sounded irrational, but I trusted my cousin and was honestly tired of struggling. I longed for a place to call my own, and to live out my introverted ways. Also, I like to wear as little clothing as possible at home and living with my cousin prevented me from doing that.

That day, I decided it was feast or famine. I could either stay on the same stagnant path or move forward. I didn't know what tomorrow had in store for me, but I knew one thing for sure: I would come out on top.

Chapter 2

KYNDALL

"Now boarding Flight 366 with services from Hartsfield–Jackson Atlanta International Airport to LaGuardia Airport."

I shook myself out of my preflight sleepiness as I hauled my few belongings from the airport lobby to the plane. After my last job, I needed a mini staycation. Since I'd joined my cousin as a "falcon," I'd been traveling nonstop. The first couple of months were terrible. I didn't have a poker face and had the shakes anytime I practiced. My cousin's boyfriend berated me and called me a naïve noob—which pissed me off, then it kicked me into gear.

Did I mention how much I hate that dude?

I trained with Alex for five months before I went at it alone. One major lesson I learned was how to hide my emotions and play my hired role. I lurked around, watched people, and copied from the guys in Marcus' crew. I became an expert at my profession within the year, and word spread in the allied gangs about me.

The Marcus cash well started drying up a couple of months into my second year. I picked up contracts in different locations and branched out from New York. Yes, I could have just stuck to New York, but I got more high-paying gigs outside of New York.

By then, I had my own furnished home, a car, a garage, which is gold in Queens, and money in my savings. With more money, I could stretch my time between gigs longer.

I looked around the small plane. A couple with their child sat next to me. As I watched, the kid read a book to his father. A smile touched my lips. I'd been on the road so long that I forgot what my primary goal was when I started, a family of my own. After this contract, I wanted something solid to return home to. No more flings. I wanted something more permanent. I wanted to find the perfect man and woman that completed me.

When I got around to exploring my sexuality, I knew something was amiss by being with one person, and it just didn't cut it for me. I wanted my cake, and I wanted to eat it, too. It was important to be in a relationship with a man and a woman. Lately, I resorted to picking them out at a club, taking them back home. We would rock each other's world, and I would be gone before the sun rises. But not anymore. I wanted to focus on my longer term goals.

It's easier said than done.

"Good afternoon, passengers, the time is now three-thirty P.M. Eastern Standard Time, and we will land in five minutes," the pilot droned.

Finally!

The best part of this type of work is when I fly home, I can truly relax and unwind. Whenever I went out, I dreamed of my bed and my Kindle. That's the ultimate introverted Kyndall dream.

As we were let off the plane, I dashed to Starbucks to get a venti French vanilla cappuccino before I headed to the luggage area. By the time I arrived at baggage claim, coffee in hand, I realized I needn't have rushed. It was taking forever and a day to retrieve our luggage. That is the reason I bring the bare minimum, but on this trip, I stopped and explored Atlanta before I returned home. I packed extra crap and was now full of regret.

I walked over to an airport worker. "Hello, my flight landed fifteen minutes ago, and we are still waiting for our luggage. Is there an ETA?"

The worker sighed and rolled her eyes. "Hello, ma'am. Sorry for the inconvenience, but we're running behind because of an unforeseeable problem. We will have your luggage out as soon as possible." Her accent was a combination of the classic New York twang with a nasal quality.

I clenched my jaw together. "Thank you, ma'am."

The one thing I missed about the South is the hospitality. If they killed you on the sidewalk, New Yorkers would step over you and keep going.

Then again, there are miserable folks everywhere. I shrugged and tried my best to stick to myself and avoid stupid conflicts.

I sat on the conveyor belt rail and waited. I watched as a group of tourists around me fumbled about with scrunched up expressions on their faces. They reminded me of myself when I first arrived in New York City by myself, after losing my family to their homophobia. I was a bundle of uncertainty, from being baffled to unsure of my future. I was so out of it; I had mistakenly gotten into the wrong taxi line that was headed into Manhattan and not the boroughs. The taxi driver let out a few curse words in Spanish that I could pick up from my sparse Spanish lessons.

The baggage carousel clunked and groaned. Shaking away the old memories, I chuckled, stood, and spotted my lonely neon green Samsonite luggage. My grandmother always said you had to buy the brightest luggage. It would ensure that no one would try to steal your bag. I missed my grandmother on days like today. If she had been alive, I believed things would have worked out differently.

Retrieving my car presented no hassle, and the drive out of the airport was uneventful. I rolled down my window, relaxed, and enjoyed Queens' older red brick buildings, the different bodegas, and local shops. I searched all over Queens for the perfect house to rent, and I fell in love with the Forest Hills area. In some ways, it reminded me of some parts of Orlando. I wanted to stay in Queens to be close to Alex.

Through the years, Alex and I had grown close—she remained the only family I had left to count on. Her best friend, Jody, had grown to tolerate me, as Jody and I became allies for once.

You know the old saying about keeping your enemies close.

I smoothly parked my car in the garage and breathed contentment. Gathering my bag, I watched the garage door rumble down and seal me in my little paradise. Gratitude rushed into my heart as I sauntered in. I was fortunate to find this rental. Three bedrooms with two full baths, soapstone counters, and hardwood floors are difficult to find here. My bedroom was the largest of the three, while I used the one as a guest room, or should I say Alex's room, and my reading room. I went to a big box store and got the most comfortable furniture I could afford on a budget. Alex called me cheap because I would not go to a local high end boutique store to get my furniture.

Of course, I just rolled my eyes.

Unlike her, I never got into the brand name obsession, and when I get that itch, I go to a discount department store like Ross, because I would forever act broke, even though I had a bit of money saved up. I would always pretend to be broke, like how I was raised.

I stripped and headed to the shower. After thirty minutes of scrubbing the airport scum off my body, I flopped down on my oversized teal sofa and turned on Netflix to watch *The Sandman*. Before the episode could finish, my phone rang. With a deep sigh, I answered.

"Hey, Alex."

"Hey, Kyn, glad you got in safely. You could have called or texted me you made it back home."

"You're right. I'm sorry. I wanted to get home and scrub the germs away from the airport." A deep sigh escaped me as I realized Alex was correct, and she was painfully aware of it. She refused to change her mind once she had convinced herself she was correct. It was usually her way or the highway. That was the primary reason I stopped taking jobs with her as soon as I was okay on my own.

In my ear, Alex murmured, "Well, since you're back, we can go out tonight to celebrate."

"I just got into my pajamas, Alex. I am not going back out." That's the cold-hearted truth. It's final once I have this bonnet on.

"Fine, I won't force it this time since you have a good excuse, but you're coming to The Little Hut this weekend. We can hang out with Jody and the girls."

I facepalmed, but I responded, "Okay, I will stop by for an hour or two to say hi to everyone."

Alex's voice lowered to a mock threat. "Absolutely not! You'll stay the whole time, and I won't hear anything about it."

I pinched the bridge of my nose because my cousin always knew how to annoy me. "Okay, I will see you then. I need to find something to eat. Kiss Maxwell for me, and I will see you on Saturday."

Maxwell was her infant son, whom she and Marcus had about six months ago. Maxwell was the best thing that happened to her. I figured being pregnant would slow her down some, but she gained this extra boost of perseverance after giving birth.

"Okay. Love you."

"Love you too, and wear something sexy. We can find a couple to knock the cobwebs out of that coochie of yours!" she snickered.

I kissed my teeth and cursed her after I hung up the phone.

"Welp, there goes my chill night." I muttered as I flipped the television off.

I gravitated towards my reading room, my eyes searched for the familiar walls. This room was my favorite room in my home. I found an oversized teal beanie chair at the thrift store and fell in love with it. I paired it with indoor hanging lights that were bright enough to read in but low enough to sleep in. On the wall opposite the bean chair, I have my prized bookshelf stuffed with books and little ornaments, which made the white walls pop. I spent most of my time at home here. Bonus points for it also being the quietest room in the house. This was the only place I could unburden myself and show my emotions because I knew no one would come here unless I invited them in, which is never. Neither Alex nor Jody had seen this room.

After I picked out a new book on my Kindle, I snuggled up on the bean chair with a comforter and read until I passed out.

The next couple of days flew by in a daze. I completed my usual post-job ritual of detoxing my brain and soul by reading all day, eating, and running errands.

Before I knew it, it was Saturday night, and I had to make myself presentable for the night out with Alex and her friends. Dread filled me as the time to leave approached. I knew I would use days' worth of my patience on this single night. My only consolation was I timed my arrival for later in the evening, which meant they were likely three or four drinks deep. I knew I had made the right decision when I spotted them.

I would be home within the hour if I played my cards correctly.

As I greeted everyone, I found a seat at the big table near Jody and Alex. Counting glasses and knowing temperaments, I guessed that Alex and her girls had already polished off two rounds of D'ussé and were heading toward a Red Stripe beer.

"Hey, Alex. Hey Jody. Y'all started early, I see." I shook my head. I mean, shit, it was only nine-thirty pm.

"HEEYY, Kyndall—" Alex, Jody, and their three friends giggled and hiccupped out in unison as they swayed in their seats to the beat of the music.

"Can I get y'all some food or water?" I asked.

"Do not come in here and fuck up the vibe!" Jody barked out. I rolled my eyes and just shook my head.

"Okay, I am sorry, Jody, I won't fuck up your vibe," I smirked while I rolled my eyes.

"Good, and don't—you—for—get, it!" Alex barely got out, in between her hiccupping.

I shook my head again and let them go back to drinking and chatting while I people watched. Jamaica, Queens, was home to The Little Hut. From the outside, the little bar was nothing special, only the neon green "The Little Hut" sign showcased the bar. They decorated the inside in the colors of the Jamaican flag. The bar was colored black with green and yellow bar stools. On the wall behind the bar was a massive portrait of Bob Marley—bigger than anything I had seen before. The rest of the tables in the bar had wide wooden benches and chairs painted green, red, black, and yellow. Light red, yellow, and green colors appeared on the wall to complement the tropical table and wall decorations. The brown stained floors were extremely shiny tonight. This bar had always been warm and inviting, and I honestly didn't mind tagging along. Though I would never tell Alex or Jody that, I would never hear the end of it.

The owner of the bar knew my family from back in Jamaica. I waved to him, and he returned the gesture. He had always been nice to me. When my family cast me out, he was one of the family friends who still treated me as a human. When he saw me a little after my arrival here, he told me he judges people by their character and not by whom they shared a bed with. I decided I liked him from that day forward.

The rest of the bar was jam-packed, typical for a Saturday. Everyone was drinking, talking, and swaying to the beat. The small makeshift stage had a local reggae artist playing their latest tunes.

"Want to dance with me, Kyndall?" Jody asked. She's drunk, so I give her a pointed look.

"No, you go ahead," I shouted over the music.

"Fine, party pooper!" she yelled back.

Alex and Jody had danced before, but this was different. As they stumbled to the floor, I watched them give their best version of dancehall moves. I could not tell if they were trying to be funny, but I sat there laughing my ass off while sipping on my beer. I caught the sight of a red dress that was the same color Melissa wore all those years ago, as I stared at the young dancer whose skin resembled onyx, black and beautiful.

I shook the silly thought out of my head before I went down a fruitless path.

When I could peel my eyes from the dancefloor, I glanced around the little bar. My neck and shoulders tensed from the feeling of someone staring a hole in the side of my head. When I glanced over my shoulder, I saw a guy with dark skin and locs that glistened in the bar's lowlight, like a God. It was as if he could see into my soul as his stare heated my core. I didn't want to give him any ideas, but I guess I gave off the wrong signal because I could only watch as his hardened body walked over to me. Frozen in my seat, I watched as he stalked toward me. I had told myself no more one-night stands. I needed to get serious about my dating habits if I wanted a family. Knowing that I was on a fresh path, I knew I had to stay away from picking up guys from bars, especially if there wasn't a girl with him. I put on my expert blank face, keeping all my emotions locked in a tiny corner of my mind.

"Hey beautiful, what's your name?" he inquired in a deep voice that made my panties moist.

"Jessica, and what's your name, handsome?" Time to play along until I could decide what to do.

"My name is Donovan, but everyone calls me Biggs."

"Well, nice to meet you, Biggs. Is there something particular I can help you with?" I requested, straight with no chaser.

"Damn, it's like that, Jessie!" He smiled. "Well, I wanted to see if you wanted to go out sometime," he joked, keeping his smile.

That smile was fucking perfect. Biggs had straight, blinding white teeth. His huge, lopsided smile could keep me trapped for years to come. He was cocky and knew it.

"Oh. Okay, I will if you bring your wife along. We can all have a good time. Do you think you can handle that?" I requested as I batted my eyes and gave him a smoldering look.

He looked at me, shocked, and sputtered. "What? I am not married—" He stopped mid-sentence after I grabbed his huge left hand and showed him the light mark from his ring. Years of being observant paid off on all aspects of my life. He snatched his hand back from me.

He kissed his teeth, "You're not worth the trouble, you sodomite."

I rolled my eyes. Same old shit, just a different day. "Damn, you're old school! Too bad it didn't work out. You're only useful as a silent extra in my post-bar masturbation session," I told him, already turning around to look for my group. Alex greeted me with a big smile as Biggs stormed off to his little group of cohorts. His arms moved erratically as he spoke, his gaze flickering in my direction, his lips twisted in a sneer - there was no doubt he was talking about me.

When the glances kept coming, I left before Mr. Homophobe and his friends tried to "teach me a lesson" or whatever. I kissed my cousin goodnight while she begged me to stay longer, but I lied and told her I was going out early tomorrow.

When I returned home, I stripped naked, as usual, in the living room and went straight to my shower. I closed my eyes in the hot, steamy water and let my imagination take me away.

As I stood in the shower rubbing my brown peaks, I heard a soft voice state, "Kyndall, you need to be punished for your filthy mouth." In my mind, I turned to see a tall, sepia skin woman with soft, dark brown eyes. Her full lips fixed into a smirk that slightly marred her beautiful face, and her curvy figure called me to run my hands down her body as she stood there naked. An equally handsome man with gray eyes and sexy down-turned lips accompanied her. He had umber colored hardened muscles and a cock that made my mouth water.

She grabbed my face with one hand and brought her mouth to my ears to whisper. "I am going to make you beg to come all over my baby's dick."

I shuddered while I caressed and twisted my nipples. I nodded yes and moaned my approval.

She delivered a hard slap with her free hand to my ample rear end. Her soft hands rubbed the heated spot. "You will call me 'madame' and use your words."

"Yes, madame!" I moaned as she released my face.

"Good, don't make that mistake again." Her hands slipped to my stiff brown nipples. Her fingers rolled one nipple while her mouth bent to suck the other. "I adore your breasts. They're perfect for my mouth." I whimpered as my core heated. "I'm going to taste you, Kyndall. Is that okay?" she inquired as her male companion approached me. He lifted one of my legs and place it on the soap dish holder. While he held me from behind.

Madame's mouth worked down to my mound, where she placed a tender kiss. "Baby," Madame called out, and I knew she was talking to the man in the shower with us. "I want you to play with those beautiful tits of hers while I fuck her with my tongue."

She wrapped one of her arms around my lifted leg and clamped her mouth around my sensitive clit. My legs wobbled and became like jelly as my orgasm built to a crescendo. Determined to tease me, she removed her mouth from my clit and dove in and out of my core with her tongue. It became too much, yet I knew I needed more.

"Please, Madame," I pleaded.

She paused and freed my leg from her grasp. "Please, what, Kyndall?"

"Please, Madame, I want to come!" I yelled out, teary-eyed.

"Baby, give her my dick, and don't be kind," she ordered.

Just then, the man—Baby—flipped and sandwiched me against the cold wet tile of the shower. He lined himself at my entrance, "Ready?" in a deep raspy voice. All I could do was nod my head. He plunged into me as he began with hard strokes. My stiff nipples rubbed raw against the tile walls. With Madame's fingertips working over my sensitive nub, and the feeling of Baby's long and thick length, I was about to have a well-earned orgasm.

BAM!

I snapped out of my daydream and nearly slipped and broke my tailbone. I popped my head from around the shower curtain to see the ever-so-drunk Alex.

"I caught your nasty ass trying to get one off," Alex hollered and nearly stumbled into the tub.

"ALEX, what the fuck!" I shrieked. "Just because you have a key to my place doesn't mean you can just invite yourself over whenever."

"Oh, Kyn Poo, I love you! I want better for you than your hand. I saved you from yourself. Literally. You should thank me." She giggled, still on her drunken spree. She only calls me "Kyn Poo" when she's inebriated.

"I seriously hate you right now. Can't even masturbate in peace." I exhaled as I got out of the tub with my towel.

"Oh, Kyn Poo, why are you mad? Who were you masturbating to this time? Halle Berry and Henry Cavill? Wait, maybe the elusive pity-fuck-and-run, Melissa." She giggled like it was the funniest thing ever.

My face heated with embarrassment and fury. With little thought, I shoved my cousin into the hallway. Hard. No one has ever disrespected me in my home. My cousin has spoken a lot of shit to me, and I let it go because someone has to be the bigger person. But that's not the Kyndall that stood before a shocked Alex.

"You interrupted my self-care time to harass me! Not only have you fucking brought up someone I haven't even thought of in years and could not give two shits about, but you thought it was funny?" I spat. I knew her judgment was clouded by alcohol, but my anger had taken over my senses.

Holding her own injured shoulder, Alex looked like she was on the verge of crying. "What the fuck?" she exclaimed. I figured I had ruined her buzz. "You would hurt me because of a joke about some old friend that couldn't give a shit about you? She hit it and ditched you years ago. Let it go. It's old news."

"You're fucking with me right now, right? Leave and give me my keys." I demanded. I spotted her bag flung on the floor and marched over to take those keys back immediately.

When I found them, I felt the cold metal of Alex's keys to my house in my grip. I lightly shoved my shocked cousin out the front door. "Goodbye, Alex! Get yourself an Uber and go back to Marcus' house," I rebutted as I shut the door in her stunned face.

I wasn't a complete bitch, or that's what I told myself—I stayed glued to that door like it became a part of my back for about twenty minutes until I heard the Uber pull up for Alex. It'd been over eight years since I had thought about Melissa or spoken her name. Okay, maybe I think about her and what happened in high school from time to time, but I wouldn't give Alex or anybody else the satisfaction of knowing that tad bit of information. I have put up every guard and wall to keep Melissa from coming back into my life and ruining the peace I'd found in my tiny home.

After what seemed to be an eternity, I pushed off the door and headed to my bed. I threw myself down into the massive beanie chair and looked at the time: one-thirty in the morning.

Great, now my Sunday is going to be fucked up. But I didn't let that throw me off. I forced myself to focus, meditate, and do the training exercises from my old therapy sessions to eliminate the negativity in my head.

I am a strong Black Woman!

I am strong!

I am worthy!

I repeated my mantras until the heavy weight of sleep claimed me. Of course, the mantras didn't work because the last thing I remembered before slipping into a nightmare-filled sleep was the image of Melissa's beautiful face telling me she loved me.

Chapter 3

MELISSA

Ten years later

"Dr. Walker, Room three is asking for an STD test because she had unprotected sex a week ago," my nurse informed me as I walked out of my last patient's room.

"Isn't that Ms. Phillips?" I asked.

"Yes, Dr. Walker."

"Okay, but please, can you go over some more safe sex practices with her and give her some condoms? I want her to be safe."

"Of course. Also, your next appointment had to cancel. After Ms. Phillips, you're free until one P.M."

"Oh gee, a whole twenty minutes for lunch. I'm so lucky!" We both giggled because I was jam-packed with patient appointments and had little-to-no time for lunch. Even when our team, which was composed of two practical nurses and three medical assistants, would take their mandatory lunch breaks, I normally worked through mines, as I scarfed down my lunch while jotting down patient notes.

"I will be in my office for lunch. You know the rules: lock up and ensure you're back on time," I announced to Sarah, the medical assistant at the desk.

"Yes, Dr. Walker," Sarah acknowledged, and bit her thin bottom lip. *Does she think that's sexy?*

Sarah had tried to gain my attention since everyone found out that I'm bisexual. No one at the office knew until one lady, my partners and I dumped, became unhinged and showed up at our clinic. Talk about embarrassing. I shook my head at the memory. As I reached my office, I sat at my desk and quickly twisted my brown braids into a messy bun. I closed my eyes and exhaled, savoring the calmness of the room.

After I graduated and passed my Boards, a family friend, Dr. Jamie Fields, allowed me to complete my residency in her *women's* clinic in the busy city of Los Angeles. This opportunity meant I could get a feel of how I wanted to run my clinic one day. In Culver City, the extensive building's warm and inviting colors helped create a calming atmosphere for the patients. While Dr. Fields was more relaxed with her staff, I wanted to be more formal with my approach. Dr. Fields encouraged her staff to wear any color scrubs. I tried to get her to change that rule, but she said, "I wanted all of my staff to show their personalities through their attire."

That's a big no for me.

Within five minutes, I had eaten my food and looked over the records of my last two patients. There was a knock on the door when I was just about to call my cousin. I sighed and flexed my hand. "Come in."

Sarah popped in with a to-go box from the small bakery around the corner. "Hey Melissa, I brought you some cheesecake," she looked elated, as she took a seat across from me.

"Sarah, thank you, but you didn't have to do that." I added a little lie. "Plus, I'm on a diet now."

"I didn't know. I'm so sorry." She looked hurt. I was so taken aback that I didn't notice the warmth of her hand as it slipped into mine until it was too late. "So, I was thinking about you and thought you might like something sweet because we've been so busy."

One of my top rules is to not play where you work. That's why I snatched my hand away. I wouldn't start now. Sarah is far from what I'm attracted to, but she refused to back down. I had to close my eyes and count to three because I was losing control over Sarah, which was a major problem. I turned my normally cheerful face blank. "Sarah, we had this conversation before and agreed that nothing would ever happen between us," I responded acidly.

"We would be good together if you give me a try. You can be happy with me. I will make a great addition to your family."

I closed my eyes and rubbed the area between my eyebrows. "Sarah, I will not give you a chance, not now, not later, never," I informed her, and I sighed because I knew I sounded like a total bitch. "Let's have a heart-to-heart off the record."

She looked hopeful. "Okay, shoot! I am all ears."

"I'm as interested in dating you as I am in contracting a sexually transmitted disease. I've rejected your flirtations and offers repeatedly, and I hate repeating myself to anyone. Yet you're still flirting and badgering me in the workplace. I think it's time for you to find a new job. I'll ask Dr. Fields to give you two weeks to find a job," I declared while I turned back to my following patient's files.

"Wait, Melissa, I'm sorry. I didn't mean to—,"

"Let me stop you right there. First, you are to call me Dr. Walker in the workplace, and second, I won't repeat myself again. Enough is enough. You may leave my office and prepare the rooms for the last two patients." I turned back to my computer.

"I—" She started, but I cut her off.

"Bye, Sarah," I told her, not looking up from the screen this time.

She stumbled out of my office, beet red and teary-eyed.

Control.

I breathed it, ate it, drank it, and lived it. This position and office provided me with that—I can control everything in my work life, the employees, office decor, and my patients. When I moved to Los Angeles, I left behind a life I knew I wouldn't be able to control. Although I wasn't too fond of how I left, I knew it was for the best.

My late Aunt Josie called my Mom the week before senior prom and asked if she would come to LA to help her prepare for her death since she had stage four metastatic cancer, which started in her breast and then traveled to her lungs. When we arrived in LA, she was halfway gone. She weighed about eighty pounds and couldn't walk from her bedroom to her favorite La-Z-Boy sofa. My aunt lasted four months and left me with the best gift. Her house and enough money for undergrad and medical school. I had no expenses throughout college. I was free of mundane responsibilities.

After my aunt's death, my relationship with my mom deteriorated to the point where we hardly spoke to each other, and when we did, it was only on a need-to-know basis. I tried to open up to my mother one night and stumbled over my words when I told her about the Kyndall situation. Which was a huge mistake. I made semi-peace with that failed relationship, and while it wasn't a simple journey, I eventually accepted my part in it, despite my Mother's haranguing. But what I hated was her constant need to blame me for being lonely. Eventually, my Mom moved out two months after my aunt passed away to live with some guy. I remembered that fight like it was yesterday.

"Mom, you can't be seriously moving out. We've been in California for only half a year! You don't know this man enough to live with him."

"I would rather live with him than with someone who might stab me in the back if I get in her way," she stated. I almost shed a tear, as if I hadn't heard her berate me over the situation before.

"I'm not an evil person," I announced to my mom, even though I didn't believe my own words if I was honest. "I was thinking about my future, and I never wanted someone or something to come between me and my goal of becoming a doctor. You, of all people, should see that even though I may have left Kyndall unconventionally, it needed to be done, regardless."

"No, none of that bullshit you said will fly with me. Your father and I taught you better, and if your dad were still alive, he would be ashamed," she spat out.

I lowered my head because that was the sore point of my life. See, my mom was right, kind of, but I would never let her know that, and she always brought up my deceased father to make me feel even crappier.

"I'm sorry, Mom, for being a disappointment to you. I'll make up for my wrongs when I'm ready."

"Make up for your wrongs when you're ready?" She turned to me and gave me the craziest look. "Do you realize a person's life isn't some toy? You can't just say one day I want to be your friend and then pause your relationship until you're ready. I know you have better sense than that."

"You're right, and I'll make it up to Kyndall sooner rather than later."

"You will never learn until it's too late." She shook her head and walked out of the room.

That was ten years ago and would be the last meaningful conversation between me and my mother for a while. Her latest boyfriend barely tolerated me since he was very old-fashioned and set in his ways.

After I had seen my last two patients of the day and completed my notes, I gathered my stuff and headed to my car for my hour and a half ride home. Just as I hit the highway, my phone rang, and I answered without hearing the caller's name.

"Hey, love, are you on your way home?" I smiled because Matt always called at the same time and asked the same question.

"Hey baby, yes, I just got on the highway, and there's traffic out the ass as usual. I will be home a bit later than usual. How was work today?" I inquired.

"It was uneventful, as usual. My favorite type of day. You want me to pick up some Chinese food on my way home?"

"Yes, please. I could eat a cow. Thank you, baby! I'll see you at home."

"Of course. See you in a few. Feel free to strip in the garage and walk-in naked." He chuckled, and I rolled my eyes.

"You're a mess. I love you. See you soon. Bye." We hung up.

Matt Walker is one of three owners of America's largest real estate firms, Walker, Jackson & Phillips. WJP, for short. When we met, I wasn't looking for a relationship with anyone. Frankly, I had hoped to find my way back to Kyndall. During my first year of college, I hid in my aunt's home, feeling lonely and wondering if the universe was punishing me for betraying my best friend. Except for one night, my classmates dragged me to a party. That is where I met Matt Walker, Aaron Phillips, and Travis Jackson.

Matt, Aaron, and Travis chipped away at the wall I had placed around my heart and mind. That night, they made it clear they wanted me as they attempted to gain my number several times, and I turned them down each time. Until I gave in at the last minute—by the end of night I couldn't remember why I didn't want to share my digits.

My words had slurred. "Why would you want to date me?"

"Why not? You're attractive, and we want you to give us lonely fools a chance," Aaron cajoled. By this hour, he had stripped off all of his clothes, leaving him in only his jeans.

"Well, I am into girls as well," I stated.

"Well, lucky for us. We love girls and girls that like girls, as well." Travis grinned. "We're equal opportunists."

I shook my head and laughed. "You wouldn't mind if I decided I wanted to have another woman in our relationship?"

Matt was the one who responded. After the three had gone quiet. "No, we're open to anything. As long as we all agree on the person, I don't see what's wrong with it. The real question is, would you be okay having a polyamorous relationship with three guys?"

"I never thought about it." I replied. I had been trying to save myself for my best friend, but I remembered I'd messed that relationship up. "So, we would do everything together?"

I'm not one to beat around the bush, but the question made me blush. I looked at the guys as they tried their best to be nonchalant, but their half smirks gave them away.

"Well, our beautiful blushing queen," Travis said. "I hate to be blunt, but we share everything, and that includes having sex with the same girl. We've done it a couple of times and it works for us."

I felt like they placed me in a furnace. But I continued, "So, you're bisexual then?"

"No, we aren't bisexual. We just love sharing," Aaron said.

I was curious, so I ended up giving the guys my number and told them I would be understanding. But after almost a month, I never heard from them and chalked it up to them changing their mind after the booze wore off.

Imagine my shock when Travis called me up to invite me to dinner. I was beside myself. When I arrived at the restaurant and saw all three gorgeous men, I got scared, but I stuck it out. I barely knew how to entertain one man, much less three. When I asked them about sharing a woman again, they gave me the same answer with a simple shrugged. Their answer was simple yet mind-boggling, even after I asked them again.

"How would you feel if I met someone that I thought would fit our relationship?" I inquired. My mind brought up the memory of Kyndall when she came over to study for our English final. There was a moment during the night, we became delirious from lack of sleep, causing me to almost slip. As I got closer to her face, I could smell the strong, sweet aroma of peppermint. Her breath caressed me as my hazel eyes stayed glued to her plump lips.

"We would date them together and see if we fit," Aaron responded, jolting me out of my memory as he finished chewing his food.

"What if we don't agree with the person?" I asked.

"Then we dump them and go from there," Matt said.

Interesting

By the time night ended, however, I was making plans for our second date.

Life hadn't prepared me for this situation.

Honestly, I felt this was a setup, because I still missed Kyndall and wondered if she would ever forgive me.

I waited for the ball to drop, but that never came. The four years we were together were a balancing act. We had our days that were so blissful I thought it was unreal. The simple movie nights we made tradition, our summer trips overseas, and the late night power study sessions spoiled me. It was the brief moments when I was sick during my sophomore year; the guys banded together to take turns to take care of me in between their classes. It's the way Travis allowed me to keep him up till one in the morning to talk about my problems or when Matt, Aaron, and I made our Sunday family dinners before Travis got back from his job.

Our rocky days were far and in-between. In those days, we fought about the simplest of things, like the toilet seat cover being left open for the hundredth time. The worst fight we had was when we got into a relationship with a girl from my physics course. Jamie was one of the top students in our class and we hit it off when we studied together. If I was being honest, she reminded me of Kyndall. Jamie's curvy body reminded me of the one I used to trace in high school when Kyndall fell asleep or the way she was dedicated to school. Our relationship was good, but when she met the guys, something shifted. Jamie and the guys clashed on everything, and I came to a point where I had to take a step back and ask what I wanted. The answer was simple. I wanted my guys. I would choose them over anyone, because I loved them.

After that, we sat down and decided we wouldn't date anyone unless we all went on a first date before anything got started. I suggested we held off from finding our fifth until we graduated. But in the back of my mind, a certain someone still occupied my mind, so it was a relief when the guys agreed with me.

Of course, the dynamics of this relationship perplexed my mom, and she was very vocal about it. I informed her of my relationship status when I felt we were in a better place in our relationship to let her back into my life slowly. I brought Travis, Matt, and Aaron along for dinner one Sunday night. It was an utter waste of time.

"You mean to tell me you ran from one girl you 'loved' to fall in love with three men? What was her name again?" She bit her lip and furrowed her brows.

"Mom," I spoke calmly. My hands were moist, and my foot bounced.

"Karissa?" she asked.

"Mom," I repeated, firmer, and I thought my foot might break off from my lower leg.

"No, it was Kyndall. Yes, that's it. I remembered when we moved from Florida. You hadn't said goodbye—" I cut her off before she could finish.

"Mom let's not stick to old news that does not pertain to my life right now."

"Who's Kyndall?" Travis inquired.

I swiped my upper lip with my hand and wiped the moistness onto a paper towel. "Mom, I'm sorry to disappoint you again, but my partners will be a part of my life. In the future, we might start a family. You're going to have to forgive me if you want to be a part of your grandchildren's lives."

"I don't understand you, Melissa, but this is your choice." She shrugged. "I don't approve of this, but you're always going to do whatever you feel like doing."

"Well, I'm just glad she's with a man and not a woman," Oscar, Mom's then-current boyfriend, who had been silent until now, spoke. "I will never understand that."

I rolled my eyes but kept my mouth shut.

We left soon after because my mom, like most mothers, had to have the last word, and I felt the weight of her disapproval on my choices.

Why did I even bother?

After that night, I had to explain the whole high school situation to my partners, which was hell. The disappointment that surrounded my past actions put a touch of mistrust into our relationship because I failed to mention it before then. We walked around on eggshells for a month before Matt, Travis, and Aaron signed us up for couple's therapy because this was a significant thing to keep a secret. The therapist told me I had anxiety issues related to my need to control everything, with some possessive traits. I didn't like her at all.

There's nothing wrong with being ambitious about what you want.

Our bond grew stronger over the four years, and we found our path back to each other. We changed our name to Phillip Jackson-Walker to symbolize our union because we could not get married legally and I didn't want to choose between my husbands. My mom and I mended our relationship. I accepted accountability for my decisions, recognizing that I had hidden that aspect of my life from my companions out of fear of relinquishing the one item that provided my life with completeness. Even though I hate to admit it, our family benefited from the sessions. Once we reached a point in our relationship to think about our future, we looked for our second female partner again. Of course, that was easier said than done, seeing that as of today, we had dated six girls in the past five years—each one a disaster.

I knew why we failed in each relationship. The guys saw through my attempts to search for a woman that reminded me of Kyndall whether they resembled my golden goddess or shared some personality characteristic of hers. They said it was unhealthy. They were right, but I couldn't help it. I knew I didn't have any business even saying her name. I guessed this was my punishment for being an evil person. There wasn't a day I didn't wonder how she was doing or what would happen if I called her old number. Would she forgive me? Had she become the fantastic teacher I knew she would be?

Melissa, snap out of your head. That was ten years ago. Come back to the present.

After spending almost two hours in traffic, I pulled into the garage and smirked as I remembered what Matt had asked me to do when I got home. *Men.* As I stepped into the kitchen, I heard the cutest voice I could ever hear—my baby, Amber Phillip Jackson-Walker. She jumped out of her dad's lap and ran to hug me. As I put her down, I felt the sticky remains of her sweet chicken on my cheek.

She's the perfect twin of her father, but with tawny brown skin. Light brown curls fell halfway down her back, but that's where my genes stopped. Amber's face is oblong, like Travis's. Those prominent round eyes are the perfect shade of jade green. She has a small button nose and dimples on her cheeks. And she's the most brilliant five-year-old.

"Hi, sweetie. Mommy missed you all day. How are you?" I asked as she smiled widely, displaying a gap-tooth grin from where she had recently lost a few teeth.

"Mommy, I missed you too much! I learned to count to fifty, and Daddy took me swimming," she rushed out.

"Oh, and was I the best daddy ever?" Matt asked as he walked over to us and kissed me.

"Yes, but not better than my other Daddies!" she shouted.

"Oh well darn; I'm second best then, Amby?" Matt asked.

"No, you're number one, too!" she giggled.

"It's just going to be you and I tonight. Aaron and Travis are running late," he mentioned.

"You guys been working late recently. Are you working on something big?"

"Yes, but we want to give you the full scoop later. Lots of details to sort through and it might all change later, anyway. If it succeeds, it might change a lot for us."

"Okay, that is super ominous."

He hugged me. "I know, but we'll reveal everything when the time is right."

"Okay. I trust you guys."

He grinned. "It's about time."

"Ha," I teased back.

Matt is such a great dad and my big softie. Matt towers over everyone, and we're not short by any means. Contrary to his personality, Matt's bronzed body is all hard, broad shoulders, with not an ounce of fat. His ocean-colored eyes peered out of a chiseled face with perfect, round lips.

Aaron, my introverted number cruncher. Aaron is the brains of the company and controls the financial portion of the company. He's willowy and has that all-American boy face without the air of ego, and instead of blue eyes, he has the most stunning hazel eyes.

Travis is Amber's biological dad. He is the spitting image of my little Amber. His jade green eyes and sexy smile would make anyone fall in love with him. But what is most eye-catching are the tattoo sleeves on both arms he got during college.

Amber and I were fortunate to have them in our lives. My partners put up with a lot from me when I was in medical school and now during residency. I constantly thought I would fail, but they swooped in and saved me every time. By the time I graduated from medical school, they knew almost everything I had learned. They gave up their time to help me study. I didn't deserve them.

After dinner, I got Amber ready for bed, which was a two-person job because this little girl was determined to have her way. Aaron and I normally have to tag team to have her settle down. But tonight, it was just Matt and me and Matt gave in to Amber anytime she batted her long lashes. As I watched them interact, it reminded me of why I fell in love with Matt. His tenderness hadn't started when Amber was born, but was there when we first met. We would sneak away from Travis and Aaron between our classes to watch movies in one of the empty conference rooms at our school. Now we just rent the theater out, but I still remember those days as if it were yesterday.

After thirty minutes, our angel had passed out—after Matt promised to buy her a new toy tomorrow.

She had him wrapped around her tiny fingers!

I closed the door to her room and opened the French doors to our oversized main bedroom. Everything was custom-purchased to fit our family. My most prized possession was the giant bed that accommodated five people.

After I got ready for bed, I jumped in the middle of the bed and turned on my trashy reality television show while Matt brushed his teeth. It was thirty minutes into the show when Aaron and Travis showed up.

"Don't you even dare think about sitting on the bed with your outdoor clothes on," I shouted before Travis could sit his butt down.

Travis froze, tilted his head back at me, grinned, and sat down. "Make me."

His jade green eyes shone with laughter against his tan skin. He was always the jokester of the three. I remember we would spend most of our dates laughing until we had migraines. He was the go-to whenever I needed to be cheered up. If we had nothing left in this world, we would have Travis to brighten our days. "Butthole," I joked, as I attempted to hit him with a pillow, but he grabbed it and pulled me in for a kiss with his hand on my throat.

I moaned against his mouth. "We can't do anything tonight," I whined. "I have a long day tomorrow and need all my energy." My lips met his, and I ran my finger along the intricate curves and lines of his tattoo sleeves. I stopped at the tattoo he got after our union ceremony.

Aaron walked in from the closet, where he took his clothes off before he came to sit on the bed.

"Hey baby," he leaned over for a kiss. "How was your day?"

"It was fine, just the same old repeat offenders today," I shrugged. "How was yours?"

"It was interesting. I got to review our financial sheets for our current projects and work on this new venture we might look into," he revealed.

I tried my best to engage Aaron with work stuff. He sometimes loses me when he gets into full accountant mode. "How interesting," I mustered. "This new project. Can you tell me more?"

"Remember what we agreed on? No taking about work in the bedroom," Travis pointed out.

"For once, he's right, baby," Matt stated as he came from the bathroom with just a towel wrapped around his trim waist.

I tried to listen to their banter about some sports score that popped up on the screen, but my poor mind was stuck on Matt and his towel.

"Melissa, please stop being a perv. All you have to do is ask me to drop the towel, and I will." I snapped my eyes back up to his face.

I must have been staring for some time because Aaron placed me between his legs and rubbed his hands up and down my arms.

"Please, I am going to be sore," I whined, but I did nothing to stop him.

"I don't think I like that type of begging," Aaron whispered into my ear while he nibbled a bit on my earlobe. "Tell us what you need," he added, as he trailed kisses to my neck.

"I. Want. To. Go. To. Bed," I moaned out.

"A wet tease, I tell you," Travis replied, from his place snuggled at my side.

"That's Matt with his towel show."

"Who lil ol' me?" He took off his towel and used it like a propeller.

"Really?" Aaron shook his head. "And he's one of the CEOs of our company."

Sadly, we were all mature adults. Thirty minutes later, we were all in bed and ready to sleep. No fooling around at all.

"I have to wait to hear about this new venture?" I whispered after the lights were out.

Travis spooned me and replied, "Yep. You know how we feel about talking about things before it's confirmed. Just know that if this goes through, we're going shopping at Hermès."

I rolled over to face him. "Okay, now I am scared if you're offering to take me shopping," I answered leerily.

"Go to sleep, Melissa, or else we'll put your mouth to use," Matt commanded.

"You're all talk," I challenged.

I knew I'd fucked up when Travis's hand gripped my neck. He growled, "Oh," I bit my bottom lip.

I'm in subbie heaven.

When I arrived at work the next day, I was barely alive; sore, and walking like a new baby fawn into the office. All the girls at the office asked if I was alright and gave me that all-knowing look in our morning huddle. I made a mental note to beat myself. Why had I begged for round two this morning, like a madwoman? I'm indeed a glutton for punishment, but the punishment was well worth it.

But was it punishment or funishment?

I smiled and went on with my merry day.

Chapter 4

MELISSA

I LOVED LIVING IN Los Angeles. No other place compared to the city's beauty; from the fantastic beaches that trumped the East Coast to the stunning scenery at Runyon Canyon Park. One major thing that kept me cemented to LA was the different cultures I could find here. Amber and I loved to spend our days visiting various pockets of culture around town.

Today we hit Amber's favorite area: Chinatown. Those enormous eyes shone from the moment the golden dragons appeared in the front window. The first time we came here, we bought her a child's cheongsam. She wore it every time we came here.

"Daddy, look at the dragons. They look better than ever!" Amber squealed.

Whenever we come here, I can hear her speaking the same words with a fondness in her tone. The beauty always amazed her.

"Oh yeah, Princess, it looks like they polished them just for you," Aaron agreed. He's a sucker for Amber as well. I bet she'll get him to buy her an entire island someday.

"That's silly, Daddy. They do it to make everyone feel good," she announced.

"You're right, Princess. What was I thinking?" he accepted.

"I don't know, Daddy," she sang, and I just chuckled.

Aaron said, "We're only spending an hour or two here today because we have a surprise for you and Mommy."

"Mmhmm," I gave Aaron the side eye.

"Don't start, mama bear. We assured you we would disclose everything when everything was finalized."

"Yes, I know, but I am a little leery as usual." I huffed. "Last time, you guys did a big reveal. You guys practically bought half of a whole town on a whim. Thankfully, it worked out for the best, but talk about stress!"

"The venture is completed and we will increase our impact and reach. I guarantee you will love this for us," he announced.

I said, "I trust you guys, and I mean it." It was true. My partners have never once been unsupportive or actively tried to harm our growing family.

He leaned over and kissed me. "Good, because you're going to love it."

"Please, no kissing when we get out of the car!" our sergeant yelled from behind us.

"Yes, ma'am," we yelled back, saluting her before we stole another kiss.

She huffed and hopped out of the car the second we parked. I chuckled softly, so that she didn't hear me. We had planned nothing and intended to just walk around and window shop. Aaron would probably buy a billion things from the shopping center for Amber. Over the course of our hour-long visit, he proved my theory half-right. Amber ran around to every store, dragging her father in each one while I sat outside on a bench. However, Aaron bought her only half a billion things. Pleased, Amber willingly settled in her car seat for the ride home. Successful skip school and workday done.

I rarely had time to do this sort of outing during a workday, but since Dr. Fields had returned from her vacation, I skipped one day while her nurse practitioner helped with the patients. Often when I had days off like this one, the whole family ditched our obligations to spend time together, but Matt and Travis had to stay back for some last-minute business with their new venture.

When we arrived home, I helped Amber put away her ten bags of new clothing and toys her dad brought. I will have to speak with her about bribing her fathers because I do not know where she got that from–okay, maybe from me, but I won't admit it out loud.

With Amber tucked away and the sitter arriving early, we were all set and ready to go to the restaurant.

The Skyline restaurant was our favorite high-end restaurant frequented by celebrities and had one of the most challenging reservation list in the city. The intimate restaurant sat on the top floor of a high-rise in downtown. Every table had a perfect view of the city and enough space to not be on top of the other patrons. We got lucky with a western view of the city. It was a breathtaking scene to see during the night, not to mention the gorgeous sunset.

As we sat at our table, our waitress took our drink orders. I ordered a single margarita since I didn't want to drink heavily when I had to work tomorrow. But the guys went all out. They opted for Armand de Brignac champagne. My eyes widened when the waiter brought the expensive bottle to the table.

"Okay, now I know this secret business venture must be extremely lucrative because you guys order nothing besides ale or Cabernet Sauvignon," I said in awe.

Matt chuckled and replied, "This is an enormous deal for the company."

"Tell me! It's been two weeks, and you guys have been keeping long work hours and being secretive and shit," I rushed out because, frankly, I was tired of waiting to know. The clinic staff asked if I was okay because I was on edge. "I'm eager to know how this will affect our family."

"Alright, love, calm down," Travis said.

While he poured himself another glass. I crossed my arms and tried to be patient.

"Well, WJ&P has been on the West coast since we started the business. For a while, we've been thinking about ways to expand, specifically to the East Coast," Aaron stated. "We reached out to a couple of our investors and sold them on the idea of several important properties."

I nodded to let him know I was listening.

"Our employees are currently maintaining and managing our West Coast investments. We're no longer needed for the day-to-day operations. We're planning on opening a corporate headquarters in New York City to get this new East Coast venture off the ground and then up and running to the same standard as our West Coast office. To achieve that, we would need to move to NYC."

I nodded, and then almost snapped my neck when I realized what he had just said. "Excuse me?" I spoke louder than I intended to.

"We would like to move to the East Coast in a month or two. Preferably sooner rather than later," Matt disclosed.

"That's not possible. I have my residency with Dr. Fields. I would have to look for another office to work for, and I would have to transition my patients to Dr. Fields, and that's if she's okay with absorbing my caseload," I voiced.

"Baby, I understand you're worried about your residency, but you have the option of finding another practice to finish your residency within NY," Aaron voiced. He's—correction—they're *all* on my shit list right now.

The waitress chose this time to come back with our food. She intentionally batted her eyes at Travis, and I gave her the side eye before she ran off, like a dog with its tail between its legs. I gave my food the utmost attention while I pretended to listen to them. Honestly, I zoned out. Shock marred my face, and I didn't know how to dig myself out of this without sounding like a major bitch.

I tuned back in just as Aaron continued, "We can talk to Dr. Fields with you. We could invite her to dinner and explain the situation."

Aaron, my lovable peacemaker. He always found the bigger picture in any scenario. When we first started dating, I didn't think we would hit it off. As I became more familiar with him, I could see the side of him he usually hides away from the world. Aaron had a tough childhood and everything we did focused on building our relationship. He opened my eyes to a love of the outdoors as we went hiking, camping, and did pottery. The pottery date surprised me, but when I asked for the reasoning, Aaron just shrugged and said, "Pottery builds patience and communication through art."

Travis cleared his throat, which forced me back to reality.

"That's unnecessary. I can speak with Dr. Fields if I need to." I folded my arms and scrunched my eyebrows. "What's the alternative if I don't want to move?"

Matt sighed. "Well, that would be extremely inconvenient for us because we would be gone for probably 11 months out of the year for the next 2-3 years. That means we would miss Amber's school events, and we would have to hire someone to help you out around the house." He continued, "Whereas in New York, you have a cousin you still talk with that can help you transition into the area and babysit. Doesn't that sound like something you would want to do?"

I stared at him because he knew I would never separate Amber from her family, and I was not too fond of the idea of a nanny raising my baby when she had three dads to take care of her. Plus, I still wanted to expand our family with another child and a new partner.

"You know I would never take Amber from you," I mentioned. "What's next? We would sell this house and rent a place in NY? I could call my cousin and ask her to find someplace for us, and I can work on finding another practice to apply for."

"Don't worry about the home. We purchased a home on Centre Island, outside of Queens. You'll love the house. It's an updated home and sits on a large lot overlooking the Oyster Bay River," Travis beamed.

"That means you guys already planned this and decided that this move was a go, even without my approval." I crossed my arms and knew I was making a bit of a scene from the way several patrons turned to stare at us. I didn't care.

"Let's take this conversation to the car," Aaron voiced, as Matt gave the waitress his card.

Twenty minutes of silence later, we pulled up into our garage. No one tried to get out. Finally, I broke the silence, "Listen, I understand the importance of moving and growing your business, but you could have given me time to decide and plan for a move. This is very inconvenient for Amber and I."

Matt was the one who replied. "We understand. That's why all you have to worry about is your residency. We're going to be dealing with Amber's school. We have movers. All you have to worry about is packing a weekend bag and getting to NY."

I sighed. Matt and the guys always knew what to say to keep me from worrying.

I pushed back. "You mean I will have to deal with a bunch of shit with my patients and my practice, since I'm still in residency."

"Okay, now you're just trying to have the last word," Travis retorted.

I humphed and rolled my eyes. "Fine, I will talk with Dr. Fields tomorrow and prepare to transition my patients. I hope this house is amazing."

It was nearly midnight before I got to bed because I spent a long time in the bathroom listening to my latest Queen Bey playlist. When I woke up, the guys were buzzing about getting Amber ready for school and preparing her paperwork to transfer to a school close to the new home. I had looked at the school's website last night—it was an excellent, diverse school. Not worth making a fuss about.

After I gave everyone my rounds of kisses and hugs, I headed to the office. I got nervous. I hated being a bother to anyone and disappointing Dr. Fields, especially since we'd been friends for years.

I pulled into the parking lot and did my five-minute meditation for the day. As I walked into the clinic, I noticed the little stuff that I would miss. It took almost a year for me to get used to everything. Now, I would have to start over in a new clinic.

I found Dr. Fields in her office after our team's morning huddle had finished. Dr. Fields was a petite older woman with gray hair that she kept in a high bun. She was highly knowledgeable in her field, and her patients loved her.

I knocked on the door even though it was open and entered when she told me to come in.

"Good morning, Dr. Fields."

"Good morning, Dr. Walker. How's it going?" Dr. Fields was more of a laid-back doctor.

"I'm doing good. How are you?" I asked.

"I am great. What's up?" she replied.

"First, I want to say thank you for letting me practice with you. For the past six years, I have learned a lot, and now I know how to care for my patients properly—"

She pushed her glasses up her nose and cut me off. "Melissa, I've known you since you were ten years old, and I know when you're buttering me up for the kill. Spit it out before I have to leave."

I chuckled and winced simultaneously. "Okay, you got me. I wanted to see about possibly ending my tenure with your office. I'm moving to New York."

"Ah, there it is. The reason for the butter," she chortled. "I would be remiss if I didn't say someone gave me a slight head's up already."

"Let me guess: this birdie's name starts with an A?" I suggested.

"Maybe, but I swore to not reveal my sources." She grinned.

Oh, it was definitely Aaron. He and Dr. Fields had had a good relationship ever since I introduced them to each other in my undergraduate years.

"Mmm," I uttered out.

"Actually, you're very fortunate, or you've hacked into my friend's list," she mocked. "Because I have a colleague looking for another partner in their women's clinic in New York. Maybe I can talk them into letting you finish up your residency and then you can decide to stay from there."

"Are you serious? Or are you just pulling my leg?" I inquired, raising an eyebrow.

She laughed. "Yes, I'm as serious as a positive pregnancy test. Let me text her and ask where the clinic is located." She pulled out her cell phone and shot a text out. Within a minute, her phone dinged with a reply. "Ah yes, in Elmhurst, New York. Are you interested? I can let her know I recommend you."

"Is she someone you trust?" I asked doubtfully, because being lucky twice was pushing it for me.

She smiled, "Oh, Melissa, never change. She's a trusted colleague, and I would send my patients to her in a heartbeat."

"Okay, I would love to check out the clinic," I nodded. "Since you already know about the move, I'm guessing you know I need someone to cover my patients. I don't want to be hit with patient abandonment on my licenses."

"We can absorb your patients until I find someone. Plus, with my NP here, we can more than handle the workload."

"Seriously?"

"Yes, work on sending out announcements to your clients and collecting all the paperwork for your New York license. They're usually faster to process than California."

"Yeah, I had my New York license randomly when I applied for my California license. I never made use of it. At least the hard part is done," I stated. I thanked Dr. Fields because I had already spent too much of her time.

Before my first appointment arrived, I walked to my office. I reflected on how I genuinely appreciated the opportunity. I'd thought that finding a new practice quickly would be an insurmountable task. This one time, I was lucky to be wrong.

I filled the following weeks with sending off my announcements, seeing my clients, and dealing with some patients upset about me leaving. I had a small dinner party with Dr. Fields, her family, and several mutual friends.

When I called my cousin Sage with the news about the move, she was ecstatic. "OMG, Melissa! We're going to be in the same state again. I'm excited. I can't wait to show you around the city, and maybe we can go wifey shopping," she screamed into the phone.

I cringed because going to the clubs to find a partner was no longer near the top of my list. Moving first. New partner later. "We'll see. Either way, I'm excited to see you and for you to see Amber again. What has it been—three years?"

"Yes, I couldn't make it out often because of my financial situation."

"You know, I totally understand, and that's in the past now. I'll be there tomorrow, and we can hang out once I get settled. Plus, my birthday is next week and it will be New Year's day. It will be perfect timing."

"Damn, I wish! It'll have to wait until after the new year. Next week I have to go to the backwoods of the US, Iowa." I can imagine her beautiful face scrunched up.

"Iowa? What's out there?" I snickered.

"Girl, I don't know, but I guess my job wants to torture me! I'm down for anything after I get back."

"Okay, sounds great. I'll plan for the following week, as long as I get to see you soon. I'll see you when you get back. Love you."

Our last night in California was sad, for me, at least. Amber was excited about the move and couldn't wait to see the snow while I silently prayed. My partners had promised we'd get a chauffeur or rideshare if we ever really needed to drive, because driving in the snow didn't appeal to me. Plus, I would have to spend my birthday in the snow now. I was not excited.

Goodbye, warm weather, and hello, new winter coat life.

As we took off from Van Nuys Airport, Amber turned to me and stated, "Mommy, I think New York will be good for us."

"Why do you say that?" I inquired.

"I just have a feeling." She shrugged and turned her attention back to the little window.

Amber had always been optimistic about everything. I wish I could have that train of thought, like the rest of my family. I seldom liked significant changes, especially when I wasn't in control.

An uneasy feeling crept up my back as I sat on the private jet, the same feeling I always get when something bad was about to happen. I pushed that feeling to the side as I completed my mini meditation to ease the anxiety, trying to push all the negative vibes out of my mind.

After five hours, we finally arrived at Teterboro Airport, and in true fashion, Travis rented us a limousine to take us to our new home. When we got in the limo, Amber ignored us to gawk at the city scene like she'd just found the lost city of Atlantis. The scene turned from the city to a suburban area with lots of lush green trees and immense homes. I wondered how much we paid for this home as each house became more grander and more spaced out from each other as we drove farther.

When we drove past an electric gate, I assumed it was part of a gated community. Then, the black road pavement disappeared and turned into a red brick driveway. I looked in amazement at the massive open yard that contained lush, evergreen shrubs, and a beautifully maintained lawn greeted us. We turned a corner and a massive French chateau-style home loomed in the distance, like something out of a French magazine. The stone façade was off-white with black shutters. Stuck in a trance, I disembarked from the car slowly and walked like a zombie to the front door. I pushed open the decorative wrought iron to see dark hardwood floors and white walls. I nearly fell on top of Amber, who clung to my leg, excited to see her new home. We passed the large formal living area—twice the size of our old one in LA—and the formal dining room. They equipped the kitchen with modern accouterments and an island big enough for us all to gather round.

As Amber and I continued our slow tour, we found two separate offices, a home theater, a fitness room, a finished basement, and a guest room off the first floor. We ran up the steps to find six medium-sized bedrooms spaced out on the second floor. Each of the rooms had their own bathroom. The main bedroom was the best room. When I opened the doors to the master, my jaw dropped, and Amber's little gasp echoed through the room. There was a massive bed that took up almost half the wall. Amber ran and launched herself on it. Aaron entered while she squealed in delight.

"Baby, did you order this huge ass bed?" I asked Aaron.

"It's an early birthday gift," he responded, hugging me from behind.

"God, this is enough to fit eight people!"

"Well, we can add four more people to our family." He beamed.

Yeah—no.

"Oh, Ha, don't even think about it. We have room for one more, and that's it." Aaron held up his hands in surrender.

Just then, Travis and Matt walked in with our suitcases.

"How do you like the home?" Matt inquired.

"I'm speechless in a good way. How big is the yard?" I questioned them.

"The house sits on ten acres. We got this home for dirt cheap. The owners had a change of mind, wanted to move to Florida for retirement, and were looking for a quick sale," Travis noted.

"Ten acres? Geez." I responded, dumbfounded.

"Yes, enough space for you to blast your Beyoncé as loud as you want because our neighbors won't hear," Travis replied as I walked into the bathroom.

I whimpered like a damn fool when I walked in. The walk-in closet was the size of a small room. The walk-in shower was on the shorter end of the wall and could hold ten people. A freestanding gold spa tub was nestled into the corner of the room, big enough for a football team. It was a marble double sink with a built-in vanity, and stocked with my favorite makeup and skincare products.

Was I in love? Yes.

Would I bless my partners for presenting me with this fantastic home? Double yes.

I had been very doubtful about the home being to my standard, because our previous house was nice, but small for our family. We had practically lived on top of each other. Whenever Amber played her sleepy-time music, we all heard it. We would catch ourselves singing it throughout the day.

I blinked, and it was already over—the weekend had gone by in a heartbeat. The movers, who must have driven here like mad people, delivered our stuff by Saturday night and had our stuff unpacked by Sunday afternoon. Amber's school enrollment was finalized. This had been the most stress-free move I had ever experienced.

We drove around on Sunday, trying to see some of upstate New York. It was extremely different from living in LA, with its sprawl. My heart ached until I remembered the view of the bay from the main bedroom.

Monday arrived way too fast for my liking. I sat in the parking lot of the Elmhurst physician's building, trying to settle my nerves. If there was one thing I hated, it was being interviewed. I silently sent a wish into the universe for positive vibes, checked my makeup in the rearview mirror one last time, and spritzed my favorite French vanilla perfume.

The building housed different healthcare specialties, from acupuncture to urologists. They gave the Elmhurst Women's Clinic the most extensive suite, even though it was tucked away in the back of the building on the second floor. When I walked in, I was surprised to see that the clinic was very welcoming, had calming lights, pretty purple walls, and comfy black chairs. The waiting room television played the home improvement channel on low volume, and the front desk had three staff members behind it. I think I liked it at first glance.

The interview was painless, and Doctors Stephanie May, and Shawn Stein, welcomed me and made me feel good about the clinic. They showed me around the office and reviewed how they divided the rooms and how they marketed their clinic. The staff was friendly, at least on the surface—time would tell what ran deeper. By the end of the tour, they had me persuaded to pick the clinic. Dr. May showed me where my office would be—the back corner, with privacy and quiet.

"Melissa, how do you feel about the clinic?" Dr. May inquired as I surveyed the room.

"Well, I'm impressed, and I would love to continue my residency with you and Dr. Stein. I want to start immediately. If it's okay with you. I've had my license to practice in New York for a while."

Dr. May beamed. "Geez, Dr. Fields was right about you. She said you wouldn't take a week off to relax."

"I would have taken some time off, but we hired movers through my partners' company. All I had to do was point."

"Oh, how nice! I wish I'd had that service when I first moved here. It was three weeks of hell. One day, we'll have to meet your partner."

"Husbands—I have three of them. They'll be happy to meet you as well. You might meet them sooner rather than later. Whenever I set up my new office, they like to visit." I smiled.

"I look forward to meeting them," she settled, as we walked me out of the building. "I will see you tomorrow? And you're positive you don't want the week off?"

"Yes, I want to set up and prepare everything for my first patients. I plan to take a day off next week to celebrate my birthday."

"It's your birthday next week?"

"No, it's actually January first, New Year's Day, but my cousin is out of town. She's the only family I have here."

"You're a New Year's baby! Well, Happy Birthday in advance. You definitely have to explore the city, at least for your birthday. Especially since your birthday is on Saturday."

I beamed. "I was thinking of something more low-key. It's been hectic, and I don't mind staying still with my family."

"I agree. Oh, and, before I forget," Dr. May perked up and her smile broadened. "We're going to have a booth at the block party we attend every year in Jamaica, Queens. That would be a perfect time to introduce yourself to clients and get a feel for the surrounding communities."

"That sounds like fun! I'll make it. When's the date?" I inquired.

"The first day of March."

After that, we parted ways, and I got into my car and headed home. The whole ride, I had a massive smile. Things were looking bright for me. This move was no longer a mistake. I was here for a reason.

Chapter 5

KYNDALL

I have a horrible feeling!

That was my one thought as I dragged my tired feet through Des Moines International Airport in Iowa. I should have stuck with my gut when Alex came over to tell me about this assignment, especially since it had been the first time we had spoken, since I kicked her out of my house about a week ago.

But I'm a money whore.

I clenched my stomach and tried to ignore the wave of nausea that threatened to overwhelm me, and gave a grunt of acceptance when I was offered the job. When she offered me the job, I could feel the tension between us, yet my heart melted and I agreed without hesitation.

What can I say? I love my cousin dearly.

After she gave me the details of the job, I had offered an olive branch, "Alex, how are you?"

"Fine," she trailed off, acting like her nails were the most critical thing in the world.

"Did you get my gift for Maxwell?" I asked.

"Yes, thanks." Her response was to the point.

"Alex, can we just—"

She cut me off. "You owe me an apology. You injured my shoulder, and you were completely out of line."

I bit my tongue and forced a smile. "I'm sorry for hurting you. That was never my intention, and I lost a bit of control."

Alex stared back at me. "Okay, I forgive you. Can I have my keys back? So that I can check up on you like a normal person?"

I counted to three and took a deep breath. "Thank you." I forced the words through gritted teeth. "I gave it much thought, and I think I will keep the keys just because I do not want a repeat of what happened last time."

"Fine." She huffed out. "I'll need to call the cops to do wellness visits for you every time you don't pick up the phone, then."

"Fine, Ms. Dramatic. I'll give you the key back, but please respect my home. My home is my sanctuary, and you disrespected me. I feel I deserve an apology as well."

She huffed. "Sorry, Kyn. I won't barge into your home when you're masturbating. I'll respect your privacy."

I never wanted to hit someone as much as I wanted to right now. I took a few seconds to calm down before I said, "I accept your apology. Let's put this past us, especially since I'll be going to the backwoods of the U.S."

"I don't know why Marcus' guys need someone to scope out there. I could have sworn it was all corn fields and cows," Alex replied nonchalantly.

"Well, the money is good. I can't refuse it," I replied.

Alex agreed and beamed. "You'll be home in no time. You're amazing at what you do. Especially since you learned from me."

"Oh, there goes that gigantic head of yours."

And we both fell into a laughing fit, like we hadn't just made up.

She's crazy. But she's my cousin, and I'm sticking beside her.

That was all I thought about as my Uber drove to the seedy motel I rented. When I opened my room door, the stench of smoke and mold made me cough up a lung. I prayed and wiped down every surface I would touch in the room. Usually, I stayed until Sunday or Monday, being here gave me "run the hell away" vibes. Luckily, I'd booked a return flight for tomorrow.

After placing my hair in a high ponytail, I quickly dressed in my black bodycon dress and black pumps and hightailed it out the door. When the Uber appeared at the club, I was astonished. The club looked out of place in this city with a modern black exterior and all sleek lines. It was like a beautiful thumb on a sore hand.

No matter how fancy, a bar was a bar. I entered the club and slid onto a bar stool. Flagging down the bartender, I ordered my usual Coke and vodka on the rocks. Of course, I told him to go light on the vodka. He found that funny as I got swept up in his smile and his brown eyes twinkled. He was hot, and if it were any other time, I would have allowed him to have me walking bowlegged through the airport tomorrow.

"Here is your Coke with a splash of vodka," he chuckled.

"Thank you," I smirked, and moved away from the bar to the tables before I got into trouble.

The club was swarming with people, and everyone was joyfully tipsy. I found a high table in the back and away from the dance floor. Perfect for me to scope out the place, dance for a few, and return to my moldy hotel room.

Thirty minutes into my assignment, the all too familiar nausea and prickling sensation set in. I quickly looked around without being suspicious, and my heart dropped into my ass. Quickly, I tried to get up to leave before Sage could spot me, but I was too late. She yelled at me. Sweat formed on my upper lip, and my stomach churned.

"Kyndall! I thought that was you. I kept saying repeatedly it was, and I was right," she yelled, a little loudly. Which caused me to squirm in discomfort.

Sage Ashford looked just like she did in high school, except she'd gained weight. Her dark skin was smooth, and her face had the same modelesque features. Her simple yellow dress made her skin glow.

"Hey, I'm sorry. I think you may have the wrong person," I asserted. I know it's irrational, but if I deny I know her, it might give me the opportunity to flee quickly. My anxiety dropped a little.

"Kyndall, come on. I know it's been ten years, but I know you remember me from high school. Me, you, Bella, Melissa, and Mercedes were best friends," she yelled over the music. My left eye twitched.

Friends?

Sigh, God shoot me now, "Oh yes, well, it was nice—"

"Come on, Kyndall, let's have a drink and catch up," Sage pleaded.

"You know what, let's exchange numbers, and we can get a drink sometime tomorrow," I told her. She didn't listen to me. Sage grabbed my hand and forcibly dragged me to her table.

My palms were sweating with nervousness. My black dress became damp with sweat. The hair on the nape of my neck and my edges puffed up. I absolutely hated this situation. I had not completed my assignment. It was a waste of a trip to this place, and now, after twenty minutes, Sage was still talking about herself. I heaved a sigh and tapped my foot while she continued to talk. "I'm living in Manhattan, SoHo specifically. I love—"

"You live where?" My eyes widened in surprise.

"In Manhattan," she repeated, oblivious to my impending heart attack. "Today is my last day here for business."

"Great, well, Sage, it was nice catching up." I stood and got about an inch away. I hurried and tried to leave with the last bit of dignity I had. Before her next sentence stopped me dead in my tracks.

"And guess what!" she yelled. "Melissa recently moved to New York with her family."

I swung back around, my eyes locked on her lips as they moved. "Excuse me, I don't think I heard you over the music."

"Melissa moved to New York...Centre Island" She looked at me funny. "You should give me your number, and I can pass it along. Maybe we can come back here to visit you. She has three husbands now!"

The news stumped me. I tried to speak, but my voice was stuck in my throat. It took me a couple of minutes to compose myself—at least enough to speak a little.

"Well, that's nice for her and you. I would rather get hit by a bus than see that bitch. You can tell her to fuck off and go back to where she came from," I managed to say as my legs were about to give out. Sage looked downright appalled and I can't say I blamed her, but I didn't care about Melissa. I'm over her and what she did to me.

Right?

"Kyndall—"

But I couldn't hear anything except the little voice in my head saying "run."

That's precisely what I did. I held onto the little purse I had brought for dear life and ran like the devil was chasing me. I didn't stop until I hit the club door and went to turn the corner and my ankle twisted. But because of my panic attack, I ran on adrenaline and kept going until I reached the end of the block. I finally slowed down, leaned against the corner building, and requested an Uber.

I never had felt more pathetic as I stood there waiting for the rideshare. With my panic winding down, the throb in my ankle became a dull pain. It reminded me it was another thing to take care of once I got home. When I wiped my face, I felt my cheeks were wet. I didn't even feel the tears coming down as I ran out of the building.

You are a mess!

I jumped into the Uber with my throbbing ankle and took out my headphones to block out the noise from the driver's car. Rude, but I decided I didn't care as I took out my last of my pain pills and swallowed the pills dry, hoping it would help my ankle. I looked at myself with my camera. The eyeliner that took me forever to do had streaked down my face. My lipstick was halfway rubbed off—long lasting, my ass. My dress had a large wet spot down the front—I must have spilled my drink a little when Sage mentioned Melissa. In other words, I looked a hot mess.

When the driver pulled up, I hobbled to my moldy hotel room.

Not caring about sleeping in my makeup or changing clothes, I dropped onto the bed and cried for the first time in maybe eight years. Once I started, I couldn't stop. I was dry-heaving and snotty. I couldn't even pinpoint the main reason I was mad. Was it Melissa? Melissa being in New York? Melissa having a family? Or me letting someone who screwed me get to me all over again?

I didn't even remember falling asleep, but when my alarm woke me up, I felt like shit. Walking to the bathroom to get ready, I got a good look at my face after last night's mess. I had raccoon eyes from my eyeliner, with bags under my eyes as big as my boobs. *A hot mess.*

As I got ready, I sent a text to Marcus that I wasn't able to complete the job. It'd been five minutes since I texted him and he was still complaining. I ignored my phone and went about my day.

Oh well, tough shit, Marcus!

Back home after five hours, I could now finally breathe for a minute. I showered and settled into my bean bag, thinking I would fall asleep reading my latest book. But ten minutes into my reading session, I'd not made it past the first page. I stared at the words.

My doorbell rang just as I finally placed my Kindle down. I would have paid a large sum of money to see the bewildered look on my face when I heard the doorbell ringing at ten PM. With my bat in my hand, I limped to the door.

"Who is it?" I tried my best to sound masculine.

"What do you mean, who is it? Who else is coming to knock on your crazy ass door! And that's the worst man's voice I have ever heard."

"Alex, why are you here so late?" I asked as I opened the door. "I just got in and wanted to be miserable alone."

"Yeah, I can see that." I glared at her, but she ignored me. She went on, "You ain't got no bra on. I know you in for the night."

I led her to the living room. "Humph, I'm going to ignore that comment. Since this is the first time you've actually rung the doorbell. I am shocked."

"See—I'm trying to be good," she huffed and flopped down on my sofa. My eyebrows shot up and my nose wrinkled in surprise when I saw her place her foot on my coffee table.

I knocked her legs down and passed into my kitchen. I pulled out the cognac that I reserved for special occasions.

Alex placed her legs up on my sofa instead. "You know I'm staying over, right? It's too late to go back home safely."

"Okay, you may stay over, but don't give me that lame ass excuse." I know Alex like the back of my hand. She always comes over late when she and Marcus got into a fight. "Where's Maxwell? I miss my baby. If you were going to drag your lying tail over here, you could have at least brought him."

Alex humphed. "Well, I would have, but he's over at his grandmother's for the weekend." She flicked on the television. "Yes, Ms. Nosy, we fought, but it was over you."

I handed her a small glass tumbler with a reasonable amount of cognac and ice. "Me? Oh, let me guess." I took the seat next to her. "I failed to complete one job, and he's going to bitch and moan about it, huh?"

"Yeah, he was doing more than a bit of bitching. I defended you because I know you wouldn't mess with your money if it weren't something major." Alex chugged her drink and then poured another to the rim of the glass. "I told him some major shit must have happened because we know how you like to nickel and dime us to death."

I rolled my eyes. There was nothing wrong with being a penny pincher, especially since I had no one but Alex to fall back on if things got rough. "Well, some of us don't have the luxury of being able to call a family member up and ask for help when times are hard. Remember, I'm the devil for being bisexual. So every penny counts."

Her eyes became glassy. I couldn't tell if she was going to cry or if it was from her chugging that cognac like it was juice. "You know I will always be there for you, like four flats on a Cadillac. Plus, fuck 'em. They're worried about the wrong damn things." She grinned. "Tell me, what happened? Seriously, this is not like you."

How do I explain this to her without sounding like a scared child? I sat there for five minutes before Alex snapped her fingers at me. "Earth to Kyndall." There was no way to make this sound good.

I told her—I told her everything. And when I was done, Alex's mouth and mind moved a mile a minute to make sure she understood everything correctly. I barely understood it myself, if we're being honest.

She went silent. I looked at Alex.

She looked at me back for a good minute.

I stared right back.

Alex's lips twitched, and I warned her, "You better not."

She did, though. She broke out in a full belly laugh. I wanted to jump up and hit her. "Yuck it up all you want. I'm going to burn your keys and kick you out again."

She snorted. "Okay, I'm sorry for laughing. I couldn't help it. Did I not tell you that pushing shit to the back of your colossal size head would come back and hit you in your face?"

I stared at her because she was right, along with the stupid therapist. Well, she wasn't stupid. I am just being whiney.

"No, you said nothing like that before." Alex made a "really, girl?" look, and I changed my tune. "Okay, fine. You did. I think the worst thing is finding out about her having a family. Which is stupid to admit because it's been over a decade since high school."

"It's okay to have those feelings, but how you deal with them matters the most. I think you should try to find another therapist and try to find a stable—keyword S-T-A-B-L-E—relationship. Not a one night stand," As she polished off her second drink.

"Okay, fine. I will try therapy again and be better this time." I looked at her, amazed that she could have a conversation with that amount of alcohol in her system. Shoot, I was tipsy if I drank more than half a glass. "I want you to get serious about your drinking as well. Since we are talking about recovering from our addictions, it's not normal to drink that much."

She pinned me with a stare that would burn the skin off my body. "We have Jamaican in our blood; plus, we're from the south. Drinking is like second nature to us." She poured another glass full of cognac. "I don't know where your tolerance for alcohol went, but you need to find it. Drinking two glasses shouldn't make you act like you had five."

"Alright, Ms. Houston, Jamerican alcohol princess. You would have only had half a glass if Marcus were here."

"Forget Marcus." She kissed her teeth and rolled her eyes.

"Yeah, uh huh, until tomorrow when y'all made up," I badgered. With a firm grip, I wrestled Alex's glass away and carried our two tumblers to the kitchen, with the clinking of the glasses echoing in my ears. I was washing them and continued, "Anyway, go to bed. I'm jet lagged."

"Yeah, I'm pretty beat as well. Maybe we can hang out tomorrow. If you're not doing anything, of course." I said, as I yawned.

"Yes, we can go down to Centre Island and drive around." She batted her eyes.

"Yes, let's go. I may take up a new hobby called ditch Alex in the Oyster Bay." I smiled sweetly.

"Okay, okay mini mafia princess. Let me lock my door tonight because you may kiss or kill me." She grabbed her breasts. "Or curse me out like you did, Sage."

"More of the killing part, I would say," I muttered. Alex may be right about therapy. As I walked into my bedroom, feeling better. Right before I dozed off, I researched the best therapist in Queens and sent a silent prayer for my savings.

Chapter 6

KYNDALL

A MONTH HAD PASSED since my return from Iowa, and I felt like I could finally think clearly again. All thanks to my amazing therapist, Dr. Anita Smith. She helped me put many things into perspective, and I gained a newfound balance. Plus, it helped that she was insanely gorgeous—I mean, fucking beautiful. She had the softest obsidian skin that I wouldn't mind wrapped around my head. Her brown-green hazel eyes were the brightest I had ever seen, and she had these heavy, full breasts that I—

"Earth to Kyndall." Dr. Anita Smith waved her manicured hand in front of me. "I lost you again for the umpteenth time. Every session, I have to snap you out of your daydream."

"I–I am sorry, Dr. Smith," I blushed. My top priority was to get laid because having a wet dream about my therapist in front of her was not it. "I'm busy nowadays. So, I don't notice when I'm zoning out, thinking about all the stuff I have to do," I lied. I couldn't tell her how I sat and drooled over the thought of bending her over her purple chaise chair and feasting on her from behind.

"Kyndall," she snapped her fingers, and I blinked back to reality. "Lost you again. You must really be busy. Is there something bothering you that is making it difficult to focus on our sessions?"

Okay, now I'm mortified. I needed to get laid soon. Staring at my therapist's body like a horny teenager was unbecoming. "Sorry, Dr. Smith."

I gave her my sweetest smile. "I've been looking into new jobs and fixing things in my library. In my free time, I'm getting to know this married couple. Their names are Zoey and Sean Rhodes. We started dating about three weeks ago."

She leaned over to scratch an itch on her ankle. I tried not to notice how the act of her leaning over put those beautiful twins on display. The moment her eyes returned to mine; I maintained eye contact. "That must be exciting." Her eyes lit up. "I know when we initially started our sessions, the thought of your ex living close to you overwhelmed you. What changed?"

"She's not my ex. She's someone I thought was a friend, and I took her kindness for something else." Dr. Smith smiled, and I don't know why but it made me want to kiss that silly smile off her face.

"I'm sure she considered you a friend as well. From what you've told me about Melissa, she acted like a friend early in your relationship." Dr. Smith looked at her notes. "A relationship ending badly doesn't erase all the good feelings that happened during it."

Dr. Smith was too sweet. This world didn't deserve someone like her. "Dr. Smith, someone who calls you their best friend or sister, doesn't leave you the way she did. I don't care what excuse someone may have. Wrong is wrong."

"You have a right to your feelings, Kyndall. Past feelings and present ones. I'm asking for you not to deny *all* of them. Until your last night together, Melissa seemed to have been one of the most important relationships in your life. It might be helpful to acknowledge, confront, and come to terms with that." She stopped writing to look at me. "I was wondering, maybe not now, but maybe soon. Would you be open to reaching out to Melissa? Hear her perspective on the events and hash it out."

There it was. Two weeks ago, I'd started suspecting Dr. Smith would suggest seeing Melissa. Yet, despite two weeks to think of one, I'm stumped at what reasonable response I could give besides "Hell freaking no!" I wanted to scream out and throw up at the same time. I made sure my voice sounded firm when I responded, "Oh, Dr. Smith, I really don't believe that would help me. Maybe if I were still that eighteen-year-old who woke up alone in my bed. Perhaps that would have helped, but I am not her anymore."

"Hmm, okay, I understand your logic. Do you think there's anything else you could do to gain proper closure from this past traumatic event?" She tilted her head ever so slightly. "I understand your go-to method is to shove it in the back of your head and go about your life, but these things always come back to light. Your recent run-in with Sage, for example."

"You're right, Dr. Smith. Talking with a skilled professional is what I need. I already feel better and don't plan to ditch therapy." I said as I smiled at her sweetly.

"I hope not. We have so much to unpack from your life." She closed her book. "Sadly, our session is over, and we will have to pick up our conversation during our next meeting. Hopefully, you won't be too distracted next time."

My cheeks grew warm. "N-No, Dr. Smith, I will be on top of yo—things next time." I ran out of her office as fast as possible.

"God! How embarrassing was that?" I muttered, as I speed walk to the elevator. Luckily, I'd been seeing this couple for about three weeks now. It was about time I knocked the cobwebs out. As I exited the elevator, that familiar French Vanilla scent greeted me. It was almost like I was back in my childhood bedroom in Orlando with my nose shoved into the pillow Melissa laid on. As soon as the memory came, I shook it out of my head. I sighed as I exited the building and went to my car.

I need to quit it.

It was the most beautiful and coldest day outside. My mind whispered not to go home yet. Instead, I drove around until I hit the Queens Zoo. Nature and animals are my solace.

I paid my entrance fee for the zoo and headed to my favorite spot, the water marsh. It was the only place in Queens you could see alligators and swamp wildlife like the ones found in Orlando. Plus, not a lot of folks sat in this area. I could shovel down my late lunch in peace.

As I munched my sandwich, I watched the latest bunch of kids ogle the gators and jump excitedly. I thought about how many hours I spent making money. For decades, I had focused on my side hustle, desperate never to be poor again, that there had been no time for a serious relationship. I had no room in my heart for true love and starting a family. For the first time in my adult life, I was secure—my finances wouldn't fall out from under me, and I could focus on my personal happiness.

It hadn't taken long for me to find Zoey and Sean, thanks to a dating app designed for polyamorous couples. One night, when boredom stuck because Alex was away on an assignment for Marcus, I had flipped through my phone's app store and there it was.

After matching with Sean and Zoey, we chatted on the app for a while, followed each other on social media, and eventually met in person. I got the feeling they were genuine. Already a hundred times better than my previous "serious" relationship. This time, I felt something new and exciting when I was with Zoey. I had shared intimate moments with people from other racial backgrounds, but I never had gone on an actual date with them.

Zoey was beautiful. Though she was white, she had skin that tanned easily because of her Italian heritage. Her big, gunmetal gray eyes sparkled in her round face, and her up-turned nose made her that much cuter. Her lips were plump and pink, with a slight gap in her teeth, which made her even more gorgeous.

Sean must have been a God in his past life. He was tall and his velvety ebony skin shined like a beacon. He had eyes that shone like black diamonds. When Sean smiled, his blinding white teeth hypnotized me. I had not gotten his complete life story, but he somehow gained a French accent that could drench my panties. He was perfection.

To be honest, things started off rocky because I was very awkward and didn't know how to navigate being in a truly committed relationship. But as time went by and we started going out more, I got more comfortable. It was now weird if Zoey didn't call to check up on me every night. Maybe they were a little clingy, but I would overlook that because I liked them. I could see myself with them long-term.

Well, I think I can.

I jumped as one of the zoo workers stopped by and told me the zoo closed in less than twenty minutes. It baffled me how fast time flew while I sat here. I discarded my trash, bought a teddy bear for Maxwell in the gift shop, and headed to my car. I would see my cousin's kiddo at the community block party next month.

The community center held the Jamaica community block party to help bring the community together and give the kids something to do rather than hang out on the streets. Alex and I usually attended because Marcus's "business" house was on the same street, which meant people in our sphere would show up as an excuse to suck up to him. It also gave me time to go check on some people I knew there for more work.

Maybe I'll invite Zoey and Sean to the block party.

Ah, yes, I like that plan a lot. A community party and then a party for three after sounded like a masterpiece. By the time I was home, I was in a much better mood. I dedicated the next couple of hours to cleaning the house until it was time for bed.

Life is good!

The following month flew by. The next thing I knew, it was March and the day of the community block party. Thanks to global warming, the weather was warm. It had almost two months since I had started dating Zoey and Sean, and to be honest, it was sucking majorly. Ever since we'd shared my birthday dinner, they'd taken to texting me almost every waking hour to check in. The clingy neediness irked me to no end.

I'd wanted to wait until the block party to have sex with them, but I caved in, and it was not good. The first time was very mediocre. I came not because of them, but because I just hadn't had time to pleasure myself in a while. After the first time, every time we had sex, I couldn't come. I would lay there, pretend, and then rush off to masturbate.

Instead of spending the morning dwelling, I hopped out of bed, did my morning routine, and hit my closet for something to wear. These tragic events call for my black skinny jeans that fit like a second skin, a leopard bodysuit with a built-in bra, and black flats. The clothes glided on over my silky skin. It was sad I wouldn't be getting anything in return for looking this good, but oh well.

Ugh, Let's get it over with before I chicken out.

The ride to Marcus' house was uneventful, and I spotted Zoey and Sean in the crowd. They stuck out like a sore thumb. Who wore designer brands to a block party? I watched them as they shifted uneasily and glanced around. A cold, sick feeling washed over me.

When I closed the distance, I greeted them with a kiss each. "Hey Zoey, hey Sean. Glad you guys could make it." I inwardly cringed because I wished they would have called and canceled.

"Of course, we made it." Like a Siamese twin, Zoey attached herself to my side. "Maybe we can sneak away and have dinner at your place."

I suppressed the sigh that was eager to come out. "Well, I may need to go to my cousin's house to help her with something," I lied. "Can I take a raincheck and we hang out tomorrow?"

"Yes, of course," she responded, looking disappointed. "Oh, maybe we can have dinner and a movie?"

Sean, the quiet God, added, "That sounds like fun. How about a Marvel movie and some cheap Chinese food?"

"Oh yeah, sounds like fun," I responded unenthusiastically. Gosh, I wanted to run right into Marcus' house and never come out, and that's saying a lot. Sean slung his arm over my shoulder, as if to match his wife in suffocating me. How did this go from good to bad in such a short time?

We walked down the block. Dozens of tables from organizations and businesses crowded the space. There was no DJ, but someone had a mix of the latest and old songs blasting from a couple of outdoor speakers. There weren't a lot of decorations, but they had a play area for the kids, and some of the vendor's tables had balloons. A banner stating, "Elmhurst Community Block Party" hung high between the two tallest houses spanning the street.

It was only noon, but people packed the block like church on Easter Sunday. The neighborhood kids were in their own world, and most of the adults gathered at the tables for gifts from the vendors. Some elders had taken up their usual spots on stoops.

One kid almost collided with Zoey, but she didn't move. She remained attached like a barnacle. Clutching me tighter, she winced. "Oh my god, this is a madhouse. There should be someone watching these kids."

Sean herded us to an open spot against a fence. "Yes, they need order here. Hopefully, our kids won't be this wild."

Don't throw up!

Don't throw up!

Don't throw up!

The thought of being stuck with them for the next couple of hours was enough to make me crazy, but the idea of 18+ years with them? Yeah, no, thank you.

I straightened and tried to shake Zoey off, but she simply readjusted to squeeze between me and Sean. The introvert in me had enough. As soon as I thought I was about to blow, I heard the saving grace of my cousin.

"Hey, my beautiful cousin!" Alex charged over with Maxwell on her hip. "How are you? And you must be Zoey and Sean!"

"Yes, it is a pleasure to meet you at last. We've heard nothing but good things about you and this handsome young fellow." Sean grabbed Alex's hand and kissed it. He playfully pinched Maxwell's arm.

As Zoey introduced herself and they spoke for a bit, I grabbed the giggling Maxwell and kissed him on his chubby cheeks. Maxwell was his mom's twin, thank God. He gave me a wet kiss and wiggled in my arms. Putting him on one hip, I used my free hand to retrieve the zoo gift shop's teddy bear from my purse. When I handed him the stuffed bear, his brown eyes shone with joy.

Holding Maxwell tighter, I excused myself and went to say hello to Marcus out of respect. Sorry, no—because I wanted the first pick of the good assignments. Basically, I was trying to kiss ass.

"Hey Marcus, how are you? You're on Maxwell duty now." I reluctantly handed him the baby.

"Hey Kyn, I am terrific. Are you ready for some more work soon?" He tickled Maxwell until he squealed. Marcus had always been straight to the chase with me—anything beyond that, he started in on sexist nonsense and annoying conspiracy theories.

"Yes, and I want a good payday as well."

"I got you. I'll send details soon."

"Alright, see ya." I left him quick, one annoying person down. I shuddered at my poor baby Maxwell. I was determined to get him over to my house as often as possible because I didn't want him to come out like his father.

I walked back to my hellish duo and my cousin. A dreadful sensation settled in the pit of my stomach and made me dizzy. Like someone was staring a hole into me. The old Kyndall would have run scared, but the new Kyndall pushed onwards to rescue her cousin, who looked about ready to shank Zoey.

Bluntly cutting into their conversation, "Alex, let's run and check the tables out." We left after Zoey and Sean kissed me.

As soon as we walked away, she let out a loud breath. "Thank God. If I had to hear them complain any longer, I would have committed murder."

"Well, at least you get to leave them here. They were making plans to come back to my place." I shuddered. "I'm trying to give this relationship a chance, but they are too clingy. If I shower for over thirty minutes, Zoey texts me to see what I did that took forever."

"Yikes. Seriously, Kyndall, why are you with them?" She looked at me. "You're better than this. They may be nice folks, but they're not for you." She led me through the crowd. "Listen, I know I've been hard on you about being in a relationship, but that doesn't mean sacrificing your happiness just because you're lonely."

"I know." And I did. Today made me realize there was no point in dragging out this relationship out, especially since I wanted a family of my own. All three of us deserved better. "I'll tell them when we leave this place. Let's look at the booths and get free shit."

"Sounds like a plan." Alex hooked her arms into mine. Unlike with Zoey, I liked it.

What I didn't like was my stomach tightening into knots. I shivered and confessed, "I feel sick and like someone is watching me."

"You're just being paranoid and maybe guilty for bringing Tweedledee and Tweedledum with you." I pinned Alex with a "don't start with me" look.

Alex and I walked the block until we were almost to the end. My phone buzzed. I became engrossed in the text I received and checking Instagram that I barely felt Alex as she tugged me along to the last table. It wasn't until we got to the front that I heard a faint but familiar voice and that haunting French vanilla scent. I snapped my head up to see the ghost of my past, someone I actively avoided. The one person who invaded my dreams on nights when I was weak and lonely.

Melissa Stella Brown

Chapter 7

MELISSA

What a shitty way to start the day!

I woke up with a foggy brain and a sense of disorientation. I felt like I'd ran a marathon while hungover. It served me right. I don't know how Amber convinced me to stay in the heated pool until almost midnight. When I knew I had to get up and go to our community outreach event today.

I dragged myself through my morning routine and got dressed. As I put on my makeup, Aaron sauntered into the bathroom, fresh from a workout in the home gym. "How long is this event? We were going to go into the city and have dinner tonight, but not if you're going to be late."

"I think we should hold off, or you guys go without me. I'll probably be there late, and I don't want princess Amber to wait to eat. She'll bite all our heads off." I chortled. "Plus, you can bring me back something, and I'll warm it up."

"Are you sure? We can just put it off until tomorrow or another weekend." He peeled off his shirt and tossed it in the hamper.

"No, you guys go. She deserves it. Plus, it's been a while since you had a father-daughter night out." I kissed him. "Okay, time to exit, or I won't ever make it on time. Bye, babe."

"Bye, don't get into trouble," he exclaimed as he stepped into the shower.

I chuckled.

As I left the house after saying goodbye, I hopped into my car and stopped by the clinic. I'd bought pens, post-its, business cards, and other giveaway items to hand out today, but I had to bring them into the clinic for Dr. May's and Dr. Stein's approval. I delighted my colleagues when they saw I personalized all the stuff with our names, clinic phone number, and address. The purchase was worth every penny. It would ensure my name, along with theirs, was out in the community.

Once I retrieved my missing items, I headed to the block party. Of course, me being me. I got lost because the GPS had a vendetta against me today.

That is strike two for the shitty day.

When I finally reached the venue, the area reminded me of back home in Orlando in a way. A bunch of colorful older homes lined the street. What stuck out more were the people lined up against the houses. There had to be over one hundred up and down the block.

The guys would have a field day with this area. I shook my head. I met Dr. May by our booth, and we set up our things and prepared for the visitors.

"Dr. Walker, are you ready for today? These free products will give us the best chance to get to know folks," As she sat in front of her half of the table.

I finally sat down. "How long do you usually stay here?"

"Maybe four or five hours." She shrugged nonchalantly. "As long as there are no problems, I stay as long as possible."

"Have there been problems before? I'm not scared of anything, but I must make it home to my baby."

"Years back, one of the rival gangs messed around here, but the one across the street kicked them out and declared they would attend the community party every year. Since then, everyone leaves safely," she said with a shrug.

"You say it like you're telling me the weather." I looked at her, perplexed.

"Well, it's New York, love. You get used to it after about your third year in." She laughed.

About two hours later, visitors visited our little table—most people wanted the gifts, but some had actual questions. I'd given out a handful of my business cards and set up a couple of new client appointments before the party was halfway done. I saw a woman come in, who was stunning. But I couldn't shake the feeling that I knew her from somewhere.

At around twelve, my stomach cursed me out for not feeding it. I told Dr. May that I would step to the side and have a quick break. I bought a burger and stood to the side eating and watched the people of the community. The stunning woman from earlier came closer and closer. Something in me wanted to run up and smother her in my arms.

Maybe I need to go on a date.

I shoved the rest of my burger into my mouth as I analyzed the woman. I knew in the depth of my heart who it was, but I just had to be sure—which I couldn't be from that angle. She had on jeans that made her ass look curvy. Her bodysuit made her waist appear smaller and her breasts scream to pop out. I definitely wouldn't have minded that, I thought as I bit my lip. Her hair was long, and it wasn't until she turned around to stand stiffly next to a Black man that I finally saw her face.

It's Kyndall. My Kyndall!

No. She was not mine, I had to remind myself, as I trampled my possessive side. When she kissed the Black man and white woman beside her, I wanted to vomit up my lunch. I was furious. But when I saw the face Kyndall made when she was sick, I calmed down. It didn't entitle me to be jealous, but oh well. Another lady with a child joined the group, and Kyndall's face lit up like they had given her water in a desert—she gathered the tiny kid in her arms and doted on him.

I lost track of time as I stared at Kyndall until Dr. May waved her hand in front of my face. "Hey, Dr. Walker, are you tapping out for the day? You've been standing there for almost thirty minutes."

"Oh yeah, I'm sorry, I just got caught up in something," As I returned to my seat. I quickly got myself in check and stopped all those stupid thoughts. I deserved nothing from Kyndall, but I found it hard to concentrate on anything else. From my seat, I caught glimpses of her circling the party with the third woman in tow. My heart raced faster and my breathing grew shallow as she drew nearer to the table. My scrubs stuck to my skin, and my mouth felt as if I had eaten a lot of salt. I was slowly but surely going to lose control of myself or the situation, which scared the living shit out of me.

Get a hold of yourself, Melissa! This isn't high school, and you're not a teenager. What are you doing?

I repeated my mantra, trying to convince myself I could keep control. When Kyndall and the other lady arrived at my little table, I jumped up like the devil himself pricked me. I barely recognized my voice when I called her name.

"K-Kyndall," I stammered like a fool.

She popped her head up from her phone and stared at me. Her eyes were a fiery reflection of her swirling emotions of anger, longing, sadness, and shame. All those emotions were gone in a blink, quickly replaced with a blank, emotionless face.

"Sorry, do I know you? I think you may have confused me with someone else." Her voice was void of emotion. She avoided my eyes and pretended she didn't know me. The lady she came with looked puzzled and lost at our interaction. That's the game she wanted to play.

I can fight fire with fire.

I turned to Dr. May to see if she was paying any attention to what was happening, and she was busy with another visitor. When I turned back, I caught Kyndall's gaze sweeping up and down my body, lingering on my breasts. When she realized I'd caught her, her cheeks turned a slight shade of pink. I don't know how I kept calm when I wanted to smack her silly and shove my tongue down her throat.

Quit it, Melissa!

I wanted to break that emotionless façade. "I thought you were living in Iowa, Kyndall. Sage said she saw you in a club there. She said you had some colorful words to say about me. I thought she was mistaken because I know you don't like clubs, Kyn." I tilted my head and unashamedly ran my eyes over her body. My tongue wet my lips.

Kyndall's lips twitched, but her friend spoke next with hate in her voice. "Excuse me, Dr. Melissa Walker." She rolled her eyes. "But you're acting inappropriately right now. I would hate—"

Kyndall cut her off. "Dr. Walker, I am glad you're doing well. I don't want to cause a scene here, but you should know one thing: you don't know shit about me anymore. I hope you and your family have a good day!" She turned on her heel and walked away.

I fucked that one up.

"Kyndall!" I shouted after her. "Wait, let's talk." But it was too late. She hauled her friend off to a house in the middle of the block, where that couple waited. Kyndall sat on the guy's lap for show because she knew I would watch her like a hawk. *She was infuriating*, I thought as I crossed my arms, but feeling sad at our interaction.

For the next three hours, I barely focused on the people who stopped by our table and instead kept my eye on Kyndall. I watched for three hours as she bounced back and forth between that one couple. Even though her body told a different story, she hugged, kissed, and giggled with them. Even with those forced actions, I could tell she was uncomfortable and stiff.

I was heading over to Kyndall when Dr. May shouted my phone was ringing as she cleaned up and took some of her things to her car.

I answered the call on the last ring.

"Hey Melissa, I know you're close to the city," Sage cheerfully spoke through the phone. "Just wanted to see if you wanted to come over after your event."

"Sage, I'll try to see if I can. I have to talk to Kyndall before she leaves," I responded hurriedly. The moment I'd glanced away, Kyndall seemed to say goodbye to her companions.

"Talk to *who*? Wait, What's—"

I hung up the phone and threw it in my bag. With only a couple of free items left, I abandoned them, not caring if someone took them or not. I breathed a silent thank you to myself for selecting my sneakers instead of my high heels.

I dashed over to the house. Oblivious, Kyndall stepped inside. The house was suspiciously fancier than the others on the block—was it some kind of trap house? I scrunched my eyebrows because I couldn't imagine Kyndall being some Queen of the North and dealing drugs. She was a straight-A student like me. I snapped out of my imagination. I straightened up, put on my big girl panties, and pushed through the silver wire gate.

A group of burly men immediately blocked me in the entranceway.

Yeah, something shady definitely happens here. I stuck out my hand to shake. "Hello," I whispered softly, because I was scared as shit. "I saw Kyndall come into this house." I straightened up. "Can I please speak with her?"

The larger guy of the duo looked me over and taunted, "Who's Kyndall? Ain't no Kyndall here. But I can get your number and take you out sometime," he grinned. He and the others laughed.

"Fine, I'll stay here and wait for her to come out," I said with my arms crossed and my back straightened.

"Okay, but you'll be waiting for a while." He took out his phone and went on, "Why don't you give me your number, and I'll give it to Kyndall?"

"Wait, I thought you said there wasn't anyone named Kyndall in the house?" I tilted my head. I knew I should leave, but I was hard-headed.

"Shit, you one-upped me. I got you, ma." He licked his lips, and I cringed. "I will get Kyndall for you 'cause I slipped up."

I prayed to whoever was upstairs. As the man disappeared through the white metal frame door of the house, others started asking inappropriate questions.

A man toward the back of the group heckled, "Yo, you letting Kyndall hit that? She doesn't keep anyone around if they ain't sharing their man. But you ain't got to share me tho. I'll be exclusive to you."

"Oh ha, Kyndall only has one-night stands with couples?" I inquired innocently.

"Yeah, she only fucks them if they're a wife and husband who wants a threesome. She's a notorious hit and runner. She won't be there in the morning, ma. But I will be there as long as you want me to." He grinned, and I got a glimpse of a mouthful of gold crowns on his teeth.

"No, thanks. My three partners are enough," I beamed happily.

"Damn, ma, you're getting dicked down already. Never mind, I think you might have got Kyndall beat." The guys laughed, and I rolled my eyes.

Men sometimes have a one-track mind.

Before I could respond to him, Kyndall came stomping down the stairs, looking ready to burn the entire block down.

Chapter 8

KYNDALL

IF SOMEONE HAD TOLD me I would never be free of Melissa Brown, excuse me, Dr. Melissa Walker, I would have laughed my ass off. But here I was, breaking my persona again because of her sudden reappearance in my life. I knew I would have acted a fool if I didn't walk away from that table, dragging Alex with me. But lo-and-behold, I acted a fool anyway. I jumped, kissed, and led Zoey and Sean on for the show. Now they were so excited about tomorrow that they plan to come earlier.

I swear, I could beat myself.

I knew once I got caught staring at Melissa's stacked body, I would either lose my shit or crumble under her, taking whatever crumbs she gave me. Luckily, when Alex finally put two and two together, I could stop the Melissa hate train because I may be a bitch sometimes, but I don't want everyone to know my business. I convinced myself that I would stay until the end of the event because I wanted to stay with Alex. In my heart of hearts, I knew I stayed for Melissa, and from the way she burned a hole in my body. She was obviously jealous.

Score one for me.

I gave myself a second point for how she stood in front of me now, fuming on Marcus' front lawn. "Kyndall, we should talk," she pointed out.

"We have nothing to talk about." I moved to leave, but I knew she was always a hard-headed person. "Let sleeping dogs lie. You ignore me,

I ignore you. You stay on your side of the island, and I stay on mine. We don't have to interact with each other."

Her hazel eyes went wide, which pleaded with me. "Please, Kyndall, I think we both need to speak and get stuff off our chests."

From inside, Jacques, a muscle man, called out. "Kyndall, I think this one might be your kryptonite!" The other guys cackled like hyenas. I flipped them off. I wasn't in the mood.

I chewed my bottom lip. I knew no good would come from this, but I agreed. "Fine, and I'll give you five minutes—nothing more, nothing less."

"Okay, that's all I need," she said with a smile and looked pointedly over my shoulder, where Marcus' men were gawking at us. "We should do it someplace private."

"Agreed," I acknowledged, and before she could respond, I grabbed her hand and led her out of the block party. We walked for five minutes in complete silence as I navigated my way through the crowd. When the crowd of people finally thinned, I spotted my red Lexus RX hybrid. She rubbed her thumb over my hand like old times, and my stomach lurched.

Get a hold of yourself, Kyndall!

I sat in my driver's seat, and she hopped into the passenger's seat. I knew better, but I noticed those tiny freckles that lined her cheeks. The same ones I stayed up to count when she was asleep.

32 on each cheek.

"Nice custom interior." Melissa commented, as she ran her hand over the custom leather seats. "I have an RX hybrid as well. Great minds think alike." She chuckled.

With a stern look, I crossed my arms. I was not giving in, no matter how good she looked in her scrubs. I didn't care one bit. Not how the scrub top strained against her heaving breasts, nor how she still wore the same French vanilla perfume. Nope, not giving in. "Your five minutes are going."

"Right." She blew out a breath. "Listen, Kyndall. I'm sorry for what I did. I was young, careless, and only concerned with what I needed to do to never become like my mother. My intentions were never to hurt you, honestly. I thought it was best if we had a clean break."

This day must be an awful joke, or some twisted fucked up dream.

"Wait a minute, was that supposed to be an apology? Melissa, do you think you were the only one with dreams and hopes? When you left, you messed up my college plans and made me become–never mind. It doesn't matter. As you mentioned, I didn't matter enough for you to tell me you were moving. I was just another one night stand, a disposal friend."

She grabbed my hands, which I must have balled up at some point. I hadn't noticed my fingernails digging into my palms until the sharp sting occurred. Melissa said, "It matters what happened. You were never a one-night stand nor someone I could dispose of. Kyndall, that night was special to me, and I fucked it up." She rubbed circles onto the backs of my hands, and I couldn't think straight. I didn't remove my hands because I was a weak hussy.

"It was a long time ago, and I'm over it," I lied. My brain latched onto those words. If I faked hard and long enough, this encounter would end, and I could return to my library haven. "I'm over you."

"Ouch, I deserve that." She looked around, ready to break down. "I thought about you almost every day during college. I always wondered what you were up to and how life was treating you. It must sound crazy, but I was going to come back for you, Kyndall."

She was going to come back for...me?

"Well, Melissa, as you can see, life has been great for me. No rescue needed." I rolled my eyes to keep the burgeoning tears from falling. "I never finished college and worked any job to make ends meet. My mom and most of my family exiled me. All I have is my cousin here in New York."

"I-I am sorry, Kyndall. Why did they throw you out of the family? That's crazy."

I stared. Why the hell was I sitting here? Seriously, she wasn't remotely sorry. "They found out I was bisexual. That was worse than sin itself." I tried to pull my hands from hers, but her vise-like grip held.

My throat was dry. She kissed the backs of my hands before releasing them to caress my cheek. I swear I nearly came in my jeans. "That's fucking horrible. You deserve better than that. I knew your family was strict, but I didn't realize it was that bad."

I need to get out of here.

I cleared my throat. "I heard you have husbands—as in more than one?" My voice was high-pitched. I never wanted to beat myself as much as I do right now.

Like seriously, Kyndall, get a hold of yourself.

She giggled. "Yes, Matt, Aaron, and Travis. I met them in undergrad, and we have a daughter, Amber." She gave me a half-smile. "I still love you, Kyndall, and as much as I try not to, I think about you almost every day." She bit into her plump, soft lip. "I dated girls that reminded me of you, but nothing compares to the real thing."

"Melissa, I don't know what type of paint you've been sniffing, but you should return to your wonderful life and family and forget you've seen me." I turned on my car to signal I was ready to go. "I'll drive you to your car. It's late, and this isn't the best place to walk at night."

I pulled out of my parking spot, and she led me to her car. As I pulled up in front of a car similar to mines, Melissa paused and turned to face me. "Kyndall, you mean to tell me you haven't thought about me since I left?"

I made the stupid mistake of looking at her, knowing I would find tears in her eyes. A bundle of pain in my throat arises. "I thought about you more than I wish I did, truthfully. But I'm over it now, and I've finally moved on with my life, Melissa. I thought stupidly that we could be a family and grow old together, but it took me a while to realize my naïveté." My mouth trembled and my eyes glazed over. "If you love something, let it go, but I don't want you to come back this time."

I did something next I would regret later. I kissed her. There was nothing lustful in this kiss. It was a goodbye kiss. I broke away from her because I was ashamed. "Goodbye, Melissa. I accept your apology and forgive you, but I won't forget. Hopefully, you and I can finally have peace. Go home and be with your family." After getting myself together, I smiled.

"Goodbye, Kyndall. Despite everything, it was good seeing you. Even though you don't want to hear it, I love you and always will."

Why would she say that?

She gave me one last kiss before getting out of my car and going around to the back. She paused briefly behind my car, like she wanted to turn around, but continued on to her car. I glanced away because I was a mess and wanted to get away so I could ugly cry.

Instead, I hopped out of my car—don't know what came over me—and banged on her window until she rolled it down. I shrieked, "Fuck you, Melissa! You don't deserve to be sad and remorseful! I hope you go home and are miserable!" I inhaled a sharp, sudden breath.

Melissa nodded.

Satisfied, I turned on my heel and hurried back to my car. I watched her peel away from my life for good.

Then why do I feel like shit? Why does the lump in my throat feel like it will explode?

Chapter 9

MELISSA

I WAS A HORRIBLE person. That was true then, and even more now. I always thought about what I would say to Kyndall if I ever saw her again, and nothing I planned came out of my mouth. As I pulled away from the neighborhood, I wiped away my tears. My hands were so shaky when I hit the end of the block that I had to pull over to gather my nerves.

I was about to pull off when I watched Kyndall's car pass by, and without thinking, I whipped out and followed her. Technically, I didn't have to follow her, since I took a picture of her license plate, but I wanted to see where she was going. According to the various signs, I followed her to the Forest Hills area. I hadn't had time to explore all of Queens yet. I got nervous because it was late, and I used my GPS to go everywhere because I didn't know the area.

On impulse, I kept a car distance away from her. I wanted to see where she was going. At each stoplight, I peeked out and noted if she turned off. She stayed on the main road until we reached the Forest Hills area. I followed her car while she made several sharp turns that almost made my car tip over. My phone buzzed again and again in my pocket—probably calls from my husbands—but I ignored them for now.

I had about thirty missed calls between my husbands, and I didn't even have the energy to call them back. The number of turns lessened as we entered a quiet neighborhood with older homes. It was a different vibe than Jamaica.

I got caught up in my head and almost missed it as she turned into the garage of a brown brick home. I parked a couple of homes away for a few minutes, shut my lights off and ducked down. Kyndall wouldn't catch me. What the hell was I doing?

I lost a piece of my mind back in her car.

It was almost twenty minutes before I came to my senses. I headed home, not before writing Kyndall's address down for research purposes.

Of course.

The trip from Forrest Hills to Centre Island took a little under an hour. I pulled up to my driveway and rested my head on the steering wheel. I didn't think I'd ever been this emotionally tired. Travis found me on our front steps with my head in my hands.

He didn't say a word. Travis just lifted me and carried me to our bathroom. He wordlessly stripped my clothes off and put me into the hot bath.

"Do you want to talk about it?" he inquired.

"No, I don't want to talk about it now or ever."

"Melissa, you know we have a rule to keep nothing from each other."

"I know. Maybe we can talk about it tomorrow? Not tonight, please. I need to be left alone."

He nodded and washed me until I was clean. I barely had the strength to get up, and he held me and dried me off. He placed me in bed, and I stayed there like a dead weight.

I heard Matt and Aaron come up from downstairs. "How is she?" Matt's question hung in the air, but I found I lacked the energy to answer.

"She must be exhausted, because I have never seen her like this. Did she say what happened?"

"No, she won't talk about it until tomorrow, when she's feeling better." I heard a grunt from someone, but I couldn't tell who made the sound.

As I drifted in and out of consciousness, I remembered how Kyndall's soft lips felt like home—like oranges and everything citrus. If I thought about it, I could still feel her velvet skin against mine.

The weekend passed by, with me barely being present for my family. I got up and followed my daily schedule before going back to sleep. I hadn't spoken to anyone or even played with Amber. I just wanted to stew in my misery until I got better. When I wasn't forcing myself to eat or use the bathroom, I filled my time with random movies on Netflix. Honestly, I just turned it on to block out the negative thoughts that raged through my head.

Everyone steered cleared of me and my depressive mood. That was rare because usually, the guys bugged me until I gave in and spilled the beans. The guys just mentioned their upcoming business trip and shuffled away. Even my mom tiptoed around me during our weekly calls. It wasn't until Sunday night that the guys decided enough was enough. They came into the bedroom with serious looks on their faces. Amber tried to come in too, but one of her dads must have called our new babysitter, because I heard the sitter's voice calling Amber away.

Matt was the first to speak as he sat next to me on the colossal bed. "Hey, love, are you hungry? We got you some terrible Chinese food." He pulled out a Tupperware with the food inside. "I brought General Tso's chicken with shrimp fried rice and crab rangoon. It's all yours since you haven't been eating much lately."

"No, I'm not hungry." I eyeballed the food. Yes, it was my favorite dish. It was also Kyndall's. We used to save our babysitting money and binge-eat it for weeks. Again, I cried. "I just want to be left alone." I returned to the movie playing in front of me—I didn't even know the title. "But you can leave the food."

"Absolutely not. We let you sit like this for too long now. It's time to talk this out with us," he demanded in between wiping my tears. "We let you stew in your shit for a day. Now it's time to talk it out."

Travis sat down on my other side. "Was it something someone said to you? Did someone touch you? Was it Dr. Stein or Dr. May?"

"No, God. No, they have been nothing but kind and helpful to me," I insisted. "It's my fault, as usual, guys. My horrible actions are returning to haunt me, and I'm not sure how to deal with that right now." My words fumbled out. I didn't want to tell them I stalked Kyndall to her house, that I wanted to drag her out of her home and lock her in ours until she forgave me. I didn't want to recount the bullshit she told me at the block party or tell them how I wanted to be on top of her, as I punished her for trying to make me jealous.

I wonder if she would like that? I could have Travis pummeling her while I rub her clit until she's on the verge of—

"Earth to Melissa." Aaron waved his arms like a lunatic in front of my face. "Where did you go? You sounded like you were about to—"

"Nothing. Sorry, I got distracted by something." I knew my face was pink. "Guys, I want to be alone for the rest of the evening. I will be better tomorrow because I have to go to work. I have new clients I'm seeing, and I want to make a good impression on them."

Aaron chuckled, and I sent him a dirty look. "That will not work at all." He grabbed the remote, paused the movie, and set the remote on the dresser by the bed—out of my reach. "Spill it, or I'll call Dr. May and Dr. Stein to tell them you won't be in for the week, and they will have to cover your patients."

I hated when Aaron got into his little power trips. When he was like this, he'd control everything until I gave in. I sighed. "Fine, I saw an old friend at the party."

That got everyone's attention. I blew out steam and told them about my messed-up reunion with Kyndall. I skipped the part where I followed her home and wrote down her address.

I mean, something is better than nothing, right?

There was a pregnant pause after I finished. Sometimes men say the craziest things because it dumbfounded me when Matt asked, "Did you know she'd be there?"

"Yes, Matt, because I wanted to meet the woman I have been in love with since I was a junior in high school. So that she could curse me out," I blurted out before I could stop and think about my words.

"What did you just say?" Aaron looked baffled at me.

"I-uh, I just over-spoke." I said as I tried to backpedal. "I'm feeling exhausted, and I think I need to get some rest."

"You just said that you're *in* love, not used to love, with your ex-best friend, and you're blaming it on being too tired." Travis narrowed his eyes. "Over-spoke, my ass. I get it if you don't want to talk to us now, but you should talk to someone about it."

I could see the direction the conversation was going, and it was not one I liked. A look of death painted my face as I stared at him. "I am fine. I felt terrible for not being able to apologize as I wanted. It's almost ten P.M. I have to get ready for my busy day tomorrow." I hopped up and went to the bathroom to get ready for bed.

When I'm finished, my body felt like I had just done a marathon from NY to CA and back. But I put on a blank face and returned to my spot in bed. I pulled the comforter under my chin and stated, "Welp, see, I feel like a new woman, and I'm ready for the new workweek."

"I'm glad our talk made you feel better. I made an appointment with the therapist in your building for Tuesday. Dr. Smith has some high reviews," Matt denoted as he turned off the lights.

The cover flipped off me, and I clenched my jaw. "I don't need to see a therapist. I just needed a weekend to recover from my mishap, and now I'm good as new."

Matt scoffed. "Oh, I'm so glad you figured it out, Dr. Walker. Ensure you're at that appointment on Tuesday at one P.M. You can use your lunch break to see her."

I covered my head and cursed out my three husbands. Until Matt wrapped his arms around me and cuddled me. I figured I could allow it for now, as the weight of the comforter combined with Matt's comforting embrace and Travis's body heat lulled me to sleep quickly.

When I woke up, I realized I was late because I had slept so soundly. I didn't hear the alarm. I rushed to do my morning routine and kissed my babies as I flew out the door. This was not how I wanted to start the work week, especially when I had new patients.

After an hour, I zoomed into the building five minutes before my first patient of the day. I quickly made my rounds of hellos and got to work. Sadly, whenever I got five minutes of peace, my mind strayed to Kyndall every time.

Would she be home if I went to her house after work?

"How was your day?" Dr. Stein asked, which snapped me out of my mind and back to reality.

"Oh, it was perfect. I have about five expecting mothers and two new gynecologists patients. They're complicated cases, but nothing I won't be able to correct."

"You're off to a good start. I heard you picked up some of Dr. May's patients as well." He fixed his glasses.

"Yes, she gave me a dozen of her patients. I appreciate it. It's important to build my roster while I'm still under residency," I told him honestly. When Dr. May mentioned she'd wanted to decrease her patient load and wanted to see how I'd handle multiple patients, I'd volunteered quickly.

"Great, well, I am out for the day. See you tomorrow."

"Goodnight, Dr. Stein,"

That Monday night sped by as I worked hard not to think of Kyndall. Which was easier said than done.

Maybe that's a good reason to go over there.... Get a grip, Melissa.

Tuesday came too fast for me, and I was in a worse mood. For the past four days—since Friday, basically—I'd dreamed of her. I stomped into my office. The staff was worried about me.

Around eleven A.M, I was looking through my patient files when I heard a knock on my door.

"Dr. Walker," one of the medical assistants called from my open door. "I have a message from your husband, Mr. Phillip."

"A message that he couldn't send me in a text?" I looked at her, perplexed.

She shrugged and handed me a post-it note. "Men operate differently."

"Trust me, I understand," I reassured her, only to look up and see the assistant had already left.

I opened the note. It was a reminder of my appointment with Dr. Smith. I mentally rolled my eyes.

After seeing two patients, I looked at the clock and cursed it. It was twelve-fourty five, and I dreaded seeing this therapist. Wasn't I pulling out of my funk fine on my own? Today I had tried to look up information about Kyndall only two times. That was three times less than yesterday. *See, progress.*

I sighed and made my way to the office on the other side of our floor. At least it was on the same floor, I thought to myself. I entered Dr. Smith's lobby five minutes before our appointment and her staff immediately brought me into her office. Okay, I was secretly jealous that her office was immaculate and filled with lavender, white, and gold colors. The scent of lavender oils lightly filled the room.

Dr. Smith entered, and I couldn't even hate her. She was a gorgeous Black goddess with boobs I would love to palm.

Okay, I am a perv even in my time of need.

"Hello, Dr. Walker," she smiled while I stewed and checked her out. "It's always a pleasure to see a fellow physician." She sat in the seat across from me. "So, I would be unprofessional if I didn't mention that your husbands called me beforehand."

Reminder to kill said three husbands.

I groaned, "Seriously?" What else is more embarrassing? "I am so sorry about that. They can be a bit controlling sometimes."

She chuckled. "Hey, I can understand why they're concerned." She pulled out her phone to record and a notepad. "So, let's get started, Dr. Walker."

"Please call me Melissa. I'm in your territory."

"I appreciate that, Melissa." She smiled. "So, tell me a little about yourself."

I sighed. I hated this part of therapy. We spent five minutes reviewing a quick rundown of my life, and then we got to the annoying part.

"Your husbands gave me what they knew about what happened on Friday, but I want to hear it in your own words."

As I recounted the story for the third time, I left out the stalking piece again. It would not be good if the medical board heard I tailed people and found out where they lived.

"You keep referring to your ex-best friend as 'she.' Does she have a name?"

I chewed my cheek for a minute, but decided against lying. "Kyndall Williams."

She paused for a minute and tilted her head to the side. She scribbled something on her notepad.

"Is something wrong?" I asked.

"No, just making some notes." She smiled sweetly. "Melissa, I want to be frank with you. Your husbands mentioned your prior therapist diagnosed you with anxiety in the past."

For fuck's sake.

"Misdiagnosed," I corrected her. "I don't need to control everything. Just my career. Everything else is fifty-fifty." This was going to be my last session with her. She was fun to look at, but I grew tired of the questions. If I had to go to therapy, it would be with someone my husbands hadn't already spoken with.

"Does your need to control extend to your husbands?"

"Ha! I couldn't control them if I wanted to, and I love them for that."

"Does your need to control extend to your daughter?"

"No, she is her own fiery little woman."

"Does your need to control extend to Kyndall?"

I snorted. "Obviously not because I would have her—" I stopped before I could finish.

"Can I ask you something, Melissa?"

"Yes, of course, Dr. Smith."

"You mentioned earlier that you and your husbands started dating for another wife to round out your family. Is that correct?"

"Yes, that's correct."

"Why did none of your previous relationships work?"

I bit back the sigh that threatened to escape. "They just didn't fit the bill."

"Because they weren't like Kyndall?" Dr. Smith smiled and tilted her head. "Were you actively seeking someone like Kyndall?"

Okay, time to go. I am not speaking to her about this. "Oh gosh, Dr. Smith, look. I have to get back to my clinic before my next appointment," I lied. I still had a good thirty minutes until my next one.

"Gosh! An hour sure goes by fast. How about we keep you on the schedule for one o'clock every Tuesday?"

I suppressed the "hell no" that was bubbling to come out. "Yeah, sure. I will stop by the receptionist and make the appointment," I smiled, knowing I would cancel each one of them.

I walked out of her office to the front desk. I slowed down a bit to listen when my keen ears heard something interesting.

"Kyndall, unfortunately, we can't fit you in today, but Thursday will work, and then you can come back to your normal schedule of Tuesdays at five o'clock."

Kyndall was not a popular name, but this was New York, and there were a lot of Caribbean families here. I crossed my arms and moved up quietly.

Maybe I would work late Thursday.

"Great, Dr. Smith will see you on Thursday at four-thirty. See you then, Kyndall." She hung up the phone, and I tried to act like I hadn't just eavesdropped on her conversation.

After making the appointment, I went back to my clinic. I made a silent promise to myself that I would not trail her footsteps any longer. I needed to get back to my life. But I shoved that piece of information to the back of my mind.

Yes, because I am not stalking her. I ensuring she got home safely and was okay.

I stuck to my guns and focused on my family life. I lasted a whole month with no thoughts of Kyndall. Not about the file I had created on her, which I stored away in my office. Everything was going smoothly until I had a late appointment on a Tuesday with one of my pregnant patients. I ended up leaving the clinic a little after six o'clock. I Locked up and used the stairs to get downstairs, when I heard the unmistakable voice of Kyndall as she flirted with someone.

I followed the sound to the elevator waiting area. The second voice I recognized as Jessica, one of Dr. Smith's front desk associates. She giggled like a maniac. "Oh, Kyndall." she placed her hand against Kyndall's arm. She was gorgeous, but I didn't like this one bit. "It was great talking with you. Thank you for walking me out."

She's fine and doesn't need to be walked out, Kyndall!

"It's no problem," my baby said playfully. "Hey, this may be inappropriate, but I was wondering if you would be interested in going out for dinner?"

Over my dead fucking body!

Without thinking, my legs led the way to Kyndall. I didn't know what I was going to say, but I knew I would die before another woman touched Kyndall.

Think of something professional to say, Melissa, and quick!

"Hey, baby," I said as I kissed her on her cheek. Oh fuck, that was not professional. If I could run somewhere and die right now, I would. Her pinched face told me she would kill me before I could run away. "What are you doing here so late, babe?"

Her face looked frozen in time as her eyes popped out of her head. I was so bold that it took her a minute to collect herself—all the while Jessica stood there with her mouth ajar. "Melissa?" Kyndall said, dumbfounded. She was pink in the face and looked like she would faint any minute.

Kyndall swallowed and continued, "Do you mind if my *girlfriend* and I have a word, Jessica?" Without a word, Jessica speed-walked to the building entrance, not bothering to wait for Kyndall, as she hightailed it out to her car.

Oh fuck, is all I thought when I'm left with a pissed-off Kyndall. "What the hell was that, Dr. Walker?" she hissed as she crossed her arms around her chest. "What are you doing here? Are you following me? Why would you tell her we were together?"

"I knew she was not right for you." I tried to do damage control. "Kyndall, I'm sorry it was a slip of the tongue, but I was looking out for you."

That's right!

"Excuse me, but we are not friends, associates, lovers, or anything for you to decide who I can or cannot see, Dr. Walker. You're nothing to me. You have your life, and I have mine." The elevator dinged, and a group of employees got out. Kyndall turned and headed to the front door with the employees. All I saw was red.

I stomped down behind her and chased after the Kyndall as she high-tailed it to her car. As soon as she was within reach of the driver's side door, I clamped onto her arm and spun her around. My chest became tight, and my mouth had taken the shape of a hard line. "You think you can just get rid of me after I finally found you?" I didn't know what I was saying, but I couldn't stop the words either. "Fine, if that's the game you want to play, then so be it. But know that you're going to be mine at the end, and there's nothing *you* can do about it." I smiled as she stood there with her mouth wide open and I kissed her.

I'm not letting anyone take what's mine.

I left Kyndall as she stood there with a dumbstruck expression. I got into my car and called the person I needed—the person who could figure out if you fell asleep in church when you were three years old.

"Hey Joey, I'm in a hurry, but I need a favor."

"Hey doc. Okay, shoot. You know I always have time for you."

Joey Han was Sage's current boyfriend and the best private investigator in the city.

"I need you to find everything on someone," I pleaded.

"Okay, can I ask why? And who?"

"It's someone I'm thinking about doing business with, and I want to know everything you can find about them. The name is Kyndall Williams."

"Wait, I've heard that name before..." He trailed off.

"Ah, it's a different person," I lied. Gosh, I'm a madwoman. This was what my life had come done to.

"Okay." He sounded skeptical. "How soon do you need it? If you want me to be thorough, you must give me at least three-to-five days. Do you want medical records as well?"

"Yes, every and anything, Joey. Sorry to push you, but I want it as soon as possible. I can pay for it as well," I said as I pulled onto the highway.

"I can see if I can get you something ASAP and slowly trickle the rest in, but you know it depends on the person. The shadier the person, the longer it takes."

"I don't think she's that shady, but she may have some ties to a gang near the Jamaica community. I met her at the annual block party, and she went into a house owned by them," I noted.

"Mmm, I'm familiar with that gang. Ran by a guy called Marcus. I have a guy I know who can provide me with some insight."

"Alright, thanks. I'm home now, so I gotta go. You can text me any further details."

"Okay, tell everyone I say hello."

We said our goodbyes. The drive home sped by after I hung up with Joey. When I drove into the driveway and went inside, I assumed the guys and Amber would be there to greet me, but the house was quiet. I checked my phone, and they went out for dinner tonight.

I ate my dinner alone. By the time I was ready for bed, the family had returned, and I put Amber to bed while my husbands did their own evening ablutions. I hopped in between a dozing Aaron and Matt and tried to sleep. It didn't work. My mind was running a hundred miles per hour, overstimulated. Luckily, Travis was still awake and willing to help me work it off.

The following day, I had a new attitude and a new goal. I stopped to talk with the guys and Amber, who were eating around the breakfast table.

"Good morning, my babies!" I sang as I kissed everyone.

"Mommy, you're in a good mood."

"Yes, Mommy is in a great mood. How about we have a spa day?"

Amber all but jumped out of her seat. "Yes! I want my nails done just like my friend Cassie."

"No, they'll be better." She giggled as I tickled her.

"When are you guys leaving for your trip?" I inquired.

"Tomorrow, after we pick Amber up from school. Our South Carolina flight is in the late evening, so we'll drop her off here and then hightail it to the airport," Travis continued. "We asked the babysitter to stay with her until you get home. We could still take Amber with us if you're not feeling well."

"OMG, Mommy, I want to go with my daddies. Please, Mommy!" She jumped up and down.

"I think your daddies will be too busy to take you out. You're stuck with me, kiddo."

"Unless you want to come with us too?"

"No, I'm so tired." I pushed for the wrong reasons. I was terrible, but I could use this weekend to review whatever Joey found and follow Kyndall. "But if you take Amber with you, I can have a self-care weekend."

Matt tilted his head. "You were excited to spend the weekend with Amber. What happened?"

Oh, hell. Why did I have to have such a perceptive husband? "Oh, you know, if I could have time to sleep the entire weekend, I'd take it." I giggled nervously. "Amber, I'll be seeing you tonight, and we can have a whole girl's spa weekend. Right now, I gotta go. Love y'all."

I ran out before they could ask me questions. Just before I closed the door, I heard Aaron mutter, "She's definitely up to something."

Although I didn't have time to research Kyndall, the weekend flew by with Amber. My husbands returned with big smiles on their faces, so the trip must have been a success. The following Monday went by in a blink, a new determination in my step which made time speed up. It wasn't until Tuesday that I received an email from the badass Joey.

Gotcha!

I quickly printed everything in the email and devoured the contents. He worked like Google. As I read the file, it mortified me, knowing I played a part in Kyndall's mental health problems. After high school graduation, she'd been homeless and suffered from major depressive disorder, though she had eventually received therapy and medication. I stopped midway through her medical records—it was too much. My vision doubled as I let the buildup of tears finally fall free. My selfish ways destroyed someone I loved. I used the back of my white coat sleeve to wipe my face clean and continued with the other information. Her last legal job information dated eight years ago, when she was a waitress at a restaurant. Joey scared me because he got her phone number, social security number, banking information, driver's license, and car registration information.

Remind me never to cross him.

I checked my watch—I had five minutes before my next appointment, and I wanted to use the restroom beforehand. Stashing Kyndall's info in a desk drawer, I rose and walked down the hall. The bathroom was on the other side of the clinic, which usually wasn't annoying, but today it was. I'd just passed the lobby when I bumped into one of my assistants.

"Dr. Walker, your next patient is a first-time client and seems very nervous. She requested a more private setting before going to the examination room." She gave me a sorry shrug.

"That's odd." I was so perplexed. "The exam rooms are not private enough?"

"She claims she can hear everything happening in the exam room next to the lobby. She doesn't want to talk about personal information where she can be overheard." Okay, that was the first time I heard anyone mention that to me in my two years of practice.

"Put her in the exam room next to my office and tell her there'll be no one on the other side." I rolled my eyes. We had some divas at this clinic.

The assistant nodded and handed me the patient's file before hurrying off.

Finally free, I made it to the bathroom with plenty of time to saunter back to the exam room, where my patient waited. Funnily enough, I noticed my office door was ajar. I could have sworn I closed that door. Oh well. I closed it again. I took a deep breath before I entered the exam room. "Hello, Ms. Grant." I rechecked the file to make sure I got her name right. "Would you prefer me to call you Ms. Grant or Alexandra?"

"Alex is fine." Her words had a harsh bite to them. She looked vaguely familiar, but I couldn't place her face with the name.

"Okay." Her attitude completely threw me off. "How are you doing today, Alex?"

She just stared at me and crossed her arms. I'm perplexed.

I broke the awkward silence. "Um, I'm sorry, but is this because of the private room issue?"

"No, it's because you're an evil, conniving bitch," she spat out, as she stared straight into my eyes.

"Excuse me?" I asked, appalled and annoyed because I didn't need someone ruining my workplace for me. "I'm sorry, but I'll be free after five o'clock if you have a personal issue with me. We can handle it like civil adults then."

"You don't even know who I am, do you?" She looked offended.

"No, sorry, you're not memorable," I tried to shake her off, while I masked my anger with an unbothered expression. "I'll see you at five if we're through."

Her jaw clenched. "You think you can come here and ruin someone's life because you feel entitled to them? Do you think you can roll into New York and fuck with someone's emotions? My cousin is not an evil person, and she bothers no one, but you came here, and you decide to fuck with her mentally. That's fucked up and unprofessional." She got up from the table and stood in front of me. She had some balls of steel.

Oh, this was the female who had accompanied Kyndall at the party. "I'm assuming you're Kyndall's cousin?" I blew air out of my nose to keep myself calm. "Listen, I understand you may think I'm playing with your cousin's emotions. But my intentions are genuine."

"Your intentions are genuine?" She pointed her finger at my chest. "You shouldn't have any intentions with my cousin, period. She gave you closure, which should have been the end of whatever sick game you're playing. But someone has been asking about her, and I could figure out only one person who would do it, you." She held up a stack of papers and, with a sinking horror, I realized it was Joey's email. "And my instinct's always right."

"You went into my private office and compromised my patient's information." I smiled. "I'm giving you a minute to return those papers to me, or I'm going to be forced to call the police. If you didn't know, that's a federal offense."

The mention of the police stopped her dead in her tracts. She looked sick. "Listen, I-I just wanted to come here to tell you to leave her alone. She's been through a lot mentally because of you and our family members already," she stuttered.

"I understand that, and I would never do that to Kyndall again." I spoke to her in a gentle, calming voice. "But I never thought I would get the chance to right a wrong, and I won't let my second chance slip away from me."

"I understand you think you mean well, but you don't. I'm asking you respectfully to leave Kyndall alone and attend to your family. Let us both stay on our sides of New York and I will forgive you."

Okay, she is annoying me now.

"Alex, I appreciate your concern for my family. But you've gotten something wrong here." I stood and straightened my white coat. "Kyndall is a part of my family. She just hasn't come to that reality yet." I crafted my words carefully so that Alex could feel my power over her and understand that I was in control. I stepped into her space as I trapped her between me and the exam table. To ensure she knew who had the upper hand, I brushed imaginary dust off her shirt. "You no longer have to worry about Kyndall. I'm going to make sure she's taken care of—I have big plans for her."

Alex's back stiffened. "What's that supposed to mean? What plans?"

"Oh, she'll be moving in with us soon. Kyndall won't need for anything." I grabbed the collar of Alex's shirt for a bit of dramatic effect, while my other hand pried Joey's email out of her fingers.

"She—she won't agree to that," she stammered, and I was officially tired of this conversation.

"Of course she will, and I can't wait until she finally realizes that," I smiled sweetly. "Because I plan to have her underneath me, begging me to make her come almost every night while my husbands fuck us until we're filled and covered with their cum. And when she can walk, I will spoil her until she forgets I've ever hurt her. If you're nice, I might invite you to our union ceremony." Releasing her shirt and with my prize in hand, I pivoted on my heel. With deliberate steps, I walked to the doorframe, paused, and glared at her. "Please stop by the front desk and pay for your office visit. I wish I could say it was a pleasure to meet you, but it wasn't. Maybe you can make it up to me in the future. Tell Kyndall I'll be seeing her soon. She better have gotten rid of Tweedledee and Tweedledum by then."

With those parting words, I walked out with my back ramrod straight, whistling my favorite tune. Later, I said goodbye to everyone and headed home with my file on Kyndall in my bag. When I got home, Joey texted me about Kyndall's "job." Yeah, she wouldn't be doing that anymore. I locked up Joey's email in the house safe and went downstairs to spend some time with my family.

Chapter 10

KYNDALL

I NO LONGER RECOGNIZED the person who stared back at me in the mirror. I used to think I was this strong woman who was invincible and wouldn't put up with anyone's bullshit. That was before my past caught up with me.

Three weeks after my disastrous encounter with Melissa and she turned my life upside down. There were bags around my red-rimmed eyes that could hold groceries. I didn't have the energy to work out, so my body was five pounds heavier. The most shameful part was the smell—I hadn't the energy to shower in days.

Today was the first time I planned to venture out of the house in about three weeks. With much effort, I completed my morning routine and got dressed in whatever clothing I had that was clean. Not ready to face the subway, I dragged myself to my car and my therapist's appointment. I found a parking spot in front of the building. I kept my eyes open wide, anxiously searching for any signs of danger the entire way to the office.

I spent the next hour with Dr. Smith as she reviewed how I felt and my current status. I mustered up a smile and tried to sound upbeat as I reassured her. So fucking wonderful. My life would make a great movie right now. I shook my head and ran out of the office and back to the comfort of my home. I hated myself for lying to Dr. Smith and to myself.

Alex called that night to check in on me and give me an update. I sighed as I listened to her recount her crazy plan and how it backfired. What deeply annoyed me was that, in the deepest corner of my mind, everything Alex told me about the situation made my panties grow moist. My nipples pebbled at the mere thought. But I wouldn't let Melissa control me. I did before, and it ruined me, but not again.

She's a possessive control freak!

"Kyndall, I'm going to be honest with you. I've never seen someone so sure of herself. I was taken aback, and that's really saying something." Alex said before she became deathly quiet.

It had been a full minute before I broke the silence between us. "Alex, come out and ask your question."

"Are you, um, shit, this is uncomfortable." I heard her as she moved around her room. "Are you into that freaky shit like BDSM and crap?"

"Yes, and no. I love being submissive in the bedroom, but not outside of it." I said as I closed eyes. It embarrassed me to admit my sexual habits to my family or friends, but I spilled the details to my cousin.

"Oh, you like to be told when to come like your girlfriend said, huh?"

And that's why I don't tell people my business. Exasperated, I responded, "Alright, Alex, that's enough now. Anyway, how's Marcus?"

Alex finally got off my nonexistent sex life and moved onto her relationship. When Alex talked about the shit Marcus had gotten into, I recoiled. I was not ignorant. I knew what he did was dangerous, but I wasn't worried about him. He'd made his bed, so he had to lie in it. I worried about Maxwell and Alex, who were stuck in that lifestyle. Marcus could be the best partner in the world, and his career would still be as toxic as fuck. That toxicity would one day spill over.

"Listen, Alex, I must go, but we'll get together soon. And Melissa isn't my girlfriend. Please stop saying it," I huffed.

"You've been really snippy since the return of your girlfriend, Kyndall. When was the last time you got your rocks off?"

And like that, I was done with Alex. After five minutes of cursing her, I finally hung up on her. Sometimes she exhausted me, and I realized why she and Marcus stayed together for so long.

Alex was right, though. I hated to admit it. Since I had seen Melissa back in March, my body seemed to be in an orgasm shutdown. Every time I wanted some "me" time, I would set the mood, and I would come, but I didn't feel the euphoria I'd usually feel after a good release. I was like a plastic grocery bag with a hole— just useless. My mind drifted to Melissa, wondering if her release still tasted sweet and salty.

Ding!

As the microwave brought me out of the depths of my mind, I jumped. I quickly retrieved my food and watched *Ghost* in the living room. I immediately regretted my choice because I remembered it was also Melissa's favorite movie. Our favorite part was coming up. It was when Sam and Molly finally said their goodbyes. Cue the water works in three. . . two. . . one.

I cried so much I couldn't hear the movie, and my vision glazed over from the tears. The salty tear drops fell into my popcorn, and the kernels became a soggy mess. What a waste of food, as I threw away the rest of the popcorn.

"You know what?" I announced to no one at all. "Fuck this, I am done with this moping. I'm shaking myself out of this funk and getting my life back on track."

I wiped the tears from my face and headed to the bathroom to prepare for bed. I decided not to sleep in my bean chair tonight—my back hurt from falling asleep there way too often.

The next three days passed so quickly that I realized I hadn't even thought of her in the past thirty-six hours. I bought new clothing to add to my wardrobe. I had a spa day by myself—the full body treatment. My hair was freshly relaxed and colored, and I waxed my face and my wild eyebrows. The gold facial treatment was worth every penny, and of course, I luxuriated in a mani-pedi. I felt like the old me again.

And I hired someone to clean my house and do my laundry because I was lazy.

On Saturday night, that little trickle of depression started to set in, but I shook it away. I was going to The Little Hut and I will find someone to knock the cobwebs out. I repeated as I forced myself to take my perfectly waxed and pampered body out for the night.

Yes, that's the perfect plan. Freakum dress time!

The soft fabric of the red mini bodycon dress glided against my skin. I skipped the bra because I loved the feel of the fabric against my full breasts. I grabbed my silver earrings, and wristlet, and then I completed the look with a pair of clear, high-heeled, open-toe shoes that clicked against the floor. When I looked at myself in the mirror, I felt my confidence soar.

I was ready to get fucked!

I did a mini-prep dance as I waited for my Uber to arrive. I think I earned a couple of drinks for the night. Fuck it, I wanted to be pissy drunk by the end of the night. When my phone beeped with the driver's arrival notification, I stepped outside and ignored the feeling of being watched. I refused to be unnerved by baseless anxieties.

Within twenty minutes, I entered The Little Hut. The energy in the room was electric, and a sea of people surrounded me. Jimmie was serving at the bar as usual, so I pushed through the crowd to shout hello. "Hey, Jimmie!"

"Wah gwan, Kyn? Long time no see," he called out, as he cleaned a glass for an order.

"Nothing much." I stole a seat at the bar. "Let me get a rum and Coke. Heavy on the Coke and light on the rum." I wanted to play it safe until I found a potential wham-bam-thank-you-ma'am for the night.

"You're drinking? Alone?" He looked at me with his beady eyes. "And without Alex?"

"Yes, I'm here by myself to have fun." I smiled innocently. "Who's the plug?"

He folded his arms across his pot belly. "You're not drinking *and* getting high on my dime. Pick your poison. It's my obligation to see you home safely."

I sighed. "Okay, just show me tonight's dealer and I'll do the rest." He pointed to an older-looking man on the back wall. "Thank you so much."

Twenty minutes later, I'd bought a blunt, smoked it, and stormed the dance floor. Now the question was, did I feel in the mood for a girl or a guy? I wish I could do both, but usually, The Little Hut's clientele was too vanilla for a submissive threesome. To be honest, I just wanted to have a fulfilling orgasm. I missed it.

On the dance floor, I lost the little chatter in my head as I danced to the music. Yes, I probably looked like a madwoman because I didn't know how to dance. But I was free, light, and high as a kite. I finally found this handsome guy with russet-colored skin and sad brown eyes. He followed my lead while I leaned on him and danced my goofy little two-step. I knew he could feel my nipples poking a hole through my dress to his chest.

It felt like I danced my little five pounds off. My only hesitation came when I thought I spotted Melissa out of the corner of my eye, but that was obviously just the weed. A second, proper look and no one was there. I shook my head, and I turned back to my partner, only to find he was gone. I searched and scanned the room again—he sat at a table with two other men.

As I approached him, he gave me a funny look. Maybe I had bad breath, or the esthetician missed a patch when she waxed. I faltered for a bit, but I proceeded. "Hey, so I didn't catch your name?"

"Because I didn't give it." He shrugged his shoulders in discomfort. "Listen, I didn't know you were a fish. I'm not into that gay shit."

And just like that...

He ruined my high. "I don't know how you would assume that since you don't know me, and I don't know you. Why would I be dancing with you if I were a lesbian?" I urged, even though there would be absolutely nothing wrong if I was a lesbian.

"Someone looking out for me told me. Now I wasted half the night on a bulldyke."

I stated, "You know what? Thank you. I was going to take you home, but you came up short when we were dancing. So, all the best, short man." As I turned to leave, I heard several people snickered. I can be petty as well.

I could go to the gay club across town or try again here.

Nah. I will not allow myself to be scared away. Plus, the gay club scene outside of Manhattan was a hit or miss. *Back to square one.* Nothing was ever easy for me. I went back to the dance floor and danced by myself for a bit when this gorgeous woman danced with me. Which usually never happens.

Setting my suspicion aside, I went with the flow, and we spent the next hour dancing together, as we whispered in each other's ears. At one point, I convinced Jimmie I wasn't high anymore, and he let me buy a bottle of cognac. Sienna—she'd divulged her name like it was the greatest secret of all—and I shared sips like we were teenagers liable to get caught.

When I was brave enough, I proposed, "Do you want to get out of here?"

Sienna flushed pink. "Yes, let me get my things from my friends, and we can leave."

I nodded, score one for me. I was going to have fun with this pint-sized umber beauty. Sienna had small breasts, but what she lacked on top, she made up for in ass. Promising to meet at the door, she stumbled to her friends, and I stumbled to the bar to tell Jimmie I was leaving.

After I reserved the Uber, I found her and her friends by the exit. As I approached her, she looked more and more panicked. Her friends stiffened their spines, like they were prepping to beat the shit out of me.

I hazarded a greeting. "Hey Sienna, I called an Uber. It should be here in five minutes."

"Hey Kyndall, listen, I changed my mind. You were sweet, but you are not my type. I'm sorry for leading you on." With that, she and her friends walked away, leaving my tipsy ass in front of the small bar.

Well, shit!

Before I could think, my phone buzzed, which let me know my Uber was outside. I stumbled into the car, opened the half emptied cognac, and chugged. By the time the Uber driver was halfway to my house, I was in a depressed, drunken state for the first time in a long time. Tonight, I felt gorgeous. The pain of rejection left me feeling like someone had sliced me open.

"My luck! I thought I-I looked good, but I guess I was wrong," I complained out loud.

"You look beautiful. Maybe it was them, or someone watching over you."

I squinted at the man in the front seat, truly seeing him for the first time. As the car pulled into my driveway, I asked, "Oh, you think I look good? You want to come in and fuck me? No strings attached."

"No strings attached?" Through the rearview mirror, his eyes scanned me up and down. He wasn't attractive to me, but I was desperate.

"Yes, you can park here in the driveway and come in when you're ready. I have plenty of condoms, and you can leave after."

He paused for a minute, then responded, "Okay, give me a minute."

I jumped out of his car and tried to run inside, but I stumbled instead. As soon as I made it through the door, I kicked off my shoes and threw the pillows off my couch. I drank some water to help me with the alcohol and used the bathroom. After fifteen minutes, I looked out the window. My buzz was dwindling, and I wanted to get my rocks off by then.

I peered out of my window, not seeing the car I had expected, and felt my heart sink. Fuck my life. It was Sunday morning, and I had no luck tonight. I was so glad I hadn't gotten off my ass drunk. I was more than sober enough to root through my fridge, retrieve some leftover pizza, and stuff it down without warming it up. After I stuffed my face, I took off everything and head to the bathroom.

Did I hear the door opening?

I shrugged and got in the shower. For the next thirty minutes, all the disappointment from this night, and this year, washed down the drain. Towel around my waist, I walked to my bedroom. A large bag sat on my bed. "Was I that faded that I forgot an entire bag?"

Someone chuckled behind me, and I snapped around, clutching my towel. My eyes were wide as saucers, and my lips fell apart.

Chapter 11

MELISSA

I NEVER WORKED HARDER than I did tonight. I was determined. Matt took time, but I convinced him in the end. I honestly knew he didn't believe my half-ass bullshit lie. The other two were easy to get on my side. But Matt made me work for it.

"Matt, I'm going to go out with Sage and then stay over at her place overnight," I told him, after I found him in his study with Amber.

"Oh, the very last minute. Sage usually has everything planned out for years," he chuckled.

"Yeah, she got a promotion at work and wants to celebrate."

"Oh, so we should all go—"

"Baby, it's a girl's night out. No guys."

"Okay, well, let me call her and congratulate her."

"No, she asked me not to tell anyone until it was official," I explained, as I tried to leave the room.

"Okay." He tilted his head.

"Okay, bye baby, bye Amber." My fake smile faltered a bit, but I needed a little more time to complete my plan. "I'll text you when I get to her place." I ran over, kissed them both. Amber's cheek was sticky as I wiped the foreign residue off my lips. I slipped out before he could ask another question.

Tonight, I needed complete control, I thought as I headed to my car. I rummaged and pulled out the bag from the adult store I'd stashed earlier.

Sage and I had made a trip to the city, and it was a heck of a conversation to explain where I wanted to go. She asked questions like a mother, which made me nervous.

As I drove to Kyndall's house, I prepared myself for the battle. I would burst a blood vessel if we continued this tension between us. I wanted Kyndall to move into my house no later than next week. And I wouldn't take no for an answer.

Forty minutes later, I parked across the street from Kyndall's home. I had just gotten out of the car when my heart seized in my chest—Kyndall stepped out of her front door. Thinking she'd seen me, I froze. But no—she hopped into a car with an Uber sticker on the back windshield. Even from this distance, she looked so good in her red mini dress. Why didn't her cousin make it clear to Kyndall that she belonged to me? That I would come to collect what's mine?

Why can't people just listen to me? It would make their lives much easier.

The Little Hut was a cute little bar, but packed. I found Kyndall twice, and she tried to pick up two people from the bar. Luckily, when she turned her back, I convinced them not to go home with her. Not that hard. I had been a little remorseful because I hated to be an O-blocker, but tonight was about me and Kyndall. After tonight, I would be the only one giving her pleasure or pain for the rest of her life.

After I dissuaded her two would-be lovers, we headed home. I tailed her Uber again, and I scratched my head when he didn't immediately leave her driveway. Slamming my car door closed, I marched up to his vehicle to find him with his dick in one hand and a wet wipe in the other—was he preparing to go into her house? Red alarms rang in my head. I banged on his car window and yelled that I'd call the police if he didn't leave. Shocked, he stammered Kyndall had invited him in for sex, that he wasn't doing anything wrong. I remained calm and informed the man that I'd castrate him.

Within five seconds, the guy peeled out of the driveway. I stood there for about five minutes while I gathered myself.

Punishment it is, then.

Thank God it was me who came in and not someone else. She'd left the door open, but before I could reach for the handle, she looked out the window for the Uber man. I jumped into the dark shadows of her veranda. When she left the window, I waited another minute before I entered her quaint home. From the first step in, I loved it, unsurprisingly; it was so like her. While she showered, I moved my car into her driveway, set my bag of adult toys on our bed, and explored her home. I even grabbed a water bottle from the kitchen.

The sounds of the shower shut off, and I hid behind her bedroom door. I watched her puzzled face at the bag. I couldn't help it—I chuckled. She turned around in her towel and almost dropped it. I kept my face blank. "Hey baby, you've had quite the night."

Kyndall's eyeballs looked ready to pop out of her pretty head. "M-Melissa, what are you doing here? And how did you get into my house?"

Her nose scrunched up, and her mouth formed an O. She was too adorable, "Well, I came by earlier, but you were going out, so I followed you so you wouldn't get into trouble. But it seems you had plans to give away what belongs to me. To think I was going to give you pleasure tonight, but I think you need some guidance first, so you know I am serious."

She shook her head. "Melissa, I'm a human being, not an object. Second, you're not welcome in my home, and I want nothing to do with you. I-I don't have any feelings for you!" She trembled at the last of her words, leaving me unmoved. *This was an act.*

"I never said you were not a human being. You are my human being, that's what I said. I want you in my bed, in my home, and in my life." I untied my teal wrap dress slowly. "Make me leave, then, Kyndall, if you hate me so much. When your cousin showed up, I thought she would have told you I'm serious about getting you back." I dropped my teal wrap dress to reveal my nakedness.

I came prepared.

"Melissa, put your clothes back on," she whispered so softly that I would have missed it if I weren't paying attention. "Melissa, I–this can't happen. I–I've been to therapy a-and fuck, you look so good."

I inched closer to her and whispered in her ear, "I taste even better." Kyndall flushed, and I don't think she could have gotten any pinker. "But if you want me to go, that's fine, Kyndall. But know what I told your cousin Alex: you're going to be mine. If you want to delay it, it's up to you, baby."

"Fuck Melissa," she breathed. Her eyes hadn't moved from my body since my dress dropped. "This is a one-night thing, and that's it."

I laughed. "Oh, baby, if you think I will let you go after tonight, you're sadly mistaken."

One minute, I had control of the situation. The next, I didn't. Kyndall pushed me against her bedroom wall and possessed my mouth. As her tongue pushed in, I tasted the remnants of the cognac she'd consumed. She kissed me like she'd waited for this moment for years. We were so pushed together that one might have been mistaken us for conjoined twins.

I trembled against her—I needed to take back control. I placed my hands on her neck. And I lightly squeezed until she backed off. When I released her, she moaned, and I wiped my mouth, breaking the string of saliva that connected us. "You're going to pay for that, Kyndall."

"Fuck you, Melissa. Leave my house. I don't need you."

I smirked. "Kyndall, let's stop denying we both want each other and be together. I'm sorry for hurting you. If I have to spend the rest of my life making it up to you, so be it. I love you. I am not letting you go."

"Fuck me." She sniffled, and her eyes filled with tears. My heart was about to break through my chest, like my lungs had stopped inflating. She stood there and stared at the floor. But after a minute, she blessed me. She dropped that towel and let me see what I've waited for since we reunited.

I could kick myself for missing out on this body. I walked a circle to admire how the curves, once hidden by baggy bell bottoms and oversized shirts, had matured and filled out. Telltale stretch marks decorated her breast, hips, and ass. Her breasts remained full and round. She lost her Florida tan, so her dark brown birthmarks stood out like beacons. She was gorgeous. I couldn't help myself as I ran a finger up the untamed stretch marks on her hips.

And all mine!

I didn't know why, but I became self-conscious about my mommy tummy and my heavy, silently saggy breasts. Kyndall must have noticed, because she suddenly held my hand. "You look amazing, Melissa.

Motherhood looks good on you." Her simple words pushed that little self-doubt voice into the back of my head.

I smiled sweetly. I knew that all the crazy things I went through to get her would pay off, and I would win her over in the end.

"You're smiling. Should I be scared or excited?" she joked.

My cheeks ached. "Oh, sweetheart, you will be ecstatic when I'm finished with you." I guided her to the bed by the hand. She sat without protest. "Aren't you going to ask what's in the bag?"

"Do I want to know?" Oh, good question.

"Do you trust me, Kyndall?"

"Is this a trick?" She chewed on her still puffy lips. "I am a complete mad woman, but yes... I trust you. Our safe word is Oranges, don't forget that."

"No, you're the most amazing woman I know, and I don't deserve you." I kissed the corner of her mouth. A smile touched my lips. "Ah, oranges. I think I like that safe word. Okay, stand up and turn around."

"Boy, you're laying it—"

I cut her off. "Close your eyes and open your mouth wide."

She opened wide, and I shoved a ball gag in her mouth. She took it beautifully. "Good girl, I knew you could open that pretty mouth wide for me. Imagine when my partners get a hold of your pretty wet mouth. They're going to fuck it until your jaw hurts."

She let out a low whimper.

As she moved a hand to touch the gag, I quickly grabbed her wrist and demanded, "Don't even think about it! You're going to take this punishment like my good little slut."

Her eyebrows almost disappeared into her hairline, but she obeyed, and dropped her hand. Defiant but submissive—my core clenched at the thought of breaking her down.

I pulled the blindfold out, and Kyndall protested around my gag. One thing about Kyndall was she hated anyone who messed with her eyes. I tenderly rubbed her soft cheek. "Baby, I know you hate your eyes being covered, but I'll give you my word: in a couple of minutes, you won't remember you're blindfolded. You'll be drooling all over that gag, begging for a release." Her chest flush pink at my words. I bent down, took one of those brown buds into my mouth, and swirled my tongue around the tender peak. I bit and sucked until she arched her whole breast into my face. As she moaned over the gag, I moved my mouth off with a pop.

She's wasn't getting out of her punishment that easily.

Devoid of protest, Kyndall allowed me to blindfold her. Next, I pulled out my bondage board. The linked soft leather boards could contort into a variety of shapes, and my husbands and I had tested out all of them. The soft, plush leather covers and the metallic clink of handcuff loops were all she needed for tonight. Whistling, I set up the board so she could comfortably prop herself up on her elbows and knees. Her legs would be wide apart and tied down, so I would have plenty of room to play.

Carefully, I guided Kyndall onto the board. The position put her beautiful ass up on full display. I kept my fingers lightly on her to let her know I was still with her. With some wrangling, I got her wrists, forearms, calves, and ankles cuffed through the board's loops. She wiggled to test the cuffs, and I delivered a sharp slap to her perfectly rounded cheek. She jerked against the board and gave a muffled yelp. I palmed the reddened cheek. "That's just the beginning, babes."

I removed the blindfold. Yes, I folded because I wanted to see all the emotions in her eyes tonight. *Weak, yeah I know.* Another brilliant idea struck. I fetched the mirror I'd seen in the other room and placed it on the other side of the bed. From this angle, I could play with her and see her face at the same time.

"Kyndall, what am I going to do with you? I told you and your cousin you're mine," I sighed with mock heaviness. "But you want to be stubborn. I can't have that. I've brought your punishment inside of my bag of mystery."

I dug through my bag until I found the perfect toy to begin with. "Ah, I got just the idea of where to start." I dipped my two fingers into the lube I brought for tonight. "Now, Kyndall, have you given anyone this tight little hole?" She stiffened when I spread her cheeks and ran a finger over her puckered star. She shook her head no, and my smile stretched out even more. I tested her out by sticking a finger all the way until her rosette rubbed my knuckle. She clenched down on my finger for dear life.

"Relax, my love," I said soothingly, and she unclenched her muscles, which allowed me to proceed.

She bucked and moaned as I fucked her ass. I watched her in the mirror. She pleaded with her eyes. Her hands trembled as she fought against her gag. I slipped in a second, lubed up finger, and she clenched so hard I thought she might cut the circulation off. "Baby, you're so damn tight. We'll have to train you before you can take two dicks at the same time."

With my free hand, I reached for her little nub and caressed her clit. As I worked her over, she clenched down as her release drew nearer. I removed both my hands from her and watched as several emotions in her eyes that ranged from shock to anger. I chuckled. If I could die from a look, I would be dead.

I whistled a long note as I grabbed my vibrating anal dildo and covered it with lube. I slowly pushed the toy into her puckered hole. "Relax and breathe," I said.

To show some mercy, I clamped my mouth around her clit. As she relaxed her muscles, I slid the toy all the way into her ass and stretched her to her limit. She strained against the arm cuffs as she arched and pushed her warm core into my face. If I died like this, I would be the happiest woman in the world.

I removed my mouth from her clit, and she whined. I gave her a slap on her other ass cheek. "You're not allowed to come until I've given you permission. You're going to learn a lesson tonight, Kyndall."

I used my two clean fingers and slid them into her warm tight core, and worked her over until I heard her moan and clench around my fingers. The dildo became too hard to push into her. Her muscles gripped me as she tried to cut off my circulation to my fingers, and I cursed because now I wondered if this punishment was for her or me. With some reluctance, I withdrew my wet fingers and pulled her head back until she could see me in the mirror. Kyndall watched me as I stuck my fingers, that were drenched with her juices, into my mouth and moan in pleasure from tasting her.

"Sweet and mine, just like I remembered."

Breaking eye contact, I dug in the bag for the next toy. "See, Kyndall, I worked out every detail of what I was going to do to you tonight. Imagine my surprise when I find my girlfriend going out to give away what's mine. I was concerned." I found the clit and nipple clamps. "And worried. I had to follow you to ensure my pussy was okay and untouched. Don't you agree?" I removed the gag so she could speak, and she whimpered.

The tears left a warm, wet trail down her face as they slowly slid off her cheeks. I pulled her head back by her hair.

"Don't you agree, my love?"

"Fuck you, Melissa."

"Well, not yet, babe. Maybe later. We have all night, Love." I smiled.

"You know what this is?" I asked innocently.

"N-No, what i-is it?"

"I can show you better than I can tell you. Lift a bit, honey." I placed the nipple clamps on as she lifted herself. She yelped in surprise when I snapped them closed.

"Melissa, I don't think I can—"

"Kyndall, my sweet love, you're going to take my clamps like I know you can." I smiled and kissed her on her glorious ass. "Look at your ass, babe. I can't wait to see it filled with cum and red from being beaten." She moaned and bucked as I slid the anal toy back and forth a little. After thrusting it to the hilt once more, I placed the final clamp on her engorged clit. She screamed. I yanked her by the hair again and kissed her until the screams stopped.

Her agonized wails turned to muffled whimpers and tears. I stopped kissing her, as I trailed little kisses to her ears, and whispered, "There you go, love. It's not as bad as you think it is. Try not to come." I bit her ear softly. "You don't want to disappoint me, do you?"

She whimpered, "N-No."

After a minute, I removed the clit clamp and slowly caressed the soreness from her little nub with my fingers and reapplied the clamp. I entered her hot, wet core again and together we established a rhythm. Whenever her muscles clenched around me, I released the clamp and my fingers and waited. For each year we were apart, I denied her release.

"Melissa, please," she finally squeaked out. She was drenched in sweat, the salty liquid dripped off her skin and onto the board.

But I wasn't done yet and because she asked so nicely, I brought out the pièce de resistance: seven inches of glorious curved dildo. As I angled the cock to her dripping entrance, I wondered how Kyndall would look sandwiched between the guys, and I had to resist getting sucked into the daydream.

Out of the blue, my phone rang. Without an ounce of regret, I climbed off the bed, silenced it, and resumed. After removing the clit clamp, I slid the cock inside her pussy. I heard her intensified moan as I caressed her abused nub, while she adjusted to being filled twice over.

She begged, "Pl-Please, Melissa, shit, I've learned my lesson! Please, I want to come. I'm so full!" Her begging transformed to sobs as I reapplied the clamp and fucked her pussy with hard, fast strokes.

I knew I couldn't keep it up forever. The warm slickness ran down my thighs and the throb intensified in my clit. Since this situation was her fault, I delivered a series of stinging slaps to Kyndall's ass. I watched as her ass jiggle, which made me more aroused. Kyndall's pussy muscles quivered around the dildos—I halted all motion and removed the clamp to prevent her release yet again. No happy ending. Not yet.

"I hate you," she said, breathlessly. After a few more breaths, she tugged on the restraints and continued, "Let me out."

"Babe, in case you haven't noticed," I took her hair and wrapped it around my hands, "I'm in charge, not you, but you're in luck because I was going to let you loose, anyway." She rolled over when I released her from the bondage board. I threw the board across the room, not minding where it landed. I got a good look at my work. Kyndall lay there, spent from being edged multiple times. The nipple clamps squashed her brown nipples. Streaks of salt from her tears painted her flushed face.

"Shit, you look so fucking good," I whispered in her ear, and I swear she nearly came from the words. Endorphins flooded my brain, and in reward, I licked, bit, and sucked her earlobe. I replaced the nipple clamps with my mouth. She sighed in relief. Leaving her tender peaks, I guided her hands to grip the sheets. "If you move your hands from this bed, I'm going to edge you again. Do you understand me?"

"Y-Yes," her words stumbled out.

She tasted like tears and cognac when I kissed her, and it made me wetter. I had officially boarded the Kyndall crazy train. Our only pause in kissing was for me to line up my dick with her entrance. Double stuffing her once again. My rhythm gained speed as I fucked her with both entrances. "Kyndall, babe, I want to make you come all over this dick of mine, but you have to say the magic words."

"W-W-What?"

"The magic words, Kyndall. Mean them, or I will know." I picked up the pace, and she arched off the bed. I couldn't resist biting lightly on the one nipple close to my face. It made her whimper. "Who does this pussy belong to, Kyndall?"

She didn't respond. So, I slowed my strokes in punishment. "I said, who does this pussy belong to, baby?"

She clenched her jaw like she was going to be defiant. I pretended I was going to withdraw the dildo entirely.

"Please, no, Melissa," she whined. I dove in with fast strokes. Her whine changed to a screaming moan as she grabbed her nipples. "Yes, more!"

"Look at me, Kyndall." Her eyes latched onto mine. She didn't complain. I loved that for myself. "Who does this pussy belong to?"

"You! It's all yours! This pussy belongs to you and no one else!" she screamed.

"Come all over my dick—"

I didn't finish my sentence before Kyndall's release struck her so hard that I thought she would die in this bed. Her back arched as she writhe in the bed. Her eyes shut to the world as she a string curse words fell from her mouth. She looked like an angel. I waited until she returned to earth, removed the dildo from her sopping wet core, and made her suck it off clean. Removing the anal dildo, I kissed her and tasted her essences on her tongue. I was so caught up in tasting her from the kiss that I didn't notice Kyndall snatch the dildo from me until she pressed it against my entrance. When I nodded, she entered me slowly, using tiny, gentle thrusts. I tried to take it from her, but she caught my hand by the wrist. "No, I want to get you off." She let go of me and moved her fingers to my oversensitive clit.

It didn't take long until I chased my release along with Kyndall's—as I fingered her at the speed she fucked me. We both laid there with our sweaty bodies wrapped up in each other like on that fateful prom night. A comforting embrace of peace surrounded us and love, something my husbands and I never thought we'd find with another woman. Right before we fell asleep, I heard her whisper she loved me, and I repeated the words I said to her many years ago. Tonight, and for the rest of my life, I planned to back up that statement. Before I went to dreamland, I dragged myself to the bathroom, grabbed two wet washcloths, and cleaned her and me. Disposing of the cloth, I cuddled up next to my girl in our bed.

As I dozed off, I was content and at peace that my plans had become a reality, not just me chasing my crazy dream.

Chapter 12

KYNDALL

I WOKE UP WITH the biggest hangover known to humankind. Well, okay, *to me*, it was the worst hangover. But it wasn't the hangover that weighed on me most deeply in my post-tipsy state. It was the fact that I had my head wedged between a pair of breasts, and one of my legs was across a woman's lower body. I squeezed my eyes shut, as I prayed this wasn't some sick joke. Hopefully, last night was not a dream.

"I can tell you're awake, Kyndall." *Shit, shit, shit, and shit.* She stroked my hair, which was kinked up because of our sweat-induced night, and kissed my head. "I was waiting for you to wake up. After our third round, I was sure you'd be asleep until next week." She chuckled.

"I—huh?" I fumbled like a middle school virgin who couldn't believe their crush was speaking to them. I tried to move my head, but my body was under Melissa's spell. There was a voice in my head that said I love this woman.

Did I just think that?

I moved to get up, but she pulled me in for a kiss that made me forget my headache. "I'll get you something for your headache and start breakfast." She gave me another quick kiss and headed to the kitchen. Naked as the day she was born. I watched as her ass jiggled until I couldn't see her anymore. There was no doubt in my mind I was in trouble. This was never supposed to happen. I was supposed to be better than this. I was supposed to live my life Melissa-free and get folded like a pretzel by someone who would crawl out the bed in the morning and never see me again.

I touched my nipples and bit back a curse as I remembered the nipple clamps from last night. Those fuckers needed to be placed in a dark corner somewhere far away from me. Melissa returned, her breasts swayed lightly, as she bounced in the room with water and pain meds. I downed the pills in one go. She responded, "Next time, don't mix drinking and smoking, babe."

"Melissa, we should talk about last night."

"We will, but we need food first." She kissed me again as she returned to the kitchen, naked.

She's going to cook naked!

I groaned. I willed myself not to think about Melissa cooking naked. As I dragged my hot and sticky body out of bed. I winced as my thigh rubbed. My clit was slightly sore from those damn clamps as well. *Yeah, I won't be putting those on again.* A hot shower cleared my mind and soothed the aches. Twenty minutes later, I was dressed and ready for the day. Well, ready to fake my way through the day, I guess. A tingling sensation worked itself into my gut, as I hoped she wouldn't pull the rug out from under me.

Pathetic... I know.

I grabbed a robe for Melissa and made my way to the kitchen. Apparently unaware of my presence, Melissa was dividing bacon, eggs, and toast between two plates on the breakfast table. When she sat down, she produced a book stolen from my library and flipped through the first few pages. I cleared my throat, and she looked up. I smiled.

Simp.

"Thank you for cooking." I blushed like a fool.

"You're welcome, baby." She patted the seat next to her, where she'd placed my food. I pulled a pile of books off the chair before sitting down, and she rewarded me with a kiss. "Come on. We should eat."

We kept the conversation light—catching up on years of changes. When we finished, I cleaned up, and Melissa showered and dressed. She found me in the living room, trying to act nonchalant.

I fiddled with the faux zipper running down the side of my shorts. "We need to talk about last night, Melissa."

"Okay, babe. I think we should go on a date on Friday. I have a heavy caseload this week, but I was thinking about going to the city to visit that famous restaurant off First Street everyone raves about."

"Melissa, I can't afford that place. I don't have that kind of money."

"Don't worry about that, Kyn. Do you remember when you worked that shitty ass babysitting job for the summer? You bought food for us every paycheck. This is me paying you back." Carefully, she straddled my lap and wrapped her arms around me. "You overthink things. I want you to sit back and let me make up for lost time."

"And what if I don't want that? What if I want this to be a one night thing? What if I want us to be acquaintances?"

Tears welled in her eyes. Melissa usually kept her emotions under wraps, so her rare outbursts of emotion always made me give in. Otherwise, I felt like the bad guy. Her voice trembled. "Kyndall, I'm trying to show you I've changed. Can you at least give me a chance?" She looked at me with those big brown eyes.

I closed my eyes and took a breath. Even after all these years, Melissa had a vise grip on my heart. "Fine, but let's go slow and take it from there." Something possessed me, as I pulled her closer and kissed her until we were both topless. Melissa shoved her hand down my shorts, and I ground myself against her palm. Her fingers slipped into my warm core while I bucked and moaned into her mouth.

"So, this is why you haven't been answering your phone," Alex scoffed, as she stood with her hands on her hip.

I jumped so badly my forehead banged into Melissa's nose. Seconds ago, my body was a on the verge of an orgasmic bliss. My cousin might as well have thrown a whole bucket of ice water on me. Melissa let loose a curse and pulled her fingers out fast.

The look of triumph didn't suit Alex's face. "Caught with your hand down your pants again. Or should I say someone's hand?"

"Alex," I shouted, as Melissa and I fumbled to put our shirts back on. She plastered an annoyed look on her perfect face like an ugly mask.

Shit, why can't life be easy for me?

"Alex, how wonderful to see you again," Melissa said unenthusiastically.

The tension thickened, and I swallowed, ignoring how my eyes shifted back and forth. "Listen, I'm sorry, Melissa, for this interruption. Alex,

I'm sorry I didn't tell you I made it home last night. We agreed to call if either of us was going to be late getting home, but umm—"

"She got caught up with me, Alex. But I made sure she was more than okay," Melissa stated smugly.

Okay, I had to nip this in the bud. I couldn't afford to have both of the people I cared about fighting. I didn't need anyone to call the police.

Did I just admit again that I cared about Melissa? Already?

Out loud, I asked, "Alex, why don't you wait out here? And Melissa, why don't you wait for me in the bedroom?"

"Don't be long, Kyndall," her voice intoned. She threw her arms around my neck and kissed me for Alex's benefit. I was no better when I stared after Melissa as she glided to the bedroom.

"If you don't drag your horny ass eyes back to earth," Alex spat out. Fury stormed behind her eyes.

"Alex, I—"

"You don't owe me any apologies. I figured you would probably give in eventually. You like to learn the hard way. If this goes sideways, I'm going to be the one picking up the pieces and gluing them back together. I may be wrong, but I pray you trust your instincts and keep your heart safe. I don't trust that whore."

"Alex." What could I say to that? She had some valid points. I continued, "I can't tell what the future will bring for us, but I want to go down this road. If I get burned, then I'll let you lock me up and micromanage all my relationships forever."

Her anger dimmed to a slow sadness. "You trusted yourself and her before," she whispered. "And you almost killed yourself because of it. I would hate to see a repeat."

My gaze fell to the floor. If this went south, I didn't know what I would do. But I had decided to no longer avoid or deny my past, but embrace it. "I can promise you, Alex, that I won't even think about doing what I did back then. I was young, and in a horrible place. Now, if crap goes sideways, I know what to do to prevent myself going back to...." I looked at the bedroom door to make sure it was closed, but it wasn't. Hopefully, Melissa hadn't heard or dug up anything to know what I was talking about. My face was so hot, it felt like I was in a sauna. "You know what," I whispered.

"You better be right, or I will rain hell and brimstone from Flushing to Centre Island, and you know I am serious as shit," she reprimanded loud enough for Melissa to hear. "If someone, I don't care who it is, fucks with you, they will have to deal with me. No one gets to mess with my family or me."

That was my cousin for you, and she meant it. The last time Jody had gotten beaten up by her boyfriend, Alex made Marcus send half of Queens to pay him a visit. That was the last time we heard from José. There was no letter, blood, or anything left, even when Jody snuck into his apartment to retrieve her stuff. I shuddered. I knew they did shady shit, but I rarely witnessed any part of the hardcore stuff.

As I hugged her, I could feel the tears welling up in my eyes and my throat tightening with emotion. "I love you, Alex, and you have always been there for me. When everyone left me for dead, you were there beside me." I struggled to say the words I had mulled over since Melissa reappeared in my life. "I don't think I stopped loving Melissa, and I want to see where this leads. Call me a weak simp, but I hope you can understand that. Heck, I hope I can understand."

Gosh! I haven't cried this much since high school.

Melissa's voice suddenly butted in. "I know I deserve the hate, but I can assure you, I love Kyndall, and yes, I once made a dumbass decision, but I have changed and grown since. Now, I know what I want, and it's Kyndall to complete my family."

I pulled away from our hug. Alex glared right into Melissa's eyes. "I'll give you a second chance, but you better know I will leave you ruined if you fuck her over again. I will take everything away from you."

Melissa nodded and smiled, as if she expected nothing less. "I under-stand, and I thank you for watching over my wife when I couldn't do so. I'll repay you by inviting you to our commitment ceremony."

"Commitment ceremony? Wife?" I was confused. What in the heck was she on?

"Yes, a ceremony for us to exchange vows, like a wedding, but for polyamorous groups." Melissa continued on. "We will exchange vows and party. It will be fun. You're my wife. There's no discussion needed on that."

"That's some." Alex spun a finger in a tight circle around her ear.

Melissa rolled her eyes. "It's intimate and special." Melissa's phone rang, and she excused herself to take the call in the bedroom. This time, she closed the door.

"She's been in Hollywood way too long." Alex shook her head. "Welp, that's all on you now, I guess. I'll be keeping a close eye on this relationship." Alex pointed two fingers to her eyes and mine.

"Aye, captain," I saluted.

"Sheesh, she already thinks you're her wife. Jesus, be a fence!"

"Yeah, I don't know about that one. We have a lot of ground to make up before any commitment ceremony, and that's a maybe, anyway." I willed myself to be stern on this point, to hold the line.

Alex teased, "Does she know that? She's one of those that means every word she says. I figured that out the other day and y'all looked pretty snuggly on that sofa just a while ago."

Well...

"Oh ha, let me tell Marcus you want him to plan out everything for you," I teased back.

Alex kissed her teeth and rolled her eyes. I just chuckled. The sound echoed through the room, as I acknowledged the toll this day had taken on me mentally.

"Since I'm over here, I think I may stay over to keep you company. Unless the poly princess stays over. I love you, but I don't want to hear you screaming for her to tongue you down." Alex twisted her face.

Only my cousin could make me want to hit her upside her head and ask for forgiveness in the same sentence. I popped into the kitchen to fetch coffee for the two of us. We sat on the sofa together, drank our coffees and chatted. Alex talked about her current Marcus debacle, and it left me with enough time to let my mind free.

I hadn't even had time to adjust to what had happened last night. No time to sit in my bean bag, alone, and turn the events over in my head. My patience for people would wear thin soon. I needed to get in some "me" time. Melissa rejoined us with her bag in her hand, and her face was flushed pink. I immediately knew something was wrong.

"Let me walk you out." I spoke in a hurried tone. The second we were in the driveway, I asked, "What's wrong?"

"Amber fell and fractured her arm. She is going to have surgery today. Her dads tried to call me last night, and I turned off my phone and forgot to check my messages and voicemails this morning."

I was remorseful instantly. Maybe this was a sign. Melissa was so wrapped up with me she forgot about her child—who was number one, above all things. I chewed a hole in my bottom lip.

Melissa pulled me into a kiss that made me weak in the knees. My heart raced. When she pulled away, she clarified, "Don't you dare think this is your fault. I know you too well. Amber will be okay and will be back to her normal self soon. I'll call you to confirm our date." She kissed me quickly before she got into her car and drove away.

I could take a lot of things, but news of a hurt child broke my heart. I sent positive vibes to Melissa and her daughter as I headed back inside.

"Is she okay? I ain't seen someone run that fast... lately," Alex inquired. She flipped through Netflix, totally ignoring the "My List" tab to find something she wanted to watch.

"Her kid fell and broke her arm. She had to rush to the hospital." Though I sat next to her, I took out my phone to not look at Alex's face.

"That's horrible. I can't even imagine what I'd feel if Maxwell broke a bone while I was bumping uglies. I would die." She knew better than to glance my way. "Do you think she was lying to get away?"

I sighed. "Alex, can you please not? I don't need that on my conscience. You can feel sorry and still be nice."

"Yeah, I can, but you need to give me something more than just this 'that's my pussy to care for' speech."

Well.... They had the worst introduction to each other so far. I couldn't blame Alex for her heated reaction. I rubbed my neck to relieve some of the tension.

Okay, I needed to get Alex to go home.

Alex propped up her feet on the coffee table. "And if you think I'm leaving tonight, you're making a sad mistake. I want every detail of your sapphic fest." She said before adding, "And Chinese food."

Welp, there goes that plan!

"Oh, and you're treating me since I had to drag my tail over here to find out if you were alive or dead!"

And there goes my money as well.

Chapter 13

MELISSA

GUILT WRECKED MY BRAIN. Amber's surgery went well, with no complications. Amber, the explorer she was, was going through my part of the closet and fell. She admitted she wanted to put on the jewelry I kept hidden away. I could beat myself up for showing her where I kept my jewelry. I moved their hiding spot lower in the closet so Amber wouldn't have to climb again.

I texted and called Kyndall on Monday after things had settled down. She wanted to know about Amber's well-being and how we were holding up. I insisted that Amber's dads set her up like a mini diva, with a private nurse and her fathers were now at her beck and call. She was on cloud nine. To be frank, I'd spied her asking Aaron to massage her feet. When I came home that night, she had a new kid's chair with a foot spa, and Travis sat at her feet, as he rubbed away her pain, as she watched Nickelodeon.

She's the Queen of the house, and we're just her servants.

It was Wednesday night. I just got off the phone with Kyndall to confirm our Friday date. She'd sounded eager for the date, but annoyance undercut her words. Her annoying—excuse me, I mean protective—cousin had likely been hounding her all week. I rolled my eyes. I couldn't be mad at her, to be honest. It was just too many hens in the chicken coop.

When I walked into the foyer, I knew some shit had happened. Our home was never this quiet unless we were asleep or out of town. I walked through the massive house and found all my moody men in Matt's office. A hushed conversation stopped when I entered.

"Hello." I kissed all the guys, but something was way off. "What's going on? Is Amber alright?" I panicked.

"No, we're concerned about you," Aaron said truthfully. He Grabbed me by the waist and maneuvered me into his lap. He hugged me from behind. "You went missing in action Saturday night and part of Sunday."

"That's not like you, Melissa." Matt leaned back in his chair. "Plus, you weren't in Manhattan with Sage like you claimed."

Well, fuck!

I meant to tell them, but I had wanted to wait for a time we could all get together. I wanted Kyndall and me to have at least one date before I introduced the guys to her.

"Well, I—"

Matt frowned. "When you start sentences with 'well,' I know you're about to downplay whatever actually happened. Try again."

"I went to see Kyndall." I held my head up, which was hard since it would be so much nicer to melt into Aaron's chest, away from their intense stares.

"And that was the second time you saw her? What did you guys do?" Aaron asked.

Oh gosh, this wasn't what I planned at all. I floundered. "Oh, I think Amber's calling me. Maybe I should—"

"She's asleep. Her pain medication knocked her out. Nice try, though." Travis smirked.

"So, you met up with Kyndall," Matt prodded. "Where did you go after that?".

"Oh, I just slept over at Kyndall's house." I looked at my phone. I yawned. "Man, I am so sleepy. Are we done here? I have an early morning tomorrow."

Matt spoke slowly, like he wanted to test out each word's full weight. "You slept over at your ex-best friend's house. The ex-best friend who you have feelings for?"

Travis backed Matt up. "The same friend you had sex with and ghosted the next day—an incident you still regret to this day," he continued. "The same friend you said goodbye to a little over two months ago and became depressed for an entire weekend?"

Travis shook his head and folded his arms.

"Yes, and it was very therapeutic." Enough of this. I left Aaron's arms and practically fled to the master bathroom.

I stayed in the shower until my skin became pruny. I tiptoed into the closet and prayed the guys were asleep, or at least Matt was asleep. Then I stopped myself.

I don't know why I'm hiding!

I sighed, went to the house safe, and retrieved both the papers from Joey's investigation and the receipt from the sex store. Using whatever husbands superpower told them I was ready to talk, all my partners had assembled in our bedroom just as I returned. I dumped everything on our massive bed.

"Listen, I know how this looks, but I can explain." Eyes closed, I rolled my neck. When I opened them up, I continued, "I'm sorry I went behind everyone's back. I went off the rails. My thought process wasn't right, and I went off with my emotions."

Everyone looked at me like I'd grown an extra head with a pimple on the nose. Aaron picked up the papers, whistled, and showed them to the other men.

Taking the silence as permission to continue, "I've been thinking about us dating Kyndall. We spoke about a lot of things last Saturday and—"

"Does she know you have every piece of information on her and bought an..." Aaron frowned at the receipt, "anal boot camp kit?"

"She's aware of the information and the toys." I looked defiantly at Matt in particular. "She knows about the toys personally."

"So that's why you didn't pick your phone up when we called you about Amber. You were too busy deep in your ex-best friend's ass," Travis smirked.

"Well, technically, I went through her anus and into her rectum..."

Travis laughed. "Okay, stalker doctor."

I knew I appeared like a stalker, but I was not too fond of the word being thrown in my face. I acted out of love and being in love makes you do some shitty ass things in the moment.

"I know I've done some crazy shit recently, but I'm trying to correct a wrong. My endgame is near." I forced my voice to sound confident.

"What's your endgame? To keep Kyndall a secret from us while you prance around the city with her?" Matt asked.

"Oh ha, no, I want you guys to meet her, and then we can go from there."

Travis raised an immediate challenge. "And what's your plan if we decide we don't have a connection with her? Are you going to let her or us go? Because we won't let you go so easily."

I clenched my fists as I tried to remain calm. "Travis, why don't I set something up after our Friday date?"

"Your date? We're supposed to date her together first, then go from there." Matt chuckled, but it sounded dark.

I sighed loudly. "I'm sorry for how I went about this, but I want Kyndall and not someone I have to compare to her. This sounds crazy, but I think we had to go through this to grow. I know you guys will love her if you tried. If you guys don't, then I don't know. I haven't thought that far down the road."

"Did you ever stop loving her?" Aaron asked. He had been silent as he observed the situation until now.

"No. I have always loved her, and I know you guys will as well."

The silence between us was a loud one. It was Aaron who made the first move—by coming over and hugging me. "I disagree with how you went about it. You violated Kyndall's privacy. You broke our vows. We're supposed to date our potential fourth together. Let alone have sex with them. You ignored these boundaries, and you lied about it—which defiled our most important rule to be honest with each other. Cheating is cheating, no matter the gender or situation."

My heart pounded in my ears. My vision swam. Was I going to faint? I clutched my husband tighter.

Aaron finished, "But I understand, and I want you to know that we're willing to make this work."

My breath punched out of me, oxygen rushing in with relief.

"But just know if we're not comfortable with Kyndall, then you're going to have to let her go," Matt stated.

"I-I understand, and I agree with your decision," I stammered. I knew I would make this work. Taking an enormous gamble, I spoke my next words. "I want her to live with us. I think it would do us good. Before you start, I haven't lost my mind."

"You want to bring a complete stranger into our home, Melissa?" Matt asked. His eyebrows were basically to his hairline and mouth was agape.

"She's not a stranger, she's my best friend—she's a part of me, as much as you guys are a part of me." The tears that were building in my eyes threatened to spill. "I love her as much as I love you guys. I have this second chance and I don't want to ruin it. Plus, Kyndall loves kids."

There they stood in the room. All of their intense eyes were on me like I told them the world would end. Matt tilted his head. My heart pounded so fast, I thought I'd collapse, but I held my ground. I knew it wasn't a coincidence Kyndall found her way back into my life and I was determined to keep her right where she belongs—with me.

Matt, out of everyone, was the first to respond. "Okay, but we have to meet her soon."

Aaron and Travis gasped. Their eyes looked as if Matt's words were squeezing their eyes out of their sockets. I breathe a sigh of relief.

Aaron asked, "Seriously?"

Matt replied, "Yes, we trust each other, and we know Melissa wouldn't do anything to jeopardize our family."

"I would never do that, ever. You have my word." I promised.

"This is about the craziest thing we've done. That's saying a lot." Travis stopped and ran his hand through his dirty blonde hair. "But I'm down."

We all let out a stifled laugh—except Aaron.

"I really don't understand what's going on right now." Aaron shook his head and stated, "It's three against one. I just hope Kyndall is with this plan, or else all of this would have been for nothing."

That seemed to put an end to the endless questions. It wasn't until after everyone was asleep that I let cold dread fill me. Failure was possible. What would happen if my partners didn't like Kyndall? How would I navigate that situation? We usually agreed on everything important. I knew in my heart they would like her, but a petty demon on my shoulder shoved my fear in my face.

Thursday was a whirlwind of activity, from the moment I opened my eyes to the moment I felt my head sink into my pillow. My nerves were so shot that I gagged and vomited three times.

As I waited for the limo on Friday night, I did a once over by the door. I shook the last of that little devil out of my head. My red ruched tulle dress shone all the brighter with my black high heels, diamond earrings, and my birthstone necklace to set it off. The necklace was the same one Kyndall had given me in high school, and it had become a source of comfort over the years. Going off the red theme, I'd chosen the red Balmain clutch—a present from Aaron on our third anniversary—and kept my makeup unremarkable except for a pop of red lipstick. My one regret was none of my hair accessories were a complementary red shade, so I'd settled for coaxing my braids into a bun.

Amber ran up to me just as the nerves filled my legs with pins and needles. Where was that limo?

"Mommy, you look beautiful!" Amber hugged me with one arm and stared awestruck into my face, her green eyes twinkled.

"Thank you, baby," I replied, even though this was her third compliment for the night.

"Can I come with you?"

"Next time, baby, we can have a girl's night and do our nails." I chuckled as she wrapped her arms around my upper thigh. It reminded me she was growing up way too fast, or I had shrunk. Both choices unnerved me.

She grinned "Yes! I want my nails to be yellow now."

I kissed her. "Of course, sweetie. Anything you want, you'll get."

"Now, who's the one spoiling her?" Matt came up and handed me a mini gift bag and gave me a peck. "Don't forget Kyndall's gift. You look amazing, by the way. Are you sure I can't escort you, beautiful ladies?"

I mock-punched his arm. He knew tonight was my first date with Kyndall, and I was nervous. The limo pulled up, and I signaled the driver to give me a minute. My palms grew clammy, and I wiped my hands on my dress.

My knees went soft as I kissed Matt. "I love you, baby. I'll see you later. Thank you for being supportive."

"I love you too, and I know everything will be okay. No more being nervous." Matt squeezed my ass to send me off. As the limo traversed our long driveway, I watched Amber and Matt fade into two black shadows through the rear window.

When the driver pulled into traffic, I called the only other person outside of my immediate family who knew about tonight, Sage. She was shocked when I first told her about meeting Kyndall at the block party. Sage admitted she figured Kyndall had something for me back in high school, but thought nothing of it because she wasn't a narc. I begged to differ, but I let her have it. The icing on the cake was when I told her about prom night and my current plans. She thought I was going crazy, and I firmly agreed that this entire experience had driven me crazy.

For the rest of the ride, I brooded. I was so lost in my thoughts that I didn't notice the driver had pulled up to Kyndall's home. Like a teen, I hopped out of the limo and rang the bell with shaky hands.

I need to get a hold of myself.

I heard her walk to the door and fumble with the locks. When the door finally opened, I stumbled back. She was gorgeous every day, but she looked like a goddess tonight. She wore a white bodycon dress that stopped mid-thigh with a split that revealed her silky, thick flesh. Like me, her hair was in a high bun, but loose strands framed her tranquil face. Besides her nude lipstick and signature white winged eyeliner, she had no foundation—and with a skin that dewy; she didn't need any. Her silver stilettos flashed in the porch light, and more silver winked from her wrist and ears.

I fidgeted with my dress over my mommy's pouch.

"Kyndall, you look amazing," I said, my voice shaky. "Are you ready to go?"

"Yeah, let's get out of here." She walked before me, and behold, Alex came up afterward.

"Don't let her ruin my dress!" Alex shouted loud enough for all of Queens to hear. "And if you guys are planning on having sex, please do it in the car. I don't want to hear y'all moaning and groaning."

"Did she have to scream that loud?" I asked, as I entered the limo after Kyndall.

"I'm sorry on behalf of Alex. She's a mess." She shook her head bashfully.

"Well, now all of your neighbors know we're messing around, so I guess I don't mind." I chuckled.

"You're a mess as well," she flushed.

The ride from Kyndall's home to the restaurant was quick. Within thirty minutes, we sat in the high end restaurant. When the waitress sat us down at one of the corner windows, I ordered a bottle of white champagne and hard apple cider for Kyndall. Since she doesn't want to drink the "devil's juice" tonight.

"Melissa, I feel awful. I just realized how sexy you look tonight," she said hurriedly. "Red looks great on you."

"It's okay, babe," I replied, truthfully. "Honestly, I feel silly in this dress."

"What? You look so amazing in that dress and without it." The waitress returned with our drinks, and Kyndall busied herself with her cider. "The little weight you put on makes you look even better, if you can imagine that." as she met my eyes, her cheeks turned slightly pink, and she smiled. "I hope your husbands tell you that you're beautiful every day."

"They do." I smiled. "I'm fortunate to have them. You'll love them as well."

She shook her head and smiled. We continued to have light conversation throughout our dinner. There would always be more to learn about Kyndall, and I had a decade's worth of knowledge to catch up on. We giggled and smiled our whole time together. I missed this type of female interaction. Just to sit down and have a conversation with another woman, with no strings attached. After we finished our dessert, I sensed it was the perfect time to strike. No need to prolong the inevitable.

I placed my hand over hers on the table. "Kyndall, this was so absolutely amazing, and I want more. We started on a weird foot, but I want you to know that I'm ready for the next step."

"Next step? Melissa, what are you talking about?" She cocked an eyebrow. "Please tell me you're not up to another one of your schemes. I'm giving you another chance here, and historically speaking, your schemes don't turn out the best."

"I know, but I feel like we're making great progress, and it's time to take the next step. No more pussyfooting around."

She looked at me like I had lost my mind. "I'm so confused, Melissa."

"Let's take this to the limo. Fewer ears around." I flagged the waitress and gave her my card.

"Melissa, what's the total?" she asked, reaching for her bag.

"Kyndall, I'm paying. Put your card back," I insisted, but when the waitress returned for my signature, Kyndall grabbed the receipt out from under me.

"Three hundred and fifty dollars? Wait, this is a joke, right? For filet mignon?" She glared at me.

I signed on the dotted line without further protest. "Yeah, it was worth the price, Kyndall. Plus, this was my treat." I handed the check to the waitress. "Nothing is too expensive for you, babe. Speaking of which, I got you something."

I pulled out the small gift bag and held it out for her. Before she took the bag, she paused. She removed the small red jewelry box and opened it. She gasped when she pulled out the twenty four carat gold chain with a custom diamond locket with our picture from our prom in it.

"Melissa, I love it," she choked out. "You didn't have to buy me this—"

"I know, but I wanted to give you something to show my appreciation for giving us another chance." As I sniffled. "I wanted to give you something special now that I can afford it."

Before she could utter a word, I quickly grabbed her hand. I got up and went to her side of the table. I pulled her into a kiss, which I knew she'd complain about later cause she hated public display of affection. We walked out and waited for the limo. When we got in, I immediately rolled up the partition.

"Spill it, Melissa," as she crossed her arms, which made her breasts push up more than usual. She cleared her throat—oops. *Caught.*

"Er... There's no rush. The night's still young, and I want to go to this popular gay dance club around the corner." I kissed her as we pulled up to the club, and she gave me a skeptical look. "It's nothing too bad. Let's go dance until our ankles hurt."

I didn't give her time to form a snarky comeback. We got into the club quickly, and I ordered a rum and Coke for the both of us. Of course, Kyndall made a fuss about the drink choices, and I ended up drinking both of them.

"Melissa, the cider already had alcohol in it. Rum will have me on my ass tomorrow," she whined, and it was adorable. Okay, maybe I was horny.

"Babe, just relax." I drank half of my drink. "Here, give me half of your drink. See? We're compromising already. Our relationship is progressing nicely."

She rolled her eyes. "You're doing *the most*." She chuckled and tugged on my arm. "Let's go dance they're playing Beyoncé's new album, Renaissance, all night."

I allowed her to lead the way to the dance floor, but I took the lead on it. With a bit of liquid courage, we danced like a couple of lunatics without a care in the world. Under the strobe lights, we left the past and the future to live in the now. When the DJ slipped into slower-paced ballads, we smashed ourselves together. We probably looked like two zombies, clawing and leaning on each other. I was too far gone even to care. The DJ's announcement about the club's closure for the night took me completely by surprise. We stumbled out of the club, two tipsy fools, into the limo. I apologized to the driver because I never expected to stay out this late.

Once we were on our way, I rolled up the partition and sat back in my seat next to Kyndall. Silently, we sat wrapped up in each other's arms, until Kyndall pulled me in for a kiss. I didn't know how long we kissed, but when we were done, we were both breathless. I wanted more, but I had promised myself to be good and to show her a good time without us having sex.

What I hadn't expected was for Kyndall to want more. Her soft hands traveled underneath my dress and brushed against my Spanx high-waisted thong. I'd worn it to smooth out my stomach. Kyndall snatched and yanked at it, like she was angry at the fabric for existing. I lifted my hips to help, but she ended up on her knees on the floor, anyway. She growled, "Don't wear this stupid, annoying shit anymore. You don't need it. You're perfect the way you are, Melissa."

My core became wetter from her words. Kyndall never took the lead anytime we had sex. I never expected or wanted her to, but I was down to try anything with her. She finally got off my shapewear and moved in between my thighs. I gasped as she licked the entire length of my drenched core. Mixed emotions filled my heart—she must have perfected this technique with someone else. Before I got lost in my head, she wrapped that little sexy mouth around my clit and sucked it until I let loose a breathy moan. She tortured my pearl, switching to swiping it with her nose as her tongue penetrated my core. I grabbed the back of her head to get her even deeper.

"Kyndall, my good girl, fuck, yes, eat my pussy." I was an incoherent mess. I tightened my grip on her hair. "Keep fucking me with your tongue while I ride your face like that."

Lost in the pace of my hips as they moved against Kyndall's face. My body stiffened as I bit my lip to muffle my moan. Kyndall licked all the come she could as I came directly onto her tongue. I held her head until I could form words again.

I felt the softness of her golden hair bun in my hand, and my nails dug deeper to keep her from moving back. "Shit, that was so good, baby. Now clean our pussy up like a good girl." My voice filled with pleasure. I kept control of her head to ensure she got every bit of my juice. When she was done, I kissed her until I couldn't taste myself anymore. Digging into my clutch, I found a wet wipe and offered one to her.

Since the limo didn't have a trash can, Kyndall threw the wipe into a cup holder. I checked to see if she was as wet as I was. Kyndall's thong was drenched. She groaned when I drew my fingers away.

"I will not give you a release because this was supposed to be a clean and fun date night, and you made a mess of yourself and me. So as your punishment, I don't want you to touch yourself until I tell you to."

"Melissa, please, I-I can't wait," she whimpered. I pulled her hair hard and suddenly, making her yelp, I kissed her and sucked on her tongue.

Our breath hitched as we moved away, transfixed.

"You can and will. Every time you think about touching your pussy while I'm not there, I want you to insert your anal toy for an hour, and I want a video of you sliding it in and removing it. And I will know, Kyndall, if you touch what's mine. Do you understand?" I pulled her head a little further back.

"Yes, ma'am," she whispered.

"I couldn't hear you, baby." I pulled her hair a little harder again, but slower this time.

"Yes, ma'am! I won't come unless you tell me to!" she shouted. I knew the driver had heard us, but I was not embarrassed.

I'm so turned on by her obedience.

"Good. Oh, and I want you to wear the nipple clamps simultaneously as well." She nodded her assent.

I didn't know how long the driver had been sitting in Kyndall's driveway, but I got out and told the driver I would be back. He dipped his head and averted his eyes. His response, knowing he'd heard us, made me blush.

I helped Kyndall out of the limo and guided her to her front porch. It startled me out of my thoughts when Kyndall muttered, "I need some dick."

I chuckled as she unlocked the door and reassured her, "Don't worry, you'll have three dicks to play with soon."

She rolled her eyes and her light, airy giggle filled the air as we kissed and parted ways.

I got to the limo door and rolled down the window, pleased to see that Kyndall was still on the porch, watching me. I smiled sweetly. "Oh, and Kyndall? I'm giving you a month to get your affairs in order and to pack."

"What?" She tilted her head.

"This is part of the plan where I compromised a little again. I originally wanted you to move in by the end of next week, but my husbands convinced me to give you a month. You have thirty days to change your permanent address and pack. I've already scheduled the movers. Goodnight, babe. I love you." I blew her a kiss and rolled up the window while she cursed me out. As the driver pulled away, I checked my phone: five texts from Kyndall and one from the guys, asking when I'd be home. I sent a quick text to my husbands saying I was on my way, texted my address to Kyndall, and added to both chats that I loved them. Kyndall replied I was a crazy, controlling hefa.

Mmm, Maybe I won't let her come for a week. Teach that mouth of hers.

Chapter 14

KYNDALL

As I opened the USPS Change of Address website form for the seventh time that day, I knew I had officially lost my mind. I was supposed to be finding another job. Instead, I'd gone back and forth with Melissa about this moving situation. Our texts ranged from "Kyndall, you better have your things in order in twenty-something days," to "you're an egotistical mad woman, Melissa."

It'd been a week since our fantastic first date and over one hundred sixty-eight hours since my last orgasm. Every time I thought about pleasuring myself, I put in my anal toy, snapped on the nipple clamp, wondered why I was doing it, and got the camera rolling.

Insanity at its finest.

Did Melissa really know a way to tell if I had played with myself? I mean, she was not a witch.

Did the method work on anyone, or was there something special about me?

Did she plan to interrogate me until I confessed to any masturbation sessions?

The thought brought a chuckle out of me.

Alex had been right on the other side of the door when Melissa yelled her demands. Which meant I got to hear her opinion on the situation every day since then. *Lucky me! Not.*

On the Saturday morning after our date, Alex and I were eating breakfast. She'd said out of the blue, "She's touched, that one. You sure you don't need me to hide you from her?" She tilted her head and sent one of her famous smirks my way. "You must have some golden enchantment between your legs."

I rolled my eyes. "Why do you have to be so dramatic?"

"We're half Jamaican. There isn't such a thing as being too dramatic." She shrugged. "You know what? She's like your twin."

"What do you mean?"

"You guys have so much alike, except for she is a bit... controlling and richer." She shrugged.

I just shook my head.

Melissa and I were supposed to meet tonight, but she had to change plans. Something about staying home with Amber. I couldn't promise I didn't feel disappointed, but I understood. When I asked if I could at least relieve myself, she asked if I'd become mental.

I really couldn't stand her sometimes.

As I typed out the news to Alex about Melissa's cancellation, I could feel her excitement as she invited me along to The Little Hut with Jody and the girls. Going out seemed a better option than moping at home, so I agreed. After four hours, we settled at our usual table, and I tried to keep our mischievous group from making a spectacle of themselves.

When Alex's face lit up, I knew there was going to be trouble.

My cousin shouted, "I'm feeling generous! Kyndall, go buy us two bottles of the most expensive drink they have for the table!"

"Truly, all good financial and health decisions are made after five glasses of Wray & Nephew's rum, with a smidgen of Coke," I replied, dry as a desert. Truly, I'm amazed she was upright.

I succumbed to Alex's badgering and made my way to the bar. Everyone, even Jimmie, started looking at something. I followed their gazes to three white men who walked into the bar. Three white men in Jamaica, Queens after, well, anytime is rare. Much less after ten P.M.

They're tall as hell and fine.

Jody hollered, "Welp, there goes the neighborhood. We are getting gentrified at night now."

"Oh, those assholes can wait for their bottles!" Jody's miserable attitude hit some inner limit, and I needed time away. I went to the bar, nabbed a spot right next to one of the white men who had sat in the three chairs nearby. I might be crazy, but one of them smiled at me. My knees nearly buckled. I looked away so fast my head almost spun off my neck. My face burned like hot coals.

I'm in a committed relationship!

"Wah gwan, Kyndall!" Jimmie came up and saved me from my wayward mind.

"Hey Jimmie, nothing. How's it been going?"

"I've been good. I spoke with your mom yesterday," he beamed. It was as if I was supposed to jump for joy.

"How wonderful." I rolled my eyes. "Can I get two bottles of whatever has the lowest alcohol content?" Trying to trick Alex into sobering up.

"Yeah, she told me she's coming here next week or month."

"Amazing, that's wonderful." When Jimmie proffered two enormous bottles of Red Stripe beer, I grabbed and turned to leave. But Jimmie's wasn't finished because Jamaican men always had to have the last word.

"Can I give her your information? I think you guys should link up." He smiled, and I wanted to throw up at the mere thought.

"Look, Jimmie. I think someone was waving for you in the back," I lied and walked away. The white boy trio tried to drop me some discreet glances—they must've overheard everything. I smiled and ignored them.

Already forgetting that she sent me for something, Alex and our friends cheered when I returned. They were happy to see me safe and happy to swipe the beer. I wanted to feel good enough to go out to dance, so I downed several big gulps before anyone could stop me. A warm euphoria traveled from my mouth to my stomach. I tried to get to the floor, but stumbled, air rushing past my ears as I braced for impact.

Instead of eating shit, I landed in the warm, muscular arms of one of the white newcomers. Thank God because I would die if I fell in front of everyone. "T-Thank you," I stuttered.

"You're welcome. Be careful when you're a lightweight." He smiled.

I knew if the alcohol hadn't turned my brain into mush, the next words would have remained in my brain. "You have a fuckable mouth."

No, that wasn't right.

"Fuckable smile, no, that's not right either."

"I meant nice smile." I smiled back. *Yeah, that was it.*

He laughed. "Thank you, that's a first. Maybe you should switch to water now."

"Mmh, okay." My stomach tightened, but I pushed on. "What's your name?"

"Aaron. You must be the infamous Kyndall, right?" He held his hand out, and I took it so loosely that Aaron might as well have shaken hands with a rag doll.

"Yes." My wide, glassy eyes continued to roam his body. "How did you know?"

"We overheard your conversation at the bar, and we've heard a lot about you. Sorry for eavesdropping, though."

I stared at him because his hazel eyes were stunning in the bar's light. So caught up in eye-fucking him I didn't remember what he just said. I replied, "That's okay."

"Do you mind if I join you on the dance floor? They can get you some water."

"Yes, that's fine." He could have asked me to drop my panties, and I'd comply.

After ten minutes of us swaying offbeat to the dancehall music, his friends joined. Introducing themselves as Matt and Travis, the way their muscles strained against their shirts, got me all hot and bothered. My neck hurt from the angle I had to hold it in order to meet their gazes. I'd had my share of white men, but they were different. You could tell by the way they strolled and how they handled themselves.

Big dick energy.

Over the next thirty minutes, they filled me with enough water to fill a small lake, which helped sober me up enough to answer their questions. I thoroughly enjoyed myself. We talked, laughed, and danced until I had to excuse myself to use the restroom. Thankfully, my stomach waited until I had my head over the toilet to expunge its contents. My senses wobbled and blurred, but I thought, with a little more water, I'd be totally fine tomorrow. My walk back to Aaron's table was steady.

The moment I approached, I knew something was up because Jody was there and her famous stern glare was currently skewering Matt. It amazed me how she could wreck a mood. Any Time, Any Place.

From her pulpit, she droned on, "I don't like real estate investors. They don't respect neighborhoods; all they see are dollar signs."

Yeah, that's enough. I interrupted, "Hey Jody, can you get me something to drink? I could go for a Coke."

She nodded and went without argument. I was part mystified and part amazed. She must really be out of her mind tonight, because I could never get her to do anything without a fight.

Reclaiming my seat at their table, I tried to lighten the mood. "I'm sorry. She doesn't have a filter. Plus, she's lived in Astoria her whole life. Nowhere near Jamaica."

"No problem. We get it all the time," Travis shrugged, as he stretched his arms behind his head as if to relieve any tension. I was proud to report I didn't ogle the sleeves of the tattoos that snaked over his muscles. *This time.*

I laughed. "Still, she's had a lot of alcohol, which makes her unbearable."

Aaron replied, "Apology accepted. We should get going anyway. It's past our bedtime."

"I should walk you out. It's not safe around here."

"Oh, so your security now, huh?" Travis laughed, and my eyes went to his lips.

Oh God, I need to get laid soon.

"Only the best security around. I don't fight, but I will yell for help," I teased back.

The entire group was smiling as I walked them out of The Little Hut and kept smiling all the way to their car. Matt told me goodbye and kissed me on my cheek. Travis followed suit and kissed me on my other cheek. I stood there—my face was on fire.

"Kyndall, this was a great night. We're interested in a second date, provided our wife won't kill us for having this much fun behind her back," Aaron grinned.

"Ah, excuse me? Your what?" The little alcohol that remained in my system all but evaporated. Shock replaced it.

"Yeah, and I'll let our wife know you were on your best behavior. We look forward to our second date."

I was still stunned by the announcement that they had a wife. But Aaron caught me even more off guard when he leaned over and kissed me on the corner of my mouth. "B-But I didn't give you my number or anything. I can't go out with you. I'm in a relationship."

"Goodnight, Kyndall. It was a pleasure meeting you, and we look forward to getting to know you more. We have your information," he smiled and winked.

About thirty seconds after they got into the car, I got out, "H-Have a good night."

This has been the weirdest night ever.

I shook my head and walked back to the bar. Alex and Jody had returned to the dance floor, but I was too tired even to think about waiting for Alex. I grabbed my cousin and hauled her off. Jody tailed us like smoke to fire. We called our separate rideshares and went home.

By the next week, I was so consumed with not thinking about sex that my mind had forgotten about that night at the bar and the guys. Plus, those guys neither had enough information on me nor likely remembered me. I meant to ask Melissa about it, but ultimately decided it wasn't worth the trouble.

What I was sure of was Melissa's seriousness about this moving in proposition. I knew this was Melissa's way of controlling me, and I loved the idea of being around her daily. It was that right now, moving in didn't seem workable. I didn't know her husbands. She had made no efforts to introduce them to me—in fact, she'd only spoken about them. My mind kept wandering back to Melissa's controlling nature. How whatever she wanted; she got by any means necessary. This part of her both scared and excited me. I had never experienced a desire for someone as strong as my desire for them.

By Wednesday, we had communicated every day. Melissa somehow got me to agree to have a lunch date with her. I was hesitant because she worked in the same building as Dr. Smith, and I hadn't seen my therapist in a while. I counter-proposed we meet in a restaurant, but Melissa insisted. She knew she had me at the surprise.

I couldn't turn down a gift.

The surprise was Melissa had me spread eagle on her desk with my teal wrap skirt hitched around my waist and my white lace camisole top shoved up my chest. My ball gag stuffed in my mouth, and Melissa crouched between my thighs, feasting on me like it was Thanksgiving. I had been ashamed, like everyone could hear me, and the shame aroused me more. I came so hard that I nearly fell off the desk. Luckily, Melissa held me so I wouldn't go anywhere. Not so lucky was that my release leaked onto her desk's fine grain wood.

The second surprise was a red vibrating thong. Melissa convinced me we needed to try it on during our lunch date, and what did my gullible ass do? Put it on. The lacy thong had a hidden pocket right above my clit, and Melissa slipped the vibrator inside with a smile.

With the damn vibrator controller in her hand, she tortured me on the way to the restaurant. When we arrived, I was so on edge that all I could do was wave to the employees. Melissa, the sadist, sensing that I was going over the edge, stopped the vibration.

"You're an evil, sick, and twisted woman. I hope you know that." I scowled at her.

"You haven't seen the worst of it, babe," she laughed.

I just shook my head. I knew what I was getting myself into when I signed up. Thankfully, she didn't turn the toy on while we ate, and instead we had an engaging chat about our day so far. I was deep in thought about how much I missed us having lunch with Melissa when I heard someone was calling my name. Melissa's lovely face crumpled into a grimace. Some shit was about to go down.

Lo-and-behold, the people I'd completely forgotten about, Zoey and Sean, walked up to our table. Zoey said, "Kyndall, I would say it was lovely to see you again, but you disappeared on us without an explanation." Zoey gave Melissa a nasty look. "I guess we didn't get the memo that you'd moved on."

Oh, for fuck's sake. I couldn't catch a break for once. In all fairness, I'd forgotten about Zoey and Sean after the block party. I owed them an apology for ghosting them. But hadn't they also ghosted me? I hadn't received a text or call from them since March.

Melissa spoke up, speaking over the apology on the tip of my tongue. "Well, isn't it lovely to see you... Zelda? Kyndall has been very preoccupied, so she couldn't get back to you."

Sean's quiet, stoic face turned to disbelief, and the expression was so comical I wanted to laugh. How dare Melissa be aloof to them?

"When you leave her high and dry, she'll come running back to us." Zoey whipped her hair back to cover how red her face was. "For your information, it's Zoey, not Zelda."

"Kyndall is where she belongs, and that's with me, not with you guys. But make an appointment with me. I'm a doctor and will happily cure a case of the sourpuss." Melissa smiled sweetly.

"I-I don't have to take this," Zoey said. "Come on, Sean."

Zoey and Sean stomped off, and I sat there with my mouth open wide. Without a word, Melissa paid for lunch. While the interaction was funny, I didn't even have time to apologize. Melissa acted as if nothing had happened.

"Melissa, that was wrong of you to do. They were nice, despite everything. I needed to apologize to them."

"You don't have to apologize for anything, babe. Things happened, and your paths didn't align. I deleted your message history with them and blocked their numbers when I slept over the other night," Melissa responded, like it was the most normal thing in the world.

"You went into my phone? How did you get in?"

"Babe, you have the same pin code from high school." She shrugged.

"So that makes it right for you to search my phone?"

"No, I'm sorry about that, but I didn't want you contacting them because, well... I don't."

Okay, she was doing the most right now. I was fuming as I charged out of the restaurant. Melissa followed, and we rode back to her work in silence. I could see if there was mistrust in our relationship, but not this. Angry about the situation. I couldn't even deal with Melissa right now.

When we made it back to her building, I stopped in the hallway, unwilling to return to her office. Sounding quizzical, Melissa asked, "Babe, are you really mad at me?"

"Absolutely. You made me seem like an incompetent adult," I stated, and I wouldn't back down. "Melissa, you need to loosen your control on me for us to work. You can have me submissively in bed, but we need to be equals outside the bedroom."

She sighed. "I'm sorry, Kyndall. I'm just worried about losing you again. Since I gave birth, I have been suffering from low self-esteem. I'm just afraid you'll get bored with me."

"What have I done to make you feel that way? I have been praising your body since we got back together. And you know what? You look so good that I don't need vibrating underwear or gifts. I get wet just knowing that I'm near you." I smiled because I wasn't boosting her ego but speaking the truth. She was gorgeous before her baby, and even more gorgeous afterward. I gave her a chaste kiss. I didn't want to start anything I couldn't finish, nor did I want one of her patients to see their doctor sucking faces in the hallway.

Before we parted ways, we made plans for the weekend. She wanted me to go to the spa with her and Amber, and I immediately freaked out. Knowing she had a daughter and meeting said daughter were two different situations altogether. I didn't know how I felt about meeting her daughter before her husbands. I supposed I could tell her.

I decided I would tell Melissa my decision on this whole moving thing after I met her little one. If the child resented me, I wouldn't push myself into their life. I hated when my mom's boyfriends intruded on our life, so I didn't want to put another child through that ordeal. It would ultimately hurt mine and Melissa's relationship too. I prayed I would be better than my mother and love my child no matter what.

The weekend was over before I knew it. The days passed by in the blink of an eye. By Monday, I could breathe with reassurance that Amber liked me. Amber reminded me so much of her mother. She was ecstatic when I allowed her to pick my nail colors and hairstyle, and even more ecstatic when I bought her a child-sized spa robe from the gift shop. As I looked back at how Melissa, Amber, and I interacted so seamlessly, it made me smile.

I'm a sucker for kids.

Monday night was restless, as my thoughts wandered all over the place. Surprising even me, those thoughts traveled back to the three men from The Little Hut. How were Aaron, Travis, and Matt doing? Had they found their perfect fifth?

I shook the wayward thoughts from my head. I hadn't met Melissa's husbands, yet I was over here daydreaming about other men.

I guess I need some me time tonight.

I gathered my plastic boyfriend, also known as my vibrating dildo, and got comfortable on my bed. As I tortured myself over and over with my toy, I imagined them pushing past my limits and taking me over the big O cliff; I imagined every hole being filled to the hilt.

A girl can imagine.

Satiated, I drifted to sleep with the biggest smile on my face and ignored my vibrating phone—everyone and their mother knew that I slept like a drugged lion. It was hard to wake me up once I was asleep, and, if you woke me up, I was as helpful as an inflatable life vest with a hole in it. I dreamed a man bounced and lulled me, the soft cadence of his shifting voice falling over me like water.

I slowly rose from my deep slumber. An extra warmth enveloped me, like a continuation of my dream. The cuddler within me wiggled closer. That is, until my brain woke up and I remembered I fell asleep alone. I'd left my toy under the sheets, but the toy didn't include manly arms or the poke of a hard penis against my back.

A very impressive penis, I might add!

I stiffened and looked down at the arms. Tattoos snaked from biceps to wrist. A large hand cupped my breast. Melissa's familiar voice chortled. "Aw, you guys look so good together." There was a flash, and I shielded my eyes from the bright light.

"Melissa, what the hell are you doing? And who...?"

I turned in the arms and screamed.

Chapter 15

MELISSA

Yeah, maybe I'd overdone it this time, but I had a great explanation of why I went to gather my girlfriend out of her house with her belongings. After our date and spa weekend, I knew she would get lost in her mind and think of little things to avoid the move. So, I took it upon myself to nip that in the bud.

Am I crazy? Yes, indeed.

I was right to kidnap–excuse me, evacuate—her from her tiny home in Flushing, with their crime-ridden streets. My bed was much safer. Kyndall's car stayed behind, but I had the keys safely in my purse. On Friday, the movers will arrive with her furniture, books, and clothes. Whenever Kyndall was ready, we would fetch the car together.

Unfortunately, Kyndall wasn't seeing the rightness of my thought process. Instead, she had murder in her eyes as she hastily covered herself with the sheets. "Melissa, what the hell did you do?"

"Well, I guessed you wouldn't be ready by Friday, and, from the looks of your house, I was right. I took the steps to ensure you made it here safely."

"You mean to tell me, with your whole chest, that you kidnapped me to force me to move in with you?" She pinched the bridge of her nose and shook her head.

She makes it seem like a bad thing when she says it like that.

"I mean, I know you would've made up reasons to not move in—"

Travis popped his head up. "If it's any consideration, I thought her plan was a mess." He released Kyndall from his hold, rolled onto his back, and rubbed his eyes. "Oh, and sorry for locking you in my arms. Melissa normally sleeps there, so my body naturally reaches out for her. But I could get used to having you as a cuddle, buddy." He smiled his most irresistible smile.

Kyndall blushed, but her tone was still angry. "Wait a fucking minute! You're one of the guys from the bar. What's going on here?"

Travis looked at her, puzzled. "Melissa told us to meet you at The Little Hut and get to know you. I thought you knew...?"

"No!" Kyndall protested. "I thought you were random guys!"

Bewilderment flashed across my husband's face. He opened and closed his mouth. "Ah. That would explain why you were confused when we mentioned having a wife. I'm going to get dressed. This situation calls for clothes." Travis climbed out of the bed and gave me a funny look on his way to the closet.

Meanwhile, Kyndall gripped the bedsheet hard enough to whiten her knuckles. "This is too crazy, Melissa. Even for you. I need to go home. I have another job lined up and all my belongings are there."

I hadn't forgotten about her dangerous 'falcon' position. Now was not the time to tell her she had to quit that line of work, so I bit my tongue. "Babe, I know how much you love your books and things. That's why a lot of your things are already here. The rest will come on Friday." I came up in the middle of the bed and tried to snuggle against her, like the prized possession she was, but she scooted away.

Slow and steady wins the race, Melissa.

I wrangled the sheet from her grip and grabbed both of her hands into mine as I tried to calm her incoming panic attack. I'd cleared my schedule for the day and worn soft, cozy loungewear to emanate comfort. "Listen, I know things seem rushed and crazy right now, but it will work out. The guys loved meeting you at the bar. Amber, the queen of the house, loves you as well. You should have seen her when she got home Sunday night. She couldn't stop talking about having another spa date with you. Just relax and let the pieces fall into place."

She stared at me like I'd told her the earth would end in the next minute. Shit, this wasn't going as I planned in my head. I continued to apply gentle pressure and circles to her hands.

"It's going to be okay. Our house has plenty of room for your books. You can have your own, bigger library."

Travis walked out of the closet dressed in his business suit. He straightened his tie and groaned, "Wait a minute, not only did you not know who we were at the bar, but you also didn't know about this move beforehand? Melissa said you agreed to move in, and that your fantasy was to be swept away." Travis frowned and shot me a disapproving look. "Melissa, we're going to talk about this later."

Kyndall's gaze darted between me and Travis. "What the fuck. Melissa, I just have to wonder what the hell is going on in that mind of yours. Granted, now that I thought about it, she did mentioned your names but I overlooked that information. But neither of us had properly discussed this beforehand."

Travis pressed his lips together into a thin line of displeasure—he was not angry with Kyndall. His next words were careful and slow. "Kyndall, I apologize for my wife's behavior. None of us condone kidnapping. I'll drive you home with all your stuff if you decided to leave. For what it's worth, Aaron, Matt, and I like you and think you'd make a great addition to our family. Plus, you're a great cuddle buddy. I'll be downstairs when you're ready." The fire in his eyes cranked up when he looked at me. "Fix this." He stomped out of the room.

Kyndall turned so pink in the face that she looked ready to burst. When the last echo of Travis' footsteps faded, she spat venom at me.

"I am so ashamed and mad at you, Melissa. I don't want to see you or your family right now." Kyndall climbed out of bed, walked naked to the bathroom, and slammed the door.

"Our family," I corrected automatically. I gathered her toiletries and sidled up to the bathroom door. "This is just a minor hiccup. Everyone is waiting for us downstairs. The guys won't leave until they see you." I knocked on the door. "I brought your toiletries."

A hand snaked out of the bathroom and grabbed the bag from my hands. After twenty minutes, Kyndall emerged in the short red sundress I had never worn. As we made our way to the kitchen, Kyndall was quiet as a mouse except for a few gasps and wows at our house. I almost forgot this was the first time she'd been to our home.

When we finally got to the kitchen, everyone was eating breakfast. Kyndall's presence made Amber's little face light up and instantly filled her with happiness. She wiggled out of her chair, hugged, and kissed me, and stopped right in front of Kyndall. "OMG, it's true you're staying with us!" She didn't give Kyndall or me a chance to reply before she flew into Kyndall's legs and wrapped her arms around her knees. "Now we can have a spa date every weekend!" She giggled and returned to her pancakes and eggs.

Matt picked Amber up and put her back in her chair. He asked, "Am I invited to the spa day as well?"

"Yeah, but Daddy, you have ugly toes. Mommy has to do them for you."

Everyone, even Kyndall, laughed. A bit of tension leaked out of the room. I served Kyndall and myself some oatmeal, and we joined everyone at the breakfast table.

"Wow, your children always make you re-evaluate your life," Matt replied while he returned to his food.

Kyndall seemed to understand we couldn't discuss our misunderstanding in front of Amber. With a sympathetic, almost apologetic tone, Aaron asked, "So, Kyndall, how did you sleep last night? I hope the bed is all right."

"It was an interesting night," she stammered. I had to lower my head to my bowl so no one could see as I smiled. Aaron was such a sweetie.

"Are you going to be my new Mommy as well?" Amber said excitedly. Her lanky frame shook with excitement.

Multiple parents were Amber's norm since birth, but she knew other kids had only one mommy and one daddy. We'd prepped her for the day she might gain another mother, and she was eager to have another adult to wrap around her finger.

Of course, Kyndall looked like we had strapped her on the railroad tracks in front of an oncoming train.

I saved my wife with gentle chiding. "Amber, remember I told you that when the adults decide, they'll let you know next?"

"Yes, ma'am, but I would love it if Kyndall were my new other Mommy. I like her." I loved my kid.

"Well, when we're ready, we will let you know, okay?" I stated firmly. Note I kept my sentence ambiguous, instead of saying "Yes, she's your new Mommy." That's what you call growth. "Now, go get your stuff.

Your dad will take you to school." Though she whined, Amber hurried off.

Kyndall looked like she'd seen a ghost. Matt spoke up before I could. "Sorry about that. Amber's been so excited since we told her we were looking for a new partner."

Finally, she found her voice. "Listen. This is the most insane thing that's happened to me. And that's saying a lot."

"We're sorry to have put you in such an awkward position," Matt responded.

I fiddled with my plate. "It would be a shame for you to leave immediately. We can tour the home and the grounds." I refused to let Kyndall go, but they didn't need to know that.

Kyndall ignored me while she addressed the guys. She stated, "Travis explained you were trying to be sweet and fulfill a romantic fantasy. Is this sort of grand gesture something you do often? It seems a lot for someone you barely know."

Aaron shook his head. "No, only for you and Melissa."

"To be honest, we know a lot about you, Ms. Williams. You love to read romance books," Matt pointed out.

"You always wanted to be a teacher and you're hard on yourself for flunking out of college. You battled depression while working at the happiest place on earth." Aaron furrowed his brows, and I knew he was ticking off entries on a mental list. "You like to masturbate at least once a week. You love listening to Beyoncé and R&B music. Your favorite place to concentrate is the zoo. You once ran naked through an orange field."

Travis continued, "You love to wear black thongs and sleep naked. Your favorite movie is *Ghost*. The only ice cream you love is Ben and Jerry's cookie dough ice cream because something about Ben and Jerry's doesn't upset your stomach. You named your dildo 'your plastic boyfriend,' which we found in your bed last night. You looked thrilled in your sleep. I'm guessing it does his job." He grinned. "There's a bunch more stuff, but those are ones that stuck with me. You told us a lot at The Little Hut."

"Oh, and you fantasize about Melissa almost every night," Travis added, and winked at us.

I was happy about how well my husbands paid attention. Kyndall, however, turned slightly green. She buried her head in her hands.

"Okay, that's our cue to go. Kyndall, for what it's worth, we would love to have you here with us. We have a good feeling about you, and Amber has latched onto you. If you'll give us a second chance, we can do a group date night. Tell us where to be, and we'll be there," Matt continued, "I want to live Melissa's dream out." My guys rose, gave me kisses, and walked out of the kitchen.

"I'm more mortified than I was before I came out. How is that possible?" She sighed. "What dream is he talking about?"

My first instinct was to lie. Then I remembered Travis' disappointed face and quiet anger. Instead, I told the truth. "I told them I wanted to see you stuffed between all of them."

"Okay, I'm so out of it. I do not know what that means right now."

I placed a hand on her thigh and slowly inched it closer to her core. "Kyndall, I want to see every hole you have filled with our partners' dicks. Sooner rather than later."

My fingers found her little clit and swirled circles around it. I entered my two fingers into her tight, wet cunt and pumped at a slow and even pace. She whimpered and rode my fingers. But just when I thought she would sit back and enjoy the ride, her eyes snapped open.

She grabbed my arm, removed my soaked fingers, sucked her juices off, and pointedly returned my hand to my oatmeal bowl. Shocked, to be honest. I'd figured she enjoyed being a submissive, but I never thought she would deny me access to her.

Well, until now.

"Absolutely not. You will not taste me. You're not getting any until you get me back home," she stated.

I laughed because it was hilarious to watch her try to be dominant. I anchored my arm to my side and hiccupped. She gave me this murderous look, and my vision blurred a bit from the tears.

"Melissa, I am done. *Done!*" She got up and carried her empty bowel to the sink.

"I'm sorry, babe. That was the first time I've seen you try to be dominant." I finally got a hold of myself. "I already contacted your landlord and paid for your broken lease. This place is ready to be your home. You can be mad, but I want to show you the space I created for you."

"You contacted my landlord? Melissa—"

I didn't want to be challenged anymore. "Yes, so this is your home now and forever. So, get used to it."

"The dumb part is I was going to text you today to say I wanted to move in, to try it." Kyndall ran a hand through her hair and laughed. "You crazy lady."

Happiness burst through me. Would I really get off that easy? I kissed her and dragged her up the stairs.

I led her to the room opposite the main bedroom. While Kyndall snoozed away the morning, my husbands and I organized this room just as I wanted it. Kyndall gasped in surprise pleasure, and that cued a surge of pride in my chest. I painted the room teal with white trim. A carpenter had built a wall-to-wall bookshelf, except to leave room for a big window seat with a view of the water. Instead of her bean bag, I'd bought a matching teal oversized cuddle chair, and the cozy vibes were complete with a sheepskin rug over the dark wood flooring. The bookshelves weren't full—not yet—but we'd placed little knick-knacks from her house on the shelves and some framed photos. I pressed a button and a white screen dropped from the ceiling. "It's a projector TV," I explained. "Through the far door is a bathroom and small closet, because I know you like to fall asleep in your library."

Kyndall moved around the room without a word as she tested and touched the space in silent awe. I tested out the cuddle chair and watched her glow. She stayed the longest by the window, looking out at the bay. I knew this move would not be an easy sell, but I'd tried my hardest.

Tears filled her eyes. "This is beautiful—no, stunning—to be honest. I always wanted to live near the water. But, Melissa, you don't have to buy me things. If you think you can buy my love, you don't know me."

"I know that, but this wasn't about trying to buy your love, Kyndall. It was more about showing that I appreciate you and that you have your own space in our home. Somewhere you can go to hide away." I raised from the chair, I slipped a bit of her dress between my index and middle fingers.

Kyndall didn't even acknowledge me as I stood there, and I felt like an idiot. Doubt reared its head, and I crushed it down. Kyndall's approach to our relationship was too slow. "Forgive me."

"Only if you promise to never do this again. No taking me places in my sleep. No making big life decisions for me. Discuss things with me—don't decide for me," Kyndall demanded. She paused and added, "And no more going through my phone, either."

"I promise."

"I love you, Melissa, but I don't want to be like my mom. She falls in love with any guy who showers her with gifts. Repeatedly, she's been 'in love' and then left high and dry when her partner got what he wanted. I want what we had in high school, where we would sneak away to be together, talking about the craziest shit ever." She smiled softly. "You remember when we took the bus to outside of Orlando and found a deserted park? We spent the whole day there goofing around and had to call my mom to get a ride back. She chewed us out in English and patois."

We both chuckled. "Yeah, I remember, and I kept asking you what your mom was saying."

"I remember you calling me, saying you didn't like my mom anymore." She laughed.

"Right, 'cause I can take an English curse out, but y'all be cursing the heck out of folks in patois." I laughed as I pulled her down to sit at the window. "When you kissed me in the classroom, I ran because I wanted to kiss you for so long. Kiss you and do, well, other things," I stated. "I ran to the bathroom to masturbate and ended up messing up my jeans and panties. My underwear stuck to me the rest of the way home."

"What? How come I'm just hearing about this?" Her eyes were nearly popping off her skull. "Wait, I knew you said you wanted to be with me since sophomore year, but we never spoke about the kiss. So, you liked it that much, huh?" She covered her mouth to hide her smile.

I blushed. "I thought about that kiss and prom night throughout college." Her soft brown eyes were too much for me. The rug was easier. "I also thought about how I should have told you I was leaving. I thought it would be easier, but really, it was just easier for me. You had to deal with the fallout all alone. How I treated you haunted me, even when I met my husbands."

Kyndall's gentle fingers lifted my chin to face her again. "Good, you deserved to feel that way. I don't feel sorry for saying that either. I've been through hell. I used to blame you for it, but I have grown and gone through therapy. Your abandonment was just one part of the trauma that made me crumble." Her smile turned sad. Wistful, even. "Depression got the best of me. I couldn't get out of bed. Eating was a chore, and I lost a lot of weight. I couldn't focus on school. It was a mess." I shook my head. "The reason I got my first job was to pay for therapy and my car."

She giggled and sniffled. "I remember the day the therapist suggested I tell my mom I was bisexual. So that one aspect of my life would be easier. What a disastrous plan that was! She kicked me out when I told her. She told me I was a demon from hell, so I was working, sleeping in my car in the Walmart parking lot, and bathing in the Walmart bathrooms when I couldn't afford a room at the cheap motels. When Disney fired me, they allowed me to work the two weeks, and a manager was nice enough to allow me to sleep on their sofa for the two weeks. Then I was on my own. I called Alex and asked if she could help me, and she said yes without hesitation. I barely had the money for the plane, even after selling my car. Alex paid for six months of therapy. After that, I was supposed to go back but never did. I was fine until you came back into my life and turned it upside down again...." Kyndall scoffed, more at herself than me. "That's a lie. I was coping terribly. Sex got me through more days than most."

I went to grab her hand, but she pulled it away. I winced at the action, but I understand.

Kyndall continued, "When you left, I didn't have a backup plan, Melissa. Everything we promised to split together—college, an apartment, a damn mobile phone plan—there was no one to take your place. Nobody stepped up. In a strange way, it made me step up before I was ready. It exposed a lot of problems I'd been dodging since freshman year. Love doesn't solve mental health problems. That shit's in your blood and bones. Genetics predispose you, and a hard life sets it off. I was dealing with my depression before I fell in love with you, and I dealt with it after you threw me away." Her voice sounded harsher than ever before, and I've heard this woman scream. "I won't allow you or anyone else to ruin what I built up for myself. I mean it, Melissa. Don't fuck with my life because you can, because you have money and status now. I am a person, not a toy to use however you want. I allow you to have full control of me in bed, but outside, we are equal. That's my peace. Take it or leave it."

Damn, if you told me Kyndall could speak to me with this much vehemence, I would have laughed in your face before today. The Kyndall before me now had a fierce look on her face, as if she could punt my head across the state of New York with one kick. I had never seen Kyndall be aggressive about anything, especially about herself. God! She was turning me on, even though this was supposed to be a serious conversation.

I cleared my throat to break the silence. "Thank you for telling me all that." As I listened to her story from her own mouth, it was so much more powerful than reading it in a dry medical file. Why had I hired Joey when I could have had this conversation? "I shouldn't have done this... kidnapping thing. It was wrong of me to stalk you as well. I should have waited for you to open up to me at your own pace." Kyndall watched and waited, so I continued, "What we have right now is the real deal. I'm trying to fight for you, but in all the wrong ways. I see that now."

I pulled her against me and hugged her from behind. "We spent five or six years dating different girls with some attribute that reminded me of you. That's the truth. If you want me to go through fire for you, then I will. As much as I've said, you belong to us, we belong to you as well. If you give us a chance."

"Keep your promises, Melissa." She placed her hands over mine and squeezed. "I want to sleep in a separate room until I think we're at a good stage in our relationship."

"Can I sleep with you some nights? And the guys as well?" I put as much innocence in my voice as I could muster.

"No." I could almost feel her huffing from annoyance. "Did you really tell them I like to sleep naked? And that I mostly wear black thongs? And about me masturbating daily?"

I giggled. "Nope, that was all you, my love. You're not pinning your loose lips on me." She facepalmed. "Trust me, the guys don't think any less of you." I spun her around slowly and kissed the look of embarrassment off her face. "Want to test out the chair? I've been dreaming of eating you from behind on it since it got here."

"Melissa!" She blushed. "No. You're sadly mistaken if you think you'll get anything today. You're on punishment until I say so." We broke apart, and she put her hands on her hips—my budding disciplinarian.

"Okay, babe." I was about to invite her on that house tour when her phone rang. "Who's calling you?"

She looked at her phone, and her mouth twisted. "It's an unknown number. Let it go to voicemail, and I'll listen to it later." She shrugged.

I bit back the urge to ask if I could listen to the voicemails with her. *No.* I had to trust Kyndall. She would tell me if Zoey, that clingy asshole, called to harass her. Instead, I responded, "Let me give you a tour of your new home."

We spent the next twenty minutes side by side. I showed off all the unique features of our house, including the garage with its roomy space for her car. In the name of our fragile trust, I returned her keys. Today was trash day, so I got to show her how that worked. Her shoulders relaxed when I explained the house's alarm code system. We made sure her phone had all the family's numbers and the emergency numbers—plus the usual hospital, shopping, and Amber's school addresses. Kyndall asked about the location of the nearest library, because of course she did. Since we were looking at our phones anyway, she checked her voicemail—the caller didn't leave a message thankfully.

It was a win for me.

Chapter 16

KYNDALL

Six months later

HAPPINESS.

I never imagined I would associate Melissa's name with happiness. If you had asked me this time last year, where do I see myself in twelve months? I would have said nothing would change except I would have more money in my savings account. Not here spending my days in a mansion with Melissa, Amber, and my partners.

Geez, I have partners!

Suppose someone had told me last year that I would have Melissa's daughter telling me my new name was "Mommy Kay," I would have shoved them off a cliff. Eight days after my abrupt move to the mansion, Amber stomped right up to my bedroom and determined, "You're my Mommy now too! I'm calling you Mommy Kay. Don't get confused, all right?"

How do you respond to a little girl who looked at you with big jade eyes and stuck out her little bottom lip for emphasis? Your answer should be yes, and you close your mouth and do whatever you can to live up to your new title. Which for me meant reading to her, helping her with her homework, and shopping on weekends.

It's what I always wanted, so why do I cry in my library whenever I am left alone?

The relationship with Matt, Aaron, and Travis was amazing. I hated to admit it to Melissa because she gloated when I did. They quickly erased my biggest fear of not being compatible with them after we officially started dating. First, we decided as a group to start with separate date nights. I got to know them individually before we did a big group date.

For my first date with Matt, I was astounded. He rented out an old movie theater with dining services. I didn't know such a thing was possible—I guess real estate pays that well. We had a deep connection with our love for old movies and books. We sneaked away into the city when we were alone to visit the museum of art. I found myself in a stupor when we sneaked into the back and danced together with no music.

We looked crazy, but we never cared.

Aaron's date was even more extravagant. He rented out a whole spa, and we received every service they provided. With our skin scrubbed, waxed, and massaged within an inch of its life. We had an intimate dinner on a private boat ride around Manhattan. We were so drunk off the champagne that we had sex on the limo ride back home. I hadn't planned to do that, but I was feeling myself and I was drunk. When we returned home, I had to wear Aaron's shirt as a dress since he tore my old dress off me.

I had never seen Melissa's eyes sparkle so brightly as they did that night when she smiled.

Travis and I had already hit it off since that first day Melissa kidnapped me. What kicked off was his personality. I loved the carefree California vibe—so different from the sleepless, ruthless New York one. I was in awe when he took me to a Broadway show.

When I mentioned I hadn't pegged him as a theater guy, he explained, "I want to show you where I go to get away from it all. When life and work get to be too much, I find a theater and pay to see whatever show I can get a seat in. It doesn't matter what's playing. I'm buying the ticket. It's the most therapeutic thing I do for myself."

"I always wanted to go to the theater but had no one interested in going with me," I admitted.

"Well, good thing you have me now. We can explore it together." His eyes shone in the dim theater light. His warm smile and how he spoke about his hobby made me appreciate him even more. Travis has always been open, but that date opened me to another side of the playful playboy.

I was so thrown off because out of all the three guys, I would have never thought Travis would have liked theater arts. After the show, we were so exhilarated that we ended up at a dance club instead of having dinner. We danced badly on my part until we collapsed in the car and ate greasy fast food before we headed home.

The sex between us was life changing. We hadn't had time to have sex as an entire group yet. Usually, it'd been a threesome between me, Melissa, and one of our partners. Our three male partners were constantly busy setting up their East Coast real estate office. They traveled up and down the Eastern seaboard, building an empire piece by piece.

Despite all the dates we went on and the fantastic sex, I cried every day when everyone was away and I found myself left behind in the mansion.

On the days we weren't going out on dates or having family outings, I made sure things were tidy in the home. Yes, we had a housekeeper, but I did stuff to pass the time. I had dinner ready for them when they came home. It was the least I could do. They had to work all day while I sat around reading books.

When I got bored, I decided I wanted to pick up another assignment. I sat my partners down and explained my job in layman's terms—check in, check out, get out. Melissa was adamant about me not returning to work for Marcus, stating she was concerned about my safety. I agreed with her on that point. Only a few falcons became as well known as me and endured. It was fine when I lived alone—Alex depended on me, but she knew the risks intimately. It was different now that I lived with people not in the life, and so many of them too. I gave up on the job with Marcus. Of course, he cursed me out for that, and I tossed my burner phone for good measure. When I mentioned this to Matt, he was relieved to hear about my decision and repeatedly stated, "We work enough for all of us, love. You don't need to work. We appreciate what you do here at home." I mean, honestly, what do you say to that?

My brain still itched for stimulation. I applied to a couple of work-from-home jobs and never heard from them.

So, what do I do? I cried about it in my teal room of tears.

Alex had been over twice since my move out to "the burbs", as she called it. Every time she acted like she was visiting a crime scene and she was the detective assigned to figure this shit out. The first time she came over, the guys were out on a business trip. Melissa, Amber, and I watched her comb over every corner of the mansion. Damn girl knew my weakness—she let me hold Maxwell the entire time. I couldn't be too mad, looking at his adorable face. I coached Amber on playing with him. Melissa took videos of her baby playing baby with another baby. With my girlfriend distracted, Alex could get me alone in my room of tears, saying, "This is a pretty jail cell, Kyndall. It's really classy."

"Alex, please, Melissa isn't holding me hostage. I agreed to stay."

"You should have gotten your ass over to my house ASAP." She shook her head. "I don't know what they're putting in their champagne or condoms, but I see you, my little cousin."

"Really, Alex? I'll be fine, and if it's not working out, I'll leave." Irritated, I started tidying the room, as I picked up piles of books and placed them back on their shelves.

"Kyndall, your girlfriend made you a library in her home before you even agreed to move in with her. Do you think she'll just let you go easily? I don't know what to tell you." She shook her head.

"I'll be okay, Alex. I love you, but I think you're overthinking things."

"For your sake, I hope so."

Since then, she stopped starting our conversations with, "Hey, how are you doing?" It turned into, "Hey, when was the last time you went to Dr. Smith?" I may have lied and told her I was okay and doing fabulous. I, of course, sent her selfies from our dates to further cement my statements.

After I had pretended that I was content, I eventually found myself in tears for the fifth time that day.

Of course, Alex only had my best interest in mind. I couldn't be mad at her for giving me crap about the whole situation. I just promised her I would make an appointment with Dr. Smith. Every week, I had the utmost intention of setting an appointment, but other things got in the way: Amber was sick; Melissa planned a surprise date; the housekeeper canceled, etc.

I had every excuse in the book.

One afternoon, I was so overwhelmed with frustration that I felt as if my brain would explode. Through two hours of furious tears, I brainstormed what to do next with my life. The local community college offered a teacher certification program. Yes. I signed up. I had enough money saved to pay for tuition, and I looked forward to the next chapter in my life.

I am making good progress!

I was so excited about school. At dinner that night, I apologized for not letting the group know, but they applauded me. This was my new lease on life, and I was on my way up. We discussed many ideas together—what grade I wanted to teach, what subjects, how I would decorate my classroom. The discussion kept up during our after-dinner movie. Matt and Melissa especially would chime in with thoughts, peppering the Marvel movie dialogue with real-life concerns. Tucked under Matt's arm and Melissa was on his other side.

"I said it already, but it bears repeating—I'm so glad you're reaching for your dream, love," Matt stressed, squeezing my shoulder and placing a kiss on my head. "Send over the invoice, and we can get squared away. Are you taking classes online or in person?"

"I think it may be both. I don't mind, though. It will give me a chance to meet some new people." Melissa almost broke her neck to pin a stare at me. "Don't even try it, Melissa."

"I wouldn't say anything." I gave her the side eye. Matt slapped her ass. "Really!"

We all laughed.

"Thank you for your support, guys. I have enough to pay for everything, though."

"Nonsense, we have more than enough money to pay for everything, love," Matt explained, his voice all tender. "I wouldn't feel right if I didn't take care of my family."

What could I say but "Okay, baby." I closed my eyes and fought back the tears. I retrained my focus on the movie. After twenty minutes, I excused myself and went to bed early, using a headache as an excuse. I lay there with my eyes closed until I heard a suspicious creaking of the floorboards.

"I know you're awake, Kyndall," Melissa declared.

I cracked an eye open and closed it again. "Just can't sleep."

"Are you okay, babe?"

I could tell her the truth and maybe find peace on my side, but I took the coward's way out and replied, "Yes, babe. Just insomnia."

I couldn't see her stare, but I could feel the weight of it. "I know you're lying, but we will always be here when you're ready to talk." She placed a kiss on my shoulder and left.

What could I say? Nothing.

I started classes at the local college without a hitch. I was so busy as I tried to get back into the groove of studying and completing homework that I had no time to cry. By the third week, I'd joined a study group, and it helped immensely. Of course, I didn't realize one of the other students, Lynda, wanted more than just my study notes, and of course, Melissa figured out Lynda's feelings before me.

I never gave Lynda any sign that I liked her, nor showed her any preferential treatment over my other new study buddies. But of course that didn't matter.

Melissa and I were eating lunch on campus one afternoon when the shit hit the fan. Spotting us, Lynda came over in her usual excitable manner. She squealed, "Hey Kyndall, how are you? Thank you so much for your notes last time. I really appreciate it. Are you coming to the session later today?" She smiled and leaned in. I noticed I could see straight down her hot pink dress.

I Ignored the cleavage, and I returned her smile. "Lynda, this is my girlfriend, Melissa. Melissa, this is my classmate, Lynda."

"Hello, Lynda." She dragged out her name without even blinking. "That's an interesting dress you have on."

Lynda blushed scarlet. "Oh, I love this dress. Pink is my favorite color." Lynda leaned over as she took out her books, again showing us her breasts.

Alarm bells banged in my head. Oh God, I didn't have the strength to deal with this. "Melissa, baby, how about we go home?"

Lynda spluttered as she realized I wouldn't take her bate. "I'm sorry! I didn't mean to intrude on your personal time. It's just—Kyndall never mentioned a partner before."

I collected my stuff as fast as possible. I cut off whatever snide remark Melissa was about to unleash. "It's okay, Lynda. I'm leaving before my girlfriend snatches you out of this realm. Bye." I rose from the table with Melissa's hand in mine, encouraging her to get the fuck out of there.

But of course, it was never easy for me. Lynda was oblivious or stupid. "Bye, Kyndall. I will see you next week then." She grabbed my upper arm and squeezed playfully.

Only a full body jerk released me. "I don't think I'll be studying with you again." Then I dragged Melissa off before she figured out how to murder a person with her eyes.

Melissa was quiet all the way to our car when I kissed her before we got in our separate cars. She gave me a look to say this was far from over. As I pulled out of the lot, I prepared myself for the ten-minute drive home. When Melissa goes quiet, there's so much shit going to go down. When I pulled up to the house, she was already inside, and the door was open.

Please let the ride have cooled her down. I don't want to deal with the arguing.

When I walked into the kitchen, Travis, Matt, and Melissa spoke in hushed tones and stopped when I walked in. Oh boy.

"Hey guys," I greeted in my most cheerful voice.

"Hey, babe," Travis and Matt replied simultaneously. I kissed them.

"We have some important documents to go over. We'll leave you ladies to talk." When they shuffled off, they left me with our irate princess.

I sighed. "Melissa, I wanted to say I'm—"

Before I could apologize, Melissa had gripped me by the throat and backed me into the wall. Melissa fixed her eyes on me and I heard my heart skip a beat in surprise.

"Kyndall, I thought I made myself clear." Her lips were so tightly pursed that it appeared as though they had been sewn together. She tightened her hand around my neck. "Right now, you are only dating us. We don't date outside of our relationship, not with Lynda or anybody else. If I see another girl touch what's mine again, I will beat their ass. Your punishment will be severe."

"Melissa. I. Never. Said. I. Liked. Her," I choked out. She relaxed her hold on me a bit.

"It's true that her feelings aren't your fault. What makes me angry is you never clarified that you have a family. You gave her the idea you were single. So single that she was bold enough to disrespect me."

Well, she had a tiny point, but still. With my little breathing space, I squeaked out, "I'm sorry. I promise you I won't study with her anymore." Melissa let go of my neck, and I rubbed my throat. I hugged and kissed her to help smooth the rift this incident had caused.

"How about we do something without the guys tonight?" I asked, and she looked at me. She paused for a minute, wiped her glassy eyes, and nodded. Dr. Smith would have something to say about this day and probably a comment or two about why my pussy drenched my underwear while getting choked.

After the Lynda incident, I tried my best to study alone, and if I didn't, I let everyone know I had partners that would decapitate them if they tried any shit.

But like the talented singer, Tracy Chapman once sung, "Still I cry."

I knew why I was so depressed when everyone and everything had been a fantasy. I hated to speak it out loud because I firmly believed that putting words into the universe could impact your life. In the dark early mornings before anyone was up, I thought to myself: why me? I brought nothing to this power dynamic. I was as beneficial as a shredded MetroCard. They made me feel wanted, but I had a hard time believing any of them. Why me? They could pick any woman, but they chose me.

Do you know what will solve this? Sex. Yep, that's it. I want to be filled to the hilt, knocking this feeling out.

Chapter 17

KYNDALL

I've got a plan in place. I need to act.

Melissa wasn't the only one who could devise a devious plan. I was determined to rid myself of the deep-seated insecurity I felt in our relationship. Well, to be honest, I didn't know if it would work entirely, but I promised myself to make an appointment with Dr. Smith afterward.

This will work, Kyndall!

A week after the Lynda debacle, I took a step back from the mirror and peered at my image. I attempted to appear "needy but not too needy;" this was the simplest look to convey, since it was the truth—I had to scratch this itch. I threw on my white crop top without a bra. My nipples perked against the fabric. The red lace crotchless boy shorts left a cool draft across my butt with its V-shaped opening. My freshly curled hair fell in soft waves down my back, and to finish the look, I put on nude lip gloss.

Everyone was home tonight except for my little Amber, who had a sleepover at a friend's house. I dashed downstairs, where I knew Travis's football game had him glued to the television.

First, I headed to the kitchen. I fetched Travis' favorite chips and let the bowl hide my boy shorts. When I got to the living room, he was shirtless from his shower and so engrossed in his football game that he hadn't noticed me until I sat down. Even then, he hadn't properly looked at me.

He just automatically scooted next to me, stretched an arm behind my head, let his hand drape down to play with my breast and nipple.

Score one for me!

Finally, he noticed something was different. During the commercial break, he looked down at me, and I gave him the sweetest, innocent look I could muster. "Hey, love."

I had his attention. His lips were gentle yet passionate as he kissed me deeply, his hands cradled my face. When we came up to breathe, his eyes roamed up and down my body, as he took in my entire outfit.

"Hey baby, is your team winning?" I asked, unconcerned. "The others will be home in five minutes, they said."

Travis smirked. "Yes, they're winning. Do you mind getting me a beer from the kitchen?"

Any other time I would have given him hell for that, but I smiled up at him, gave him a chaste kiss. The heat of his eyes on my ass as I made a show of walking to the kitchen made me feel bold.

Score two!

I returned with the beer. The game was back on, but Travis' gaze followed my ass as I reclaimed my seat next to him.

He cleared his throat. "Never seen you in that underwear before." His hand found my ample cheek. "Is it new?"

"Oh, this old thing? I've had it forever, and I had nothing else to wear." I shrugged and smiled.

We heard the door unlocking and the clinking of keys against one another. Melissa, Matt, and Aaron were home. I willed myself to stop the slight tremor in my hand. My plan only went this far. I mentally slapped myself and put on my big girl panties.

I can do this!

Travis's hand found my bare pussy. He almost snapped his neck to gape at me. His jade green eyes turned dark. "Oh, my little Kyndall, did you want to get fucked tonight?" he asked, and there had been no way he didn't feel how wet I was.

YES! YES! YES! I want to ride your dick while someone rides my ass. Tomorrow, I don't want to walk. I want physical pain to drown out the noise in my head.

Coyly, I looked into Travis's blown pupils and said cunningly, "I don't know what you're talking about, babe." He raised one of his eyebrows.

As Melissa walked in, she stopped and stared at us. Travis conveniently had stuck his fingers deep into my wet pussy and thrust into me, knuckles deep. My teeth sunk into my bottom lip, but a moan still escaped. That was when Matt and Aaron entered the living room. "Well, shit." I heard someone mutter, but I was so lost in Travis's fingers I couldn't tell if it was Melissa, Matt, or Aaron.

My pussy clamped down on Travis's fingers, but he wiggled them free. "Open up, Kyn." I did so, being a good submissive, and he stuffed his soaked fingers into my mouth. I took my time cleaning both fingers off as I swirled my tongue and cherish the salty, sweet taste of my arousal. Melissa came up behind me, wrapped her arms around my middle, and pulled me halfway into her lap. She cupped my breast and caressed my nipples. She pinched and rolled them while she planted wet kisses down my neck.

This is what heaven must feel like 'cause I was flying already.

A deep rumble crept out of my chest that I couldn't hold back. Sensing I needed more, she pulled my hair to yank my mouth to hers. Her lips were soft and passionate as she kissed me like she was ravenous.

Travis, the madman, returned his two thick fingers to my dripping wet core and continued to bring me to the edge as I moaned into Melissa's mouth. When Melissa pulled me away, something between a whine and a moan escaped my mouth.

Melissa's eyes glazed over with lust. Wordlessly, she stared at me, and in my mind, I imagined her command to come. I clenched down on Travis' fingers, finally finding my release for the first time in four days. My body turned to rubber as I leaned back on Melissa.

From out of nowhere, Matt lifted me up and kissed me, my lips swollen.

"Travis, hold her over my face so that I can taste her," Melissa spoke in a voice so innocent I was in awe.

Matt placed me on my wobbly legs, and Travis lifted me up. My back pressed into his front, and each leg slid into the crook of his elbows. I froze. I wasn't a small girl by any means. Matt whispered, "He's got you, love."

My muscles relaxed. Melissa arranged herself on the room's carpet. Travis straddled Melissa's waist, angling me above Melissa's mouth. Matt kneeled within reach, and I placed my hands on his shoulders for balance.

Melissa thrust her tongue deep inside of me and caressed my clit with her fingers. There I was, a sweaty mess as I clung onto Matt while Travis held me and swallowed my moans. My thighs burned, and Melissa's tongue worked me over until the pain and pleasure made my release dripped down into her mouth and onto her face.

Melissa wiggled out from under me so I could see the big wet smile on her face. "That's the best meal to come home to," she said passionately.

I couldn't even respond because I was gone from this realm. Spent and too tired to move, Matt took me from Travis after one last kiss. He sat me on his lap, so we'd be face to face.

He grabbed my face and his voice rough with need, "You want me to fuck that tight little pussy of ours, don't you?"

I nodded, which earned me a sharp stinging slap from Melissa.

He stroked my pussy lips. Aaron teased, "You know better than to nod. Be a good girl and tell us what you want."

"I think she needs to be taught how to answer again," Melissa the dictator's breathy voice, carried in the room.

"Please, I want to be fucked!" I whimpered.

Aaron helped me flip around. Matt gripped my legs and spread them so wide I thought Aaron, Travis, and Melissa could see my wet core. Matt's long, hard dick pressed at my entrance turned me on so much my essence leaked down my cheeks and onto his thighs.

"Melissa, do you think our girl could be wetter?" Aaron grunted. His sneaky fingers found my swollen clit. My vision grew hazy.

Hands removed and ripped my clothes. Melissa pumped Aaron's dick, and Matt established a bouncing rhythm. Travis' thumb circled, swiped, and pressed my sensitive button. I licked my lips as I watched Aaron's dick grew harder. The mere fact that I could have that cock inside me sent bolts of arousal through me.

Matt spoke the filthiest promises into my ears while my other lovers put on a show. My eyes couldn't handle the glorious vision of Melissa fitting both Travis and Aaron's cocks in her mouth. My orgasm strangled out of my body.

Travis grabbed Melissa by the hair and removed her from his wet dick with a pop. "Melissa, help me get our little slut ready. I want to see our cum running down her thighs by the night's end."

Travis' words made me clench down a bit on Matt's cock. He grunted and Matt fucked me harder, again and again, as he drew out my orgasm.

Suddenly I maneuvered upward, and my breasts bounced forward in the empty, cool air. The movement prompted me to open my eyes again—the moment I did, Melissa licked along where Matt and I joined. Her tongue traced a path to my clit, and she sucked my sensitive nub. I screamed. I was on the verge of coming again when Travis wrapped Melissa's braids around his hand and pulled her back. Matt surged upward. His hot cum painted my insides. Panting, I lay my head back on Matt's shoulder, nuzzling the parts of him I could reach. He pulled out, and his soft cock nestled against my cleft. Matt pressed a soft kiss on my neck and shoulder.

His hands still wrapped in her braids, Travis asked Melissa, "Should I allow you to taste my pussy again, Princess?"

Aaron chose this moment to thrust his dick into Melissa from the back. Melissa grunted, and I, mesmerized, watched her breasts spring forward. Between Aaron's thrusts, Melissa said, "Yes, Daddy, please let me taste our pussy."

Aaron stopped moving inside her and smacked her ass so hard I felt the sting. "You know better, Princess. Now answer Travis correctly." He laid a smack into her other cheek, which earned a hiss from Melissa.

She corrected herself. "Please, let me taste your pussy."

Travis assented, and immediately Melissa returned her tongue to my pussy. Every time Aaron thrust into her, she thrust into my core, and her nose banged against my sensitive clit. That's how we stayed until I came again for the umpteenth time tonight. I slumped against a grinning Matt, spent and sweaty.

Melissa cried out as she came from Aaron's cock buried deep inside her, and he pulled out of her, still hard as nails. She licked some of my release and kissed a kneeling Travis. Melissa kissed my stomach as she sucked and bit my nipples. She raised to her knees. She became level with my face. "Are you ready to get fucked, baby?"

"Oh God, yes! I'm ready to get fucked!" I cried out. Delirium and delight had settled in as permanent fixtures to my reality. If my partners didn't fuck me soon, I might die.

"Good," Melissa said, want filled her voice, as she smiled. She nodded to Aaron. "She's ready, daddy." as she kissed me and then him.

My legs were barely operational, but Matt, the gentleman, did the work. My mouth watered as Melissa teased Matt's soft dick back to hard. From the happy greed in Melissa's expression, I wasn't alone in my appreciation. Melissa splayed herself on the sofa and fingered her pussy like we were about to put on a special porno just for her. In a sense, we were, I supposed.

Aaron, meanwhile, took matters into his own hands. He Produced lube from somewhere and he lubed up his cock and lay on the floor with his head on a pillow. He beckoned me over. "Take what's yours, love."

Hunger gnawed at my insides. I stumbled and positioned myself. I had my hands on his knees and legs straddled Aaron. His cock pressed against my rosette. His lips skimmed my shoulder. "Relax, love. You know I would never hurt you."

My legs shook as I lowered onto Aaron's stiff dick. My knees framed his, and he whispered, "I love you" over and over. Aaron was a little smaller compared to our other partners, but what he lacked in length, he made up for in thickness. He gasped when I reached his hilt, and my pussy gushed arousal downward, as if to bless our union.

Yes!

Ever attuned, Matt slipped between us and rubbed his tip up and down my pussy lips. Aaron had me filled, but my hips jerked forward on their own, ready for more. "That's right, baby, take all of that dick," Travis taunted and praised. Matt dug his nails into my waist and slid home inch by inch.

God, I am so stuffed.

I gave a weak nod and a soft plea to move when I was ready. They worked together in sync. Almost like they were one person, they worked to transcend me to a higher place than heaven.

"Oh god, yes!" I screamed.

"Fuck, she looks so good sandwiched between you guys. Give me that pretty mouth of yours, baby," Travis demanded. His unrelenting fingers squeezed my jaw and turned my face to his dick, which dripped with precum. Standing, his cock perfectly aligned for me to take him into my mouth.

He fed me his dick inch by inch. The corner of my mouth ached, but I relaxed my jaw until he hit the back of my throat. He fucked my mouth fast, which made me gag a bit. I'm no wimp. I pushed him deeper down my throat, and, while tears multiplied in my eyes as all of my men filled my burning desire.

This! This is what I've been missing.

We moved in perfect harmony. The guy's hands brushed against my exposed skin as we moved together. Our movements were in tune, connected by the warmth of our movements.

Being overstimulated got the best of me as I tried to hold out as long as possible. I came so hard that black dots blurred my vision. I moaned around Travis's cock, which made him let out a string of curses.

Travis removed his cock quickly when his cock twitched in my mouth. "This load is for my pussy, not your mouth," he stated.

I couldn't muster a response beyond a whimper. I slumped backward into Aaron. As if they were telepathic, Matt and Aaron picked up their tempo. Aaron's dick twitched, and he grunted a curse as his hot cum shot out of his dick and dripped out of my ass. I could feel his heart pound against the flesh of my back. Four more thrusts, and Matt and I came together. Aaron's and I's sweaty bodies were stuck together, and I didn't think I had enough energy to move.

Travis, the sadist, stated, "Oh, it's my turn now, my good little slut. It's time to pay the piper." An electrified threat. His dark promise had Melissa moaning and squirting on the sofa.

I smiled because if it's one thing Travis knew how to do; it is to fuck. Matt climbed off, and Travis replaced him, hard cock at the ready. "You think you can handle me, baby?"

"Yes, give me everything you've got." I didn't know where I mustered the strength. I struggled to push a strand of wet hair out of my eye.

"I won't last long because I was ready to come from your pretty wet mouth," he declared. He sucked one of my nipples, sending a heated spark to my sore clit. My whole body jerked, and Aaron groaned. Travis' red, angry cock entered me in one full swoop. I gasped and moaned from the new stretch and slight pain. He was the biggest of them all. He was longer than Matt and thicker than Aaron.

I felt stuffed with Matt and Aaron, but with Travis and Aaron, I thought I would split in two.

Travis' hand sneaked to his favorite spot around my neck. Each slam of his massive cock reminded me that Aaron was still inside of me, getting harder and harder. Heat built and burned its way from my stomach to my core.

Travis pressed his fat thumb against my pulse, sending blinding panic through my brain. When he saw me fade, he would loosen his grip every couple of seconds and slap me lightly to keep my focus on him. My awareness ebbed and flowed. A foggy haze descended over my mind.

In the distance, I heard Melissa moan, and I only could assume she had found another release. Either way, she sent me an extra energy boost from her passionate sounds.

"You love getting fucked like a good little slut, huh?" Travis' voice was unlike him. It was rough and void of the joking light tilt.

"Yes—fuck. Daddy! Faster! More!" I barely squeaked the words out, but I meant them. I loved it! All of it. I begged him to go faster and harder, even.

I came with a scream-less shout, as I clenched down on Aaron and Travis both. Aaron bit my shoulder to muffle himself, and a second wave of cum burst and flowed through my ass.

Travis wasn't done with me yet, and my tired, sore pussy got wetter when he removed me from Aaron and laid me on my back on the empty side of the sofa. I was so removed from reality that I didn't hear when Travis asked Melissa to hold my lifeless legs up by my shoulders—I only felt her hands on me as she held me securely.

Did I mention this man is a menace to society?

With my legs in place, and Melissa whispered words of encouragement. Travis entered me and resumed his relentless speed. He whispered sweet and relentless praises, saying he loved me, that my pussy was his to fuck up, that my windpipe ought to be grateful to be crushed.

We came apart together. Melissa released my legs. He dropped onto me, crushing and holding, and kept the shattered parts of me together. Peace flooded between us in those moments, just him and me. We stayed like that until strength returned to my arms and I kissed his head. Travis gathered me up and carried me to the bathroom, where a steaming hot bath waited for all of us.

As we cleaned up, we kept the conversation light, and somewhere between, everyone took a turn to help cleanse each other. Of course, I fell asleep in the tub.

I awoke partially to Travis, who pulled me into his arms while Melissa kissed me. I drifted off to sleep in the middle of the bed, surrounded by my loved ones.

Chapter 18

KYNDALL

CAN I REALLY DO this?

One morning, I woke up and my stomach came alive. It started two weeks ago and came back sporadically. I scrambled to the bathroom, sweat dripped down my face, and attempted to vomit up whatever was in my stomach. When I stood up, I could feel the sweat trickling down my forehead as I approached the mirror. I grabbed a towel, quickly dampened the cloth, and wiped my face. I stared into the mirror as I stood there until my legs allowed me to walk again.

Time to get ready for the day.

When I went back into the bedroom, I was alone. Everyone else had an early start for the day, thank God. Even though I wanted to spend every second with them, the pressure was returning steadily. Between mid-finals at school and the holidays just around the corner, I felt like I was in a state of disarray. I would meet the guys' family for the first time. Melissa's cousins Sage and Mercedes were coming for Thanksgiving. I invited Alex and Maxwell as well.

I told her to leave Marcus home.

I repeated my daily affirmation about three times and did my meditation. By the time I reached the kitchen, I could eat a small village. My appetite had been weird lately from all the stress. I searched the fridge and pantry to find everything I could get my hands on. I settled on pancakes, yogurt, fruit salad, a piece of cake from Amber's birthday party, a sausage biscuit, and orange juice. Greedy and I had no regrets as I scarfed it all down within twenty minutes. I could go for seconds, but I didn't want to throw up again.

When I was anxious, I ate like a prisoner on death row and snapped at the slightest provocation. The other day I snapped at Melissa because she took my favorite shirt, and she just looked at me and asked me, bug-eyed, "Are you okay?"

My cheeks burned with embarrassment. We ended up in Manhattan for lunch to make up for my outburst. I really was a mess.

I got some more snacks to hide in my library for my study session and dragged myself upstairs. I laid out all my stuff and reviewed the books and notes. It wasn't until afternoon I took my first break. I chowed down on my snacks and pointedly did not think about how I had developed a gut. My bloated little belly demanded Oreos wrapped in pepperoni today. I promised myself to start my workout tomorrow—maybe.

I demolished my pepperoni wrapped Oreos. About ten minutes after, I had to race to the toilet and fight down the vomit reflex. Thick tears rolled down her face and dripped from her chin and onto her chest.

Well, I lasted until a little after noon this time.

I didn't know how long I sat there crying, but I moved when I heard someone in the library. When I emerged, the library door stood ajar, when I knew I had closed it.

My chest was tight, and my stomach bubbled because I was home alone and forgot to turn on the alarm. My mind filled with what-ifs. I grabbed a heavy book holder to use as a bludgeon and tip-toed down the hallway.

I heard voices in the main bedroom.

Hopefully, this doesn't backfire on me, and I die.

I could see it now: a girl from the Orlando projects killed in a New York mansion. My mom would read the article and muttered how she knew my "lifestyle" would kill me.

As I creeped closer to the voices. I relaxed a bit when I heard Matt's and Aaron's voices in hushed tones.

"She won't talk to anyone about what's bothering her," Matt tapped his foot, "Just went to check on her, and I heard her crying in the bathroom."

"Yeah, I know. It's getting worse, from what Melissa has said," Aaron commented. From my angle, I saw him shuffled around our bed. "Do you think she doesn't trust us or something?"

"No, I don't think it's that. I think she's used to coping with her problems alone. That's why we need to sit down with Dr. Smith."

"Melissa and I are coordinating with Dr. Smith to have an at-home visit. Melissa wants to get her to her office. She wouldn't say for what...." I quickly walked away before they had a chance to finish.

Nauseous heat coursed through my body. I made it back to my library and sat on the floor with my head between my legs, counting breaths. After five minutes, I was normal again, shaky but normal.

I didn't remember falling asleep, but when I woke up, I was in bed. I could hear the gentle thump of Aaron's heart. My cheek stuck to his chest as he read something on his phone. Peace ruled me until I remembered the conversation I overheard. Just like that, my anger resurfaced.

"Hey, sleepyhead." Aaron placed a kiss on my forehead. "I thought you would like to sleep in bed rather than on the floor." His signature lopsided smile made my heart pound.

How could I be mad at Aaron? His little smile eased whatever mood I was in. When he started rubbing on my shoulder, I smiled, "Thank you, babe. I appreciate it."

"It's no problem. How was your day?" He was so calm, but I knew he was watching for clues. I couldn't hide from any of them, especially Matt and Aaron.

"You know, a little frustrated with mid-finals, but it will be over soon," I replied nonchalantly. I escaped his arms and fled to the bathroom.

"Well, I can help you if you need it. Just say the word."

Oh God, the last thing I needed was to be holed up in the room with Aaron. I wouldn't be able to think about anything but crying, eating, and having sex. Well, maybe the latter would be nice right about now.

Snap out of it.

"Hey." Aaron came up behind me and put a hand around my shoulder. "I know something's been eating at you for a while. Why don't we talk about it?"

I stiffened. I had felt the same pang of anxiety every time someone asked me this, and I had always tried to ignore it. As the first thing that came to mind rolled out of my mouth, "Oh, I think it's just that time of the month, babe. Nothing serious." I avoided his eyes.

He sighed heavily. "We both know that's not true, but I'll be here when you are ready."

Disappointed, Aaron padded back to bed. For the past two weeks, it'd been harder to keep up appearances. Just the thought of having to sit across from Dr. Smith and tell her about my inadequacies caused my throat to close up.

My phone rang, and I answered on reflex.

"Hey, Kyndall," my mom answered in a cheerful voice. "How are you doing?"

My lungs constricted as I drew in a breath. My muscles were frozen, and I can't seem to get them to respond. Rigid fingers held the phone, and my first instinct was to cut them off. My mother, who hadn't spoken with me since I came out to her, had called me and acted as if she had never cast me away.

"Uh, I'm great. How are you?" I caught myself. I didn't want to give her any idea of my mental health. Or anything else.

"Oh, I'm glad to hear that...." I didn't respond, so she continued, "I spoke with Alex the other day. She told me about how well you're doing. I'm going to be in New York this weekend. I want to meet up so we can talk."

After all this time, what does she want from me?

I pulled the phone away from my ear and stared at the device as if it could tell me what to do. A cold tremor swept through my body. What did Alex tell her?

I was at a loss for words with this woman. I heard myself telling her the address to The Little Hut and saying I'd be there on Saturday night. Closing in on the holidays, Jimmie served dinner and half-price drinks early in the evening. After we hung up, I returned to the bed and Aaron. Better for his arms to close in around me than these suffocating walls of panic.

When Saturday rolled around, every sound I heard made me jump. I decided not to tell Melissa and the guys about my visit with my mother because I was already on pins and needles. I didn't need to hear Melissa's mouth about this being wrong. Maybe it was, but I still messaged the group chat, saying I was going into the city tonight. With the guys on a business trip and Melissa having a mommy-daughter night, it was easy to slip out of the house.

When I arrived at The Little Hut, I snagged a parking spot in front of the club. A chilly wind swept down the New York street as I exited my car. I shivered, despite wearing a wool sweater, boots, and a winter coat. I breathed in deep, and the cold air burned my lungs.

You can do this!

Few patrons filled the bar, so it was unfortunately easy to spot my mother. I said hello to Jimmie, and he replied. He was happy to see me and got me my usual to-go plate of oxtail, rice, and peas.

My mom hadn't aged a bit—not a lick of fat or wrinkles. Though her attire had changed. The new reality of a long blue skirt, white long-sleeve shirt, black flats, and a blue headscarf replaced my memories of her vibrant wardrobe.

While I stared in disbelief, she got up and hugged me. "Well, you look good. Turn around, let me see." On instinct, I turned a circle. Thank God she couldn't see that my sweater was stuck to my back. When we sat down, my leg started bouncing and wouldn't quit.

"You've been eating well. You gained weight," she teased.

I mentally rolled my eyes as I tore into my food because a nervous Kyndall is a hungry Kyndall. "I guess. Thank you, Mom. You've changed."

"I've converted to being a Hebrew Israelite. About five years ago, I found the true path and never turned back."

I had not the faintest idea what she spoke of. "Oh, that's great. Why don't you tell me more about it?" Her eyes lit up, and my stomach flipped.

That was when the descent started. I should not have asked her to explain her new religion. Thirty minutes later, I'd attempted to change the conversation a few times, but all roads led back to her new 'way' being the only way. I reverted to my prior habits and kept my facial expression indifferent.

I finished my plate of food to go. However, I still felt hungry and wanted to leave the bar and find something else to eat. Something with bacon.

"I heard you're engaged to a guy," my mom mentioned suddenly. "I'm glad you turned from your wicked ways and got back to what's normal, what's natural."

I stiffened. Alex may die by my hand. "Mom, I don't know what Alex or Jimmie has told you, but—"

"She told me you had a wealthy business fiancé taking care of you. Well, she said 'fiancés,' but I think she over spoke." She smiled.

Fuck me sideways. I promise to kill Alex with a butter knife.

"Mom, I am in a loving polyamorous relationship with four individuals," I specified, as my stomach felt woozy.

"Four men! Well, that's not natural, but I guess it's better than being with a woman." She visibly shuddered. "I don't even know how you could like a girl. I can't even say it."

Bile crept up my throat and burned my eyes. "No, Mom, three men and Melissa."

She sat with her mouth agape. I told her about everything. I couldn't tell you why. I guessed I wanted to let my tumultuous love life drive her away once more.

When I finished, her reply was a long time coming. "You went from bad to worse, Kyndall. This lifestyle will be the death of you." Her next question stunned me. "So, you're 'engaged' to three businessmen and a doctor. What do you do?"

"I'm in school to be a teacher." My damp sweater and jeans have all but conformed to my skin. I took a napkin and wiped the moisture from my upper lip.

"Oh, you're in school? You are too old to be in school. You should just go get a job. Do you work?"

Oh, God! Kyndall, get up and leave!

"I cook, help around the house, and help with Amber when I'm not busy with school." My mouth tasted like acid and dust.

"You're a maid and a cook, then." She took a sip of her soda. "Let me guess, and you get paid for opening your legs? That's what my child brings to the table, huh?"

"T-That's not—I'm—"

She laughed like it was the funniest thing ever. "You're basically a sex slave." She gasped for air. "When Alex told me about your new life, I thought you had bettered yourself and finally seen the evil in your abnormal lifestyle, but you went back to that girl who didn't want you." She laughed so hard that other bar patrons stole glances at us. "You became a sex slave with nothing to show to a bunch of rich people. What do you guys talk about? You bring nothing to the relationship but your vagina, cooking, and cleaning."

I ducked my head as everyone nearby tried not to eavesdrop, but I caught several people in the act. Jimmie watched from the bar with a sad expression on his plump face. I had never felt humiliated by my life choices until today. Of course, my mom would know what to say to push me over the edge.

I bring no value to the relationship. I am just there, living but not living.

I jumped out of my seat and announced, "I have to go. Bye."

I flew out the door before I heard her laugh again. I ran to my car but veered into the garbage can by my car to vomit my dinner. The winter air bit my lungs and skin—I'd forgotten my coat at the bar. Like a zombie, I shuffled into my car. My brain was a fogged mess all the way home.

The more space between me and The Little Hut, the more I could breathe. The little voice in my head was back, but it screamed a new message. It screamed to get as far away as possible.

When I got home, everyone's home in the neighborhood was dark. Melissa and Amber hadn't returned. I was famished and tired, but was driven by the need to get away. I dialed Alex's number with shaky hands and hung up about four times before I let it ring. She answered and cursed me for ringing her phone and not answering it. She stopped when she heard me sob. When I told her I had to leave, she offered me a room in her apartment, but the thought of seeing her and Marcus was enough to churn my stomach. She told me that her mother—my aunt from Houston—left her the house in her will. It stood vacant and waiting. She gave me the door code and told me to call her when I got there.

Common sense would have told me not to run, but I could no longer think rationally.

I ran to our bedroom, threw on anything I could find, and stuffed my luggage. My eyes were still watery, and I could barely see what I packed away. I ran downstairs and threw everything into my car. Headed back into the kitchen, I found the fruit mixture from that morning and ate it with my hands because they were shaking so much that I couldn't hold a utensil.

I was in my little mental hell, with my mind howling for me to run. The breathing exercises I did helped and made me more centered—enough to not make a scene. My tenuous calm shattered again when I heard Melissa and Amber coming through the garage.

I stood like a statue next to our kitchen island while I finished the leftover fruit salad from the night before. After ten minutes, Melissa entered the kitchen. I gave her a twitchy smile while the beads of sweat reappeared across my upper lip.

"Hey baby." She was in a good mood. She kissed me before she headed to the fridge. "How was your day studying?"

"It was good. How was yours?" I asked with my voice hoarser than an old man's. I sounded as if I had been screaming all day. She stopped rooting in the fridge, closed it, and faced me with a serene expression. I knew she was about to piss me off.

"Cut the bullshit, Kyndall. We're all worried about you, baby. You won't talk to us, and Matt heard you crying the other day. These feelings are normal—"

I walked backwards with my jellied legs as I tried to get away, but she grabbed my arm and pulled me back. "You're not okay, and it's not okay to ignore the people who love you. You can't keep your feelings bottled up."

I don't know what came over me, but I yanked my arm out of her hands. "You know what, Melissa? You have been asking for weeks if I'm okay, and I am, I promise you." I took a deep breath. "I'm so good that I went to meet my mom today."

Oh, shit. I didn't want to tell her anything about that meeting because it was so awful.

Melissa's expression darkened. "Tell me you're lying. She's not invited into our home unless she apologizes to you and me for disrespecting us and abandoning you when you needed her. I won't have her around Amber spewing her bullshit."

I knew she was right, but the depressed, panic-ridden bitch who operated my body had me saying, "Oh, so your mother can disrespect you and the guys, but you forgave her! You're a controlling, manipulative bitch, and all you want to do is control me and my emotions." Her eyes flashed with anger before being replaced with hurt.

Nothing made sense anymore. The words I spoke made me feel disgusted, especially with how hard Melissa had worked to curb her possessive streak. Stomach acid and fruit threatened to make a reappearance, but I swallowed them back down. Melissa hated anyone throwing shit in her face. My mood was so off and on now. As I looked at her face, bitter regret washed over me.

I tried to apologize for my outburst. "Melissa, I am—"

"Save it, Kyndall." She walked away and went upstairs.

My body found new tears from whatever little water source I had left. My salty tears flooded my face. I didn't deserve any of them. I was a little uneducated college dropout.

I ran out of the house, to my car, and straight to LaGuardia Airport. I booked the last ticket to Houston, which was a red-eye flight.

It wasn't until I placed my feet on Texas soil that my sleep-deprived brain thought...

Maybe this wasn't a good idea.

Chapter 19

KYNDALL

Yeah, this is the craziest thing you've done.

It had been two weeks, and I was in, what you call, my own personal hell.

A beautiful hell, but a hell, nonetheless. Alex and my other cousin had turned their mom's three-bedroom home into a short-term rental. The place matched all the other big houses on the block, and I'd felt small and lost when I stumbled in the wee hours of the morning two weeks ago.

It must be nice to not feel small.

Big or small, lost or found, it tethered me to the place—only going out for the bare necessities. I got my professors for my in-person classes to allow me to take my tests online and emailed my classwork. I barely passed all my classes, but as long as I passed, it was okay.

If possible, my cousin Alice, Alex's sister, was wilder than her. She'd come around occasionally to keep me company and recount her latest adventures with her girlfriend, Lashonda. Turns out I wasn't the only queer cousin in the family. With her bright green hair and bright green contacts, she made Alex look like a meek church girl. When I came out, Alice had been young and told no one nothing, so it was great to connect with the queer-positive adult. She invited me to the club—to dance my problems away—but I politely declined. I was tired twenty four-seven.

So that would be a no.

I sequestered myself mainly in the living room and didn't move from that spot. I'd established a daily routine. After waking up, eating breakfast, and dressing, I studied until I couldn't hold the waterworks. Then I got my ice cream, watched a show, and cried some more when I was done. I tidied up the living area and made a list of junk food I craved. As I checked my phone and looked through the thousands of emails, texts, and missed calls I received from Melissa and the guys, asking me to come home. I did my best to ignore them.

I don't know why, though.

I missed everyone: the dates, the house, the family dinners, the conversations, Melissa's possessive ass; Amber's tiny voice. Everything.

On days Alice visited, I bathed and ate lighter, not wanting to throw up in her lap. My little belly had expanded, and the nausea was less frequent, but persisted.

Today was an Alice visit day. I could easily tell when Alice had arrived, by Megan Thee Stallion's "Her" blasted through the air. I shook my head, sighed, and mentally readied myself for the drama, praying Lashonda wasn't visiting too. She liked to stare at my chest, and I was self-conscious about my boobs lately. They were more tender than usual.

"Kyndall!" It has begun, "Get yo' ass up! We're going out to find out what's going on with you," Alice yelled from the front door.

"I already told you what it is. Y'all don't listen." Lashonda threw her two cents in as the pair walked into my living room space.

"Can you please not?" I asked, because I was already at my limit. "Let me go to a medical professional. They can diagnose me better than the YouTube Doctor Shonda."

Lashonda peered at me with a critical eye before nodding. "Okay, sis, I've been around a bunch of pregnant ladies before, and I can tell you that you're pregnant. But what do I know?" She shrugged. "You got insurance? It's $180 without insurance. That's a lot of money to throw away when you could have taken a pregnancy test."

I cried because, well... I don't know why I was crying. Maybe I was pregnant. That would explain everything.

"See! You don't need to go to any doctor to see if your cousin is pregnant. Let's go buy a pregnancy test and call it a day." She crossed her arms. Alice took my hand and practically dragged me out into the Texas winter. The slight chill had nothing on New York City's blizzards.

As we walked to the car, I tamped down the desire to punch Lashonda back to whichever area of Houston she was from. She was friendly, to be honest, but the way my moods switched frequently now, I wanted to drop-kick someone.

In the car, I pretended to be interested in my phone. I listened to Melissa's voice message, and I was instantly guilty. I was such a horrible person for leaving the way I did.

What if I'm pregnant? It would be selfish of me to keep our baby away from their family.

I mean, I would know if I were pregnant, right? The last time I had my period was... Oh gosh. I clicked open my period calendar and swore.

Alice and Lashonda jumped in their seats. Alice scolded, "Kyndall, what the fuck! I am driving. Unless you want to end up a pancake, please quit yelling!"

I didn't want to point out we were in bumper-to-bumper traffic. Instead, I whispered, "I might be pregnant."

Lashonda shook her head. "Not might, you are. I have lived in a house where I have been through five women being pregnant, and you're like all of them. When was your last period?"

"Well shit, I-I um...." I'm a basket case.

"Spit it out, KyKy." I hated when Alice called me that, but she insisted on it.

"I forgot to update my calendar." I held my head down and mumbled.

"Okay, you're definitely pregnant, KyKy. I am siding with my baby now." We pulled into the grocery store parking lot.

"Shit. Shit. Shit." I repeated, as I cried again.

But I also feel so happy.

"Kyndall," Lashonda turned in her seat. "It's none of my business, but I consider you family since you're my girl's family. I want to be frank with you."

Oh, hell, here we go.

"I know we just met, and it may not be my place to tell you this, but I always try to help the ones I love, even when I know it may hurt." She mulled over the words for exactly one second before shooting her shot. "You need to call your therapist and make it right with your family. They still love you, even after you betrayed them, which you did. You're not supposed to run out on the people you love. Yes, I know you'll be mad at Alice and Alex for speaking about your business, but they chat all the time. Your girl and guys are worried sick about you. Alex is worried sick. I don't want you to miss out on love because your brain's fucked up."

Quieter than I'd ever seen her, Alice slipped out of the car and headed into the store. Lashonda gripped the leather of the passenger door hand rest a little tighter before she continued, "Alice kept me a secret until your aunt got sick—she'd figured out what happened to you, and she didn't want to lose her mom. It wasn't until your aunt lay dying that Alice told her she was madly in love with me. Your aunt called her so many negative things she had said broke her, no matter what I said or did. She had to go through therapy and still goes every week like clockwork. I'm trying to say that it's okay to need help. It's okay to screw up. It's what you do afterward that counts. Crying alone on the daily and holding in your feelings in doesn't help anyone, not yourself especially."

She was right. Honestly, I was tired of feeling like this. I missed my little family. Sliding back into the driver's seat, Alice placed a pregnancy test kit on my lap.

I stared at it and swallowed. "You're right, Lashonda. I'm glad Alice had someone to love her like you do. When I go back to New York, let's stay in touch." We all nodded our heads. "I'm going to make an appointment with Dr. Smith because I can't—no, I don't want to feel like this anymore. This depressive state is holding me hostage, and I'm through being a victim. Plus, I want to be mentally healthier for my baby." I smiled for the first time in weeks.

My mind drifted to the text Melissa sent me the day after I fled New York. She apologized and told me I should come home, and we could talk about it. She knew why I had been moody, but wouldn't repeat it through a text. This time, I couldn't blame Melissa. This was all my doing. I felt like crap on the bottom of my favorite shoes. Happiness was in my grasp, and I fled scared, reverting to my old unhealthy ways. What was the point of partners if I didn't let myself depend on them?

I wiped the tears, exited the car, and headed toward the grocery store bathroom, even though I knew Lashonda was right. Pregnancy would explain my overeating, strange food combination, bloating, and mood changes.

Within fifteen minutes, I returned to the car with my pregnancy con-firmation. Lashonda looked smug, and I couldn't even be mad at her. I caused all this mess, and I knew I needed to fix myself before my baby got here.

Afterward, they dragged me to eat out and go sightseeing around Houston, a beautiful, immense city, but I was too busy mentally to enjoy the moment. We went home, and Lashonda, bless her heart, followed me in and made me call Dr. Smith's office. The receptionist placed me on hold for a few minutes and let me know that Dr. Smith would see me at 6 pm at her time. Less than thirty minutes to go. I watched Alice text Alex about it, so my cousins swore I'd be ready for this appointment, come hell or high water.

After I promised them, I would make the appointment, they left. I showered and changed and was ready.

When Dr. Smith came on, she looked as relieved to see me as I was relieved to see her. We spoke for about thirty minutes, talked about everything that transpired from our last meeting, and I didn't lie or try to water down the story for the first time in a while. It wasn't until the end of the session she made a remark that made me want to burst out in tears.

"Kyndall, I was worried about you. You haven't seen me in about three months, and then your wife told me you ran away because of something she did. So naturally, I got worried, and I thought the worst. I hope you know I am here for you whenever you need to talk. You're not alone in this. You have a family that is worried about you." She cleared her throat. "I rarely do this, but I spoke with Melissa, and she asked me if I heard from you to tell you she loves you and she'll wait for as long as you want to come home."

That's when I wailed like a banshee in front of Dr. Smith.

"I am so sorry, Dr. Smith," I told her honestly. "The sorriest individual in America right now is me. I'm pregnant and alone. I don't know how to fix this situation. Sometimes at night, I hear my mother's words telling me I'm nothing more than a sex slave."

"It's easy to hear the negatives, especially when looking for them, Kyndall." She smiled sweetly. You can call me crazy, but as I looked at her, I knew everything would be okay.

We talked for the rest of the appointment and ended it with a follow-up appointment for the next week.

One step at a time, Kyndall!

After the upheaval of the day, I more than earned my rest. I propped my feet up on the sofa and watched videos on being pregnant and what I should eat and stay away from. I prayed I ate nothing that would harm my baby. Around midnight, I got the urge to text them a quick message.

Me: Hey, I'm so sorry for leaving you guys without an explanation. Hopefully, you can find it in your hearts to forgive me. I want to work on being a better person for our family. I love you always. - Kyndall

My phone vibrated a minute later. Usually, everyone was asleep by now, but not Melissa.

Melissa the diva: We love you, and we will always be here for you, no matter what.... Also, I will give you two months, and then I will search every corner of America to retrieve what's mine. Goodnight, Kyndall.

Fuck, that was a turn-on.

Jeez, I squeezed my thighs together. I repeated to myself that I was in recovery and pregnant.

Okay, maybe I will masturbate once. Yes, all I needed was one, and then I could sleep.

After round three, I fell asleep. Hopefully, my baby has its ears closed, and they can forgive me.

Melissa POV

I meant every word in my text back to Kyndall. The very night we'd argued, I'd tried to see if I could get our private plane to sneak me away. But I stuck to trusting she would come back. I'd known she was pregnant and high-strung, and I'd pushed her, anyway. If I knew one thing, it was Kyndall loved to bottle things inside instead of working them out. I blamed her crappy ass mother for that shitty coping mechanism.

I hated her mother with a passion.

I knew deep in my soul that she played a part in Kyndall, leaving us. I would get revenge on that old bitty for messing with my family.

The morning after Kyndall's text, I was spacing out over my breakfast cereal, thinking of revenge plots. Matt noticed. "Melissa, you have that look on your face again."

"I was just thinking about something." I went back to my now soggy breakfast.

It shocked the guys to wake up to the text message from Kyndall. We've been distressed over Kyndall's disappearance, even without knowing about the baby. I hadn't told them about Kyndall's pregnancy because it was her secret to tell. Amber was the most affected one. She cried and moped around the house and school. I had to sit her down and tell her Kyndall had gone away for a while and would be back.

Kyndall is in deep shit when she gets back.

Travis muttered, "You look like you're plotting to shank someone."

"I might, and it'll be Kyndall's mother," I concluded.

"Melissa!" Aaron reprimanded, as he covered Amber's ears.

"Sorry I said it out loud, but it still applies," I shrugged.

Matt shook his head, Aaron sighed, and Travis nodded and smiled in agreement.

"Don't encourage her to do something that will land her in jail... again," Matt chided in.

He always brought up my arrest in college, where I got arrested for streaking on campus after losing a dare with my friends. Totally unrelated!

"When Kyndall returns, we'll deal with her mother on Kyndall's terms. She gets to direct that fight." Matt pointed out.

"Absolutely not. I'll be manning that situation. Kyndall's going to be focused on packing and getting here by the end of the week." I wiped my mouth, got up, and placed the bowl in the sink.

"Mommy Kay is coming back soon?" Amber shrieked, hope quavering in her voice. Her sticky hands almost knocked my glass over.

"Yes, your Mommy Kay is coming back, and she has a gift for you." I picked Amber up and out of her chair and squished her close.

"Did she tell you what the gift is?" she asked excitedly.

"No, but I know whatever it is, you'll love it."

"Okay!" I set her down, and she ran over to Matt. "Daddy, I'm ready to go to school! I want this week to go by quickly."

Matt took our little girl's hand and escorted her out. Travis asked, "How do you know she's coming back this week?"

I smiled sweetly because my dear husbands consistently underestimated me, even after all this time together. "Because I know where she is." I smiled and tried to look innocent.

"You knew where she was all this time and didn't tell us?" Travis appeared dumbfounded. He narrowed his eyes. "Okay, spill."

"You already know I need to know where every one of my babies is at all times. So, I was giving her breathing room. Two weeks is plenty of time. Plus, she's going back to Dr. Smith."

Aaron smiled as he shook his head. "She knows... but how?"

"Her cousin Alex told me. We've been in constant communication," I said innocently, with a sweet smile on my face.

The long version was I rolled up to Jamaica, Queens, stuck my foot in Alex's door. I wouldn't take "no" for an answer. My cousin-in-law, Alex, the meddler—excuse me, caring cousin—let out a string of curse words when she opened her door and saw me on her stoop. I pushed past, sat my butt on her sofa, and explained I wouldn't leave until she told me about Kyndall's location.

I was slightly mad when I found out she was in Houston. I forgot her horrible dead aunt lived there. She used to tell Kyndall that romance books rotted her brain and were a gateway to hell. I rolled my eyes every time she called and I was around.

I decided I would give her a week to come to her senses, but I got busy with my caseload at work and held off. More than overjoyed when she tried to do one of her sneaky late-night texts, thinking no one would be awake. I took it as a sign to let her know I was coming, and she better be ready.

We also needed her to start prenatal vitamins and run some tests to confirm her and the baby's health.

I'm always right.

Friday morning came, and I was a mess. I couldn't sleep for more than an hour, and I shook so badly that I couldn't put my makeup on. The guys were up earlier than usual and more on edge than they had been when Kyndall left us. They tried to play it off, but Matt was nervous. He dropped the coffee carafe, sending glass everywhere. Aaron snapped at me for no reason, and Travis was in the sulkiest of moods. Today was the first time I hadn't cried from missing her.

I'm going to trust her. She'll be back by dinner.

A large part of me wanted to fly to Houston in a rage, to drag her back by the hair and edge her until she promised to never leave the house again. Instead, I put on my big girl panties and walked into our home gym. I left my feelings on the treadmill. Sensing my good idea, my husbands joined me. Matt called a babysitter for Amber because the adults needed to have room to talk.

As the sun went down, my hopes dwindled, and I hated myself for my role I played in Kyndall's departure. If only I didn't force her...

The doorbell rang, interrupting my thoughts.

We ran to the front door like the devil himself chased us. I threw the heavy wood open, and there she was. She looked good. I could cry. She wore the light blue tank bodycon dress I brought her for our three-month anniversary and blue flats. I forgave her for the flats because of her condition. But it was her little stomach that made me smile. I'd waited to see her with her little stomach for weeks now, even though it wasn't noticeable to anyone but me.

Or so I thought, but Matt glanced between Kyndall's baby tummy and me with a smile. He knew our surprise.

Kyndall placed her hand on her stomach in pride.

Chapter 20

MELISSA

FINALLY, I GOT TO hug her, and I knew how heaven felt. I missed her citrus perfume, her soft skin, the way we were wrapped around each other, and the way she wrinkled her nose when she laughed at Travis' inappropriate jokes. We held each other until Kyndall broke the silence. "Melissa, you're going to rub my ass away." She giggled and allowed me to kiss her.

"I was just making up for the lost time," I mentioned, releasing her, and letting our husbands get their own hugs and kisses in. Without letting her leave our sight, we guided her to the living room, and all sat down together on the sofa.

Kyndall cleared her throat. "I want to apologize to you, Melissa. I was horrible to you that night I left. It wasn't right, and I take back everything I said that night."

"No need to apologize. It was partly my fault. I should have pushed you to go to therapy more. I wish we all had pushed harder to find out why you were unsatisfied."

Turning to the men, she continued, "I'm sorry, Matt, Travis, and Aaron, for leaving the way I did and not sticking it out and working through my problems. But I am not sorry I left because I needed to leave to get myself together, even for a bit. I hope you can forgive me."

"We could never hate you, Kyndall. In a family like ours, no one should spend their days crying alone. We told you we were there for you, but we should have intervened when things were clearly not getting better with time," Matt explained.

Travis pulled Kyndall into his lap. "I already know how you can make it up to me, but you must make it up to Amber. She was heartbroken when you left."

"I never meant to hurt her. Gosh, I feel like shit," she groaned with unshed tears in those brown eyes I loved.

"We can all learn from this and grow as a family," I noted. "Kyndall, do you have anything else you want to get off your chest?"

"Well, I hate to admit this, but I left because I thought I was useless. It had nothing to do with any of you guys. It was me. In my mind, it made no sense for you to love me. I wasn't worthy of your love. I felt out of place." Kyndall made this speech with her eyes glued to her fingernails, as if afraid.

"If you can't see how much we value you, then we're not doing something right. We love you, Kyndall, and we would never string someone along if we didn't feel you fit into our lives," Matt asserted.

"I know, and I promise to keep my therapy appointments from now on. Next week, I have two sessions with Dr. Smith. I'll probably start with biweekly sessions and move on to weekly ones when I'm ready."

"That's great, babe," I said with a smile. "We want one of those days to be a group session, either in person or video."

She stiffened for a minute and then relaxed. "I think I would like that, to be honest." She wiggled in Travis's lap, and they smiled at each other.

"Nope, you're going to be edged for maybe a month, or until I can't stand not being inside you." He pulled her in for a kiss. "Or I think I'll tease you by fucking Melissa while Aaron and Matt edge you. Yeah, I think I like the latter." He gave her a lustful look.

"Wait, I don't think I like that too much. Plus," she gave us the most innocent look, "you have to be nice to me because I'm pregnant."

"We were right!" Aaron high-fived Matt. "You're pregnant! We're adding another baby to our family." Broad grins split their faces.

"Finally, I can now tell everyone!" I beamed, rubbing her stomach.

"Yeah, I found out Monday." Her grin matched the men's, making her cheeks round and glow. "Part of my bizarre behavior was just this little one settling in," she stated, rubbing her little tummy. "Wait, what do you mean 'finally?'" She arched a perfect eyebrow at me.

"I suspected you were pregnant for a while." I shrugged, "I mean, I know what I know, babe."

She rolled my eyes and shook her head. "I need to find an obstetrician."

Everyone went silent in the room. I just stared at Kyndall. "Really, Kyndall?"

She just shrugged and challenged me. "Maybe that will be my decision. Do we have a problem?"

The room went totally silent as the guys peered at the power struggle going on.

I folded my arms and nodded, "That's your decision to make and I will be right here to support you, babes."

Her brown eyes shone with hope and love.

"Thank you, Melissa. I love you." She smiled as she bit that plump lip I loved.

"See, growth," Travis joked, and we all laughed until we fell silent.

Kyndall's stomach chose this moment to emit the loudest growl on the face of the earth. She blushed and muttered, "I'm kind of hungry...."

That sent us spiraling again so much that our insides ached.

Since none of us had the patience to cook, we went to feed our growing baby at this restaurant that had a rooftop dance floor. We ate and hit the floor, our bodies singing for joy as we dance to the dance music. As I stared at our little family, I sent nothing but positive vibes into the universe.

Epilogue

One year later
Kyndall POV

"Mommy Kay, can we take Maxwell and Nixon to the Thanksgiving party with us?" Amber asked.

"Well, sweetie, your brother is only four months old, and the party is for big kids like you," I said, trying to sway Amber from the idea of bringing her brother. Tonight was the guys' company party, and it was no place to bring a child without all his immunizations. In fact, I'd been super careful not to take Nixon anywhere unnecessary.

"I guess you're right. Mommy Kay."

"Yes, baby." Kids, you gotta love 'em.

"Do you love me as much as you love Nixon?"

"I love both of you the same. You're one half of my heart, and Nixon is the other. I can't live without you or your brother," I repeated, looking deep into her beautiful green eyes.

"Okay, I will accept that." She grinned and skipped out of her brother's room.

I shook my head and continued to feed Nixon. As he looked up at me with his big baby blues, I thought he was the perfect baby. He was my twin except for his father's eyes, nose, penetrative stare, and fawn skin color. Okay, he was more like his dad. A girl could dream. When Matt held him, Nixon really looked like his Mini-Me. His favorite activities included staring at people like he's saving their image for later analysis and sleeping. Despite his young age, he slept straight through the night. When I told Alex that she told me I was lying; I invited her and Maxwell for a sleepover. Lo-and-behold, Maxwell kept her up all night and Nixon slept soundly. Alex was madly jealous.

When we first brought Nixon home, I'd been afraid to let him out of my sight. I pushed myself to perform all parts of his care, but you try doing that after pushing a human out of your vagina. Yeah, it was no fun for the guys or me. Travis threatened to edge for three months if I didn't let them help, and Dr. Smith encouraged me too—albeit in a much less sexual way.

When I'd returned from Houston, they made me pay for running from them. It was a torturous month of being edged. The night before they ended my punishment, I broke the coffee maker Matt brought to replace the one he broke when I was away. He observed, "Oh, I think you need something stronger than coffee," as he fucked me over the stove. I came so hard I thought I saw my ancestors.

Oh, the joy, and a great joy indeed.

Therapy was a lifesaver for me—for us. My sessions with Dr. Smith have grounded me, and I found a more effective way to deal with my low self-confidence. I mean, who would have thought talking to people about my problems would work? What do you mean it's not good to bottle emotions until they become fear and panic?

My mother, or the woman who gave birth to me, believed I never existed. Dr. Smith wanted me to have a session with her about how she treated me, about my upbringing, and how it made me not know how to lean on people. I tried to call her phone but got a disconnected number, which was weird because she's had the same number forever. I even asked Alex and Alice for her number, and they told me she had changed her number and told them never to call her again.

The family sessions worked equal, slow wonders. Our relationships weren't perfect, but we worked hard to repair and build an unshakeable foundation. We had our union ceremony and my baby shower party at the same time. It was a phenomenal night filled with our family, who supported and loved us. We exchanged rings with our birthstones and initials, and we signed documents that tied us together. I changed my name to Kyndall Phillips Jackson-Walker—a mouthful; I know. But I was happy to change the old me for the new me. Alex teased that we'd always be cousins, no matter how many surnames I added or subtracted.

I aced my first year of college while pregnant and finally found a part-time online job. I was super proud of myself for sticking with the program. We planned to celebrate my achievement by going to Paris when Nixon turned six months. I couldn't wait. Since Houston, I had wanted to travel more.

Sage and Joey broke up, and it was like the Hoover Dam crumbling. Mercedes flew in and both cousins lived with us for a month. Mercedes kept saying she knew we were bumping uglies, and that she gave us her blessing long ago to have a relationship. Melissa ate up her lies, but I knew she was full of shit. She was a mental one, for sure.

But I was at peace. As Drake once sang, "Life is good."

And that was when my little teddy bear decided he'd had enough and threw up on me. Lovely.

Welcome to the joys of motherhood.

Melissa POV

I walked into Nixon's room and relieved Kyndall with a kiss, as she went to go clean herself up after Nixon vomited on her for the second time that day. After taking the time to clean my Nix, I changed his outfit. I counted the blessings that led to my life right now.

I promised my family and myself that I would keep going to my therapist, which I changed from Dr. Smith to avoid a conflict of interest. My possessive spells came and went, but they were less these days. We planned on expanding by next year. It would be Aaron's turn to get us pregnant—preferably both of us in a single night. That was my second secret goal.

Goal check:

Dream career - Check

Dream Husbands - Check

Dream Wife - Check

Dream Children - Check

Dream Life - Check

Getting what I want - Check

Visiting that lady that birthed Kyndall and giving her a piece of my mind - Check

Getting pregnant along with my wife - Pending

I won - Check

About Author

Teal Rose is a why choose paranormal romance addictive that took her wild ideas from her hippocampus and placed them into her writings. Her primary goal is to share her vision with as many people as she can touch with her books.

When she's not writing, we can find her in front of her TV, watching movies and shows about witches, vampires, and things that go bump in the night. You can also lure away her from her books with any Grand theft auto, the last of us, and any multiplayer game she can get her hands on.

Come stalk me!

https://teal-rose.com/

a amazon.com/author/tealrose

f facebook.com/TealRoseAuthor/

instagram.com/author_teal_rose/

 tiktok.com/@authortealrose

 goodreads.com/user/show/157108661-teal-rose

Books by Teal Rose

Running from love Early 2024
Letting go can be as easy as giving in.

Jasmine Grant is a world renowned singer. Well, that was true until she retired early to fulfill her next goal in life, finding herself outside of her career, which her devoted Christian mother had been running until now. An extraordinary opportunity presents itself, allowing her to live out her craziest fantasy.

Will this be her great awakening, or will she revert under her mother's dominances?

Gabriele Sabino, Antonio Russo, and Wren Costa are all the three tycoons that are closer than family. Their parents gave them an easy life with a thriving family business. Everything seems perfect in the trios lives except for their love lives. With nothing to lose, they decide to shake up their relationship lives. But will things work out for the trio?

Will their pact to stay together last? Or will they find themselves in the same endless spiral? What happens when the foursome connects? Will they ignite a connection, or will the relationship fizzle out?